Pentrich – England's Last Uprising
(A novel based on real events of 1817)
by
Peter Darrington

Copyright © 2017 by Peter Darrington

All rights reserved. This book or any portion thereof may not be reproduced or used in any manner whatsoever without the express written permission of the publisher except for the use of brief quotations in a book review or scholarly journal.

First Printing: 2017

ISBN 978-0-244-60892-7

Reckless Yes Publishing

RY006

www.recklessyes.com

FOREWORD

"Pentrich - England's Last Uprising" began life in 2011 while I was doing freelance recording work for an independent radio drama production company based in Manchester that did a lot of work for Radio 4. I pitched the idea of a one hour radio drama about the Pentrich Uprising of 1817 to the company's producer. She thought the story had radio potential and we worked closely on developing the script for the best part of a year - most of that time was spent researching as much about the events and those involved as factually as possible.

Having been through the machine that radio people call 'script development' the final play was turned down for commissioning. Determined to not let the story die there and then, I re-wrote the radio drama as a stage play and resubmitted it to a BBC playwriting competition.

This led to the staged production being commissioned for the Belper Arts Festival. Two sold out performances later and the production was snapped up by a further two arts festivals, being performed four times in total during 2014.

The feedback from these performances was overwhelmingly positive and so with one eye on the two hundredth anniversary of the Pentrich Uprising - 2017, I decided I would novelise the entire story. This meant a great deal more research as a novel and a stageplay are two very different animals. This took me another two years to complete.

While I've done my very best to follow the real events as closely as possible I've also used a certain amount of artistic licence when it comes to breathing life into the characters and how that story is told. I hope that as a writer I've managed to strike a balance between telling a story that is character driven and full of drama while remaining faithful enough to actual events that took place, but ultimately this book is my interpretation of those events and the people involved.

P. Darrington, 2017.

Close by the ever-burning brimstone beds
Where Bedloe, Oates and Judas, hide their heads,
I saw great Satan like a Sexton stand
With his intolerable spade in hand,
Digging three graves.
Of coffin shape they were,
For those who, coffinless, must enter there
With unblest rites...

Pentrich – England's Last Uprising

CONTENTS

Prologue - 9

1. The Flame is Lit - 13

2. An Emissary Calls - 23

3. Comrades in Conspiracy - 31

4. A Spider Weaves a Web - 47

5. The Nottingham Captain - 61

6. The Night of the Rising - 71

7. Death in Pentrich - 85

8. The Siege of Butterley Ironworks - 95

9. Flashpoint - 109

10. Ambushed! - 121

11. Hunted - 139

12. The Net Closes In - 155

13. Gone to Ground - 163

14. A Sanctuary of Sorts - 175

15. Full Circle - 187

16. The Death of Freedom - 201

17. From Persecution to Prosecution - 213

18. The Trial Begins - 229

19. Defences Breached - 241

20. Verdict - 249
21. Facing the Inevitable - 253
22. An Unexpected Turn of Fate - 261
23. Execution - 277
Epilogue - 287
AFTERWORD - 291

Prologue
Port Macquarie, New South Wales, Australia.
October 21, 1822.

George Weightman's day began the same way that every day had begun for the last five years - with an ear piercing cry of terror, jolting him awake from the recurring nightmare that left his heart pounding and his bed sheets soaked with sweat. It always took him a few moments to realise that the scream was his own.

He found himself bolt upright, blood whooshing loudly in his head in time with his breathing. He gasped for air, like someone drowning. Which in a way he was. Drowning in a dark, murky subconscious lake of the horror of it all...

He threw back the covers and sat on the edge of his bed, gathering himself for a moment. His breathing slowed as he blinked himself awake. The summer morning sun cut through the gap in the tatty curtains of a single window, illuminating his thoughts as once again it all came flooding back.

The unrelenting rain. The dark foreboding sky with its pregnant clouds. The creaking of the rope in time with the rasping hoarseness of someone's dying breaths. But not his.

It haunted him. Every night. Idly he wondered if it would ever go away. Probably not. But one could argue that was a small price to pay, considering what had happened.

As the nightmare faded, replaced by the serenity of his surroundings - a single roomed wooden cabin built by his own fair hand - he silently praised God for his humble but heavenly surroundings. He was in paradise by any man's standards, but in light of everything, George took little comfort from this. It felt more like purgatory.

The sudden squawk of a Kookaburra mocked him loudly, finally bringing him to his senses. He stood, yawned and stretched in his night shirt. The heat was already bordering on enough for any native English man to bear, but the sea air that filled his lungs was oddly refreshing. He staggered over to his makeshift stove, located a battered kettle, filled it from a nearby water jug and hung it squarely over the remains of last night's fire.

Although he often roasted during the day, night time by the sea could be chilly enough for anyone to require the bone thawing heat that his modest stove provided for him. He added a few pieces of wood from a nearby sack and stoked the embers with a poker.

Wearily he prepared black tea and a small bowl of porridge which he devoured hungrily. Rummaging through a selection of small metal containers on the single sorry looking table in the shack, he found a fist sized chunk of slightly stale bread which completed breakfast.

Without pause, he dressed in a light muslin shirt, work breeches and his sawyers' boots, rinsed his face from a wooden bowl with the last of the water from the jug and set about carrying out this morning's task. He'd procrastinated enough. It was time to write the letter. He scraped a tatty chair out from under the table, pulled one of its drawers open and took out a piece of paper, a quill and a small bottle of ink.

He sat down, carefully removed the lid of the bottle, dipped the quill in the ink and tentatively began to write.

"My darling wife Rebecca. It is with mixed feelings of excitement and trepidation that I write to you on this beautiful summer's day. My heart is heavy, as so far you have not replied to my letters. However, I have such great news this time that I am sure you will finally forgive my part in the terrible tragedy that was June the ninth, eighteen seventeen. But more of that news later. There is something I must impart first. I understand why you wish to remove the entire sorry affair from your memory - you lost so much, including your home - our home. But you must read my story if we are ever to reconcile our differences. You need to understand why I was the only one of us who did not hang. Also, of the children, Mary and Joseph are now old enough to know the truth from their own father. I owe them that much, as do you. Perhaps they might read this themselves? I hear there is now a school in Pentrich – built on the site of Uncle Tommy's house, paid for by Devonshire himself! I hope they attend.

If he, who stood for everything we sought to destroy, can show sympathy with such a grand gesture... surely you can? My redemption lies with you, so please... allow me this chance to explain how, in trying to bring down an unjust government I instead brought death and misery to everyone dear to me. It began not in our native Derbyshire, but in Wakefield, Yorkshire. The eve of May fifth, eighteen seventeen. One month before that terrible, terrible night. My Uncle Tommy had travelled to a secret reformists meeting, in the back room of a tavern called the Joiner's Arms..."

And in that cathartic moment, as the catastrophic sequence of events that had led to George Weightman finding himself a pariah and an exile twelve thousand miles from home began to unfold in his mind, he was back in Derbyshire in the Spring of 1817...

1. The Flame is Lit
Wakefield, West Yorkshire. May 5, 1817.

Thomas Bacon, or Tommy as he was known to his friends, was a tough old boot – dogged determination alone drove him through the torrential rain that was currently battering the quiet Yorkshire town he'd just arrived in. Although now in his sixties, he was still every inch a fighter and would probably remain so until the day he died, such was his resolve.

When he'd left Derbyshire, the weather had been fair and it was daylight. But now it was pitch dark, and the weather had taken a decided turn for the worst. Turning into a familiar street, he paused to catch his breath – leaning on his stick during a momentary respite from the relentless wind that had constantly threatened to take his feet from under him.

He wiped the rain out of his eyes with a tatty coat sleeve and smiled. There it was, finally, not more than a hundred yards down the street.

Sanctuary, in the form of the Joiner's Arms, a humble little ale house much like any other in this town, except this one was hiding a huge secret.

He approached his destination with renewed vigour. Leaning on his walking stick, he opened the door gingerly while taking a precautionary glance back up the street, making sure he had not been followed. He then slipped inside, the door rattling shut noisily behind him.

Inside, he took a moment to let his eyes adjust to the dim lighting. The bar was thick with smoke and noisy with revelry. The perfect cover. Old Tommy huffed, shaking the rain from his beard and long silver hair. No one had even noticed him enter. Smiling wryly, he snaked his way through the crowd to the bar. A busty, swarthy looking woman no older than thirty stood behind the counter, pouring ales from a large pail. She spied Tommy out the corner of her eye and gave him a knowing wink. Tommy nodded back.

"Evening Betsy," he said, smiling.

"Old Tommy! We were gettin' worried! Can I get you owt?" she bellowed, over the din.

"Have they started?" he replied.

"Aye. Just now. In the back room, as usual," she replied, handing over three tankards of frothy brown liquid to a clearly inebriated patron.

"I'll go straight in then, I reckon. Perhaps something afterwards?" he replied cheekily.

"Right you are Tom," she cackled.

Old Tommy weaved his way through the throng, to a door at the rear of the room. He knocked tentatively, placing an ear up against the wood.

"Who is it?" he heard from inside.

"An army of principles can penetrate where an army of soldiers cannot," he replied.

The door opened a crack. Old Tommy immediately recognised the familiar face that peered pensively out. It was that of Benjamin Scholes, the Inn Keeper.

"Tommy Bacon!" he exclaimed. "We were getting worried! A few of the lads thought you might have been arrested!"

Bacon smiled. Scholes beckoned him in. Old Tommy stepped inside and the door closed firmly behind him.

Around thirty men of varying ages were crowded into a small meeting room. There was a low furtive buzz of chatter. Some smoked, most were sipping ale of some sort or another. A single wooden table sat in the middle of the room. A small group of men were seated around it, also talking. One of them caught Tommy's eye immediately, simply because he stood out like a sore thumb. Everyone else in the room was without doubt a working man, their clothes as weathered and worn as their faces and hands. But this fellow was definitely of a different class. His smart black frock coat and ruffled white shirt complimented his neatly groomed fair hair and healthy complexion. An expensive silver pocket watch chain adorned his waistcoat. His shoes showed no signs of wear whatsoever. By the looks of things, he was a gentleman of some considerable standing.

After scrutinising him for a moment or two, Tommy remembered his manners.

"Arrested? No Ben, I apologise for my

tardiness. It's just this wretched weather. The coach made slow progress in the rain and even my stick was struggling to keep me upright in this damnable wind. Have I missed much? Who's here?"

"No. Just getting started. 'Bout thirty in tonight. Good turnout. Wolstonholme from Sheffield is here, Smaller of Horbury, John Dickenson..." he gestured round the room at faces familiar to Tommy. Some of them caught Tommy's eye as he looked round. He smiled and nodded.

"We also have someone very special here tonight, Tom. A London delegate – and he brings great news!"

"Who? I may know him from the Crown and Anchor meeting!" Tommy mused.

"That's him there," Scholes gestured towards the seated gentleman who was now deep in conversation with Wolstonholme.

"Can't say I've seen him before... Bit of a dandy, by the looks..."

Scholes smiled. "Aye. He's a gentleman alright, an acquaintance of Sir Francis, he says. Not a grafter like us, granted, but well connected in reformist circles. Travelling with Joe Mitchell, so he can be trusted, I'm sure."

Tommy nodded. "What's his name?"

"William Oliver."

"I see. Where's Mitchell now? I don't see him."

"He went calling on Huddersfield members this afternoon, to take them the news... I think he's keen to make a start. I'll introduce him. Excuse me, Tom."

Tommy nodded, taking off his wet cloak. Scholes took the centre of the room by the table.

"Gentlemen. Your attention, please!" he said loudly. The room hushed. "So, as promised, our guest speaker from London. Please give a warm Wakefield welcome to Mr William Oliver."

The room applauded. Oliver Stood and faced his audience, nodding his appreciation. After a few seconds, he gestured for them to stop.

"Thank you. Thank you so much. I feel most welcome." His voice was that of a well-spoken educated man. "It is an honour to be here. My name is William Oliver and I am new to you, so I understand you doubt my credentials. But judge me not by my appearance. I believe all men are created equal and like Sir Frances Burdett, our friend in Parliament, I will not rest until we have achieved universal suffrage!"

The room gave a rowdy cheer. He continued. "Now, as you know, Sir Frances is to lobby Parliament with a bill of reform. This bill proposes that all men, not just men of wealth, be allowed to vote for who should govern this land. But this petition will fail."

He paused dramatically, to let the news sink in. There were a few hushed murmurs of disapproval.

"Because our government is not ready for such change. But change is coming - and soon, my friends, it is God's will. They may stop the bill, but they cannot stop the working men of England. This is why Mr Mitchell and I have been travelling the country these past weeks, spreading the reformist word from London. The time for talk in stale halls is over. It is time to make a decisive blow! London feels the distress of its country... but we need the support of our brothers across the land to remove the canker from its heart and I hope I can rely on you to join us. Like our American and French cousins before us, the working men of this country are to rise up and crush our government - who dine at the table of privilege, while you scrabble in the dirt for their crumbs! You defeated Napoleon for them and what did you get in return? Poverty! Starvation! Unemployment!" he banged his fist on the table in time with each word. "But no more! Soon, there will be a new flag flying over England! The flag of the New British Republic! And our leader, Sir Frances Burdett will hoist it!" The room cheered. Oliver was both captivating and charismatic.

It was Tommy who spoke first. "And just when is this uprising planned for?"

"In one month," said Oliver, boldly. "I know the time seems short, but we have to move quickly, the government is trying to infiltrate us with spies and informants. I and other delegates from London will be moving among your groups over the next few weeks bringing instructions. On the night in question, the men of the north and the midlands are to meet in Nottingham, with whatever weapons can be procured for the struggle. We will then take the canals to London, where we will seize Parliament." He gestured with a raised clenched fist, smiling wryly.

"How many do you expect will rise?" Tommy asked, "We will need many to facilitate such an insurrection."

"So far, based on the groups I've visited already, I estimate near two hundred thousand men," Oliver said, confidently. "Birmingham and district are ready with about a hundred and fifty thousand, Sheffield has ten, Huddersfield eight. Leeds and Wakefield's surrounding parishes estimate a further twenty thousand."

"Impressive." Tommy conceded.

Oliver smiled again. "You'll excuse me sir, but I do not know your acquaintance?"

Old Tommy was not fazed. He was a respected spokesman for the movement. "Thomas Bacon. I speak for the men of Derbyshire."

"Will you join us? I am to visit your nearby Nottingham soon." Oliver asked.

Old Tommy shrugged. "If what you say is true, then yes. We will join you, of that I'm certain – there is much unrest with the men of our counties, just like the people of Wakefield." He gestured round the room.

"Numbers?"

"Difficult to say. Ten thousand from each county is a possibility, if we can prepare them all in time."

"Will you lead them?" Oliver queried.

"I might, though I am a man of three-score years who walks with a stick. But I will do what I can for the cause. We have plenty of good men, any of which might captain our force. We won't let you down. I have long dreamed of this day."

There was a sudden unexpected knock at the door. The room tensed.

"Excuse me, gentlemen," said Scholes. Bracing his body behind it, he opened it about a foot.

"Betsy! Is there a problem? Tell me we're not running short of ale already tonight?"

Betsy could be heard speaking in a hushed tone. "No, no. There's plenty of ale. I've just served old Bill Wainright. He took cattle to market in Huddersfield this afternoon."

"And?"

"He says everyone's talkin' 'bout Joe Mitchell!" she continued. "He was arrested, for treason - this afternoon, as he got off the coach!"

Scholes looked visibly disturbed. "Right. Thank you, Betsy. You'd better get back to the bar."

She nodded silently and he closed the door, turning back towards the tense group of conspirators.

Oliver spoke first. "Is there a problem, Ben?"

"I'm afraid there might be. Joseph Mitchell has been arrested."

"So it begins," Oliver nodded with affirmation, "they will hunt us down like vermin! Constables could be on their way here as we speak!"

"Betsy would warn us if they entered the tavern," Scholes assured him.

"That may be, but by then it will be too late!" replied Oliver.

"He's right Ben. We must adjourn elsewhere," Tommy urged.

Oliver nodded. "If we are caught here, London will falter and all might be lost, especially if I do not return. The flame mustn't die tonight!"

"Old man Braidsby's here," Scholes nodded towards a member of the group, "we meet in his barn if numbers are high. I'll ask if we can go there. It's no more than half a mile."

Oliver beamed. "Excellent! We should make haste!"

"Let me speak with him." said Scholes. "Thomas - tell everyone."

Tommy nodded. "Of course." He turned to address the crowd, while Scholes and Oliver moved to talk to Braidsby. "Settle down everyone. We have a plan!"

And so, despite the rain, the fire had been lit on that dreary night in May. The flames were quickly fanned by the reformists' own hysteria – a fear that if they were caught now, it would be over before it had begun. Civil unrest was escalating throughout England. War with Napoleon had left England scarred. Men who fought for their country had been forgotten, having returned home to failing harvests, unemployment and poverty. Mills and workhouses had sprung up, but they were symbols of slavery and oppression, driving cottage weavers out of business while mill owners became rich.

The workers of England were looking to the revolutions of France and America with envy. Secret reformist groups, or 'Hampden Clubs', named after radical John Hampden, were forming countrywide. Previously, the objective had been reform through lobbying. Now radicals called for more direct action. That night in Wakefield, the group did indeed relocate to Old Man Braidsby's barn, debating late into the night. Finally, a vote was taken. The men found overwhelmingly in favour of an uprising. The next day, Old Tommy took the news home to his native Derbyshire village of Pentrich and when he knocked on the door of his nephew, one George Weightman, the young sawyer's life was changed forever.

2. An Emissary Calls
Pentrich, Derbyshire. May 17, 1817.

The village of Pentrich lay at the very heart of Derbyshire, between the industrial cradle towns of Ripley and Belper. Its streets lazily meandered down from atop one of the foothills of the Peak District. George Weightman, a twenty-six year old woodcutter by trade, lived in a cottage to the north of the village, with his wife Rebecca and his three young children, Mary, Joseph and George.

It had been a glorious spring day, but now the sun had gone down and there was a chill to the evening typical for the time of year. The Weightman's cottage was a humble abode, sparsely furnished with a combined living and kitchen area. A few tired rugs did their best to cover the harsh flagstone floor. A single rustic looking table with four chairs dominated the room. A black metal cooking pot hung over a meagre looking fire.

George's young wife, Rebecca tiredly chopped what few vegetables she had left at the table and scraped them into the pot. She was a pretty, slight woman with blonde hair, but a hard life with three young children made her look older than her twenty four years.

She stirred the contents of the pot with a wooden spoon, then wiped it on her apron. George appeared at the bottom of the stairs, having just washed the grime of a hard day's lumber work from his hands and face.

"Not much of a stew my love – just potatoes really. I gave the last of the bread to the children for their supper," she said as she placed two plates on the table.

"It's alright. Mother gave me some bread for helping in the tavern last night," he replied. "There's some left in my knapsack."

Rebecca sighed. "Bread's all well n' good George, but we need money. I know she's family, but you can't keep working there for nothing."

George rolled his eyes and collapsed into one of the chairs. "She'll pay me when she can," he said, tersely.

"Oh Aye? And just when will that be?" she retorted.

"Rebecca, please – "

A sudden knock at the door cut George's response short.

"Who's that at this hour? If they knock like that again, they'll wake the children," Rebecca tutted.

George stood up, went to one of the cottages' tiny windows and peered out.

"It's Uncle Tommy!" he exclaimed, his mood instantly lifting.

Rebecca turned, visibly annoyed. "Oh no. Not

now! Get rid of him George!"

"Get rid of him? He's my uncle. I can't just get rid of him!"

The knock came again, louder this time.

"He's trouble, George. I bet he's come to fetch you to one of his meetings. There's a big one tonight. Send him away!"

George huffed. He was already by the door. Shaking his head, he slipped outside, taking care to pull it to, behind him.

Old Tommy stood with his back to the cottage looking down into the village, leaning on his stick. He turned at the sound of the door unlatching and smiled at the sight of his nephew.

"Uncle! Good to see you! You look well," George beamed back. Old Tommy threw his arms wide and the two men embraced.

"And you too, young George, my lad!"

Tommy paused, and looked nervously back at the cottage. George caught his eye.

"What is it, Uncle?"

Tommy spoke in a hushed tone. "Is the door closed?"

George nodded. "Go on…"

"Well, I've not seen you at our meetings lately George. We need you -"

George sighed. "You know what Rebecca thinks of all this -"

Tommy held up his hand, George fell silent. "You need to tell her that we meet to plan for a better future for our community. We meet so that the children of the working man no longer lie crying in their beds from hunger."

"I do Uncle, I do. But she fears the worst – that

we will all be arrested or even gaoled!"

Tommy smiled. "Well, you can tell her that soon she need not fear anything," he fixed George's gaze. "You *must* come to tonight's meeting," he implored. "Your family's future – in fact, the future of all England depends on it. I told you it would come one day and now that time is here!"

"Surely not? An uprising?" George looked visibly stunned.

"The very same... I will explain tonight, but we will need every man we can. I was in Yorkshire this past week and a delegate from London brought us the news."

George looked reticent. "I don't know -"

"For your children! Don't let them down. We meet at ten tonight. Asherfield's barn. Please George..."

The moment of silence seemed to last forever. Old Tommy's gaze did not falter. Eventually George conceded.

"I will try."

That was all the old man wanted to hear. He knew his nephew very well. "Good," he smiled, "I hope to see you later. Now, I must be on my way. I need to round up as many men as I can. You won't regret this, George. I promise." Old Tommy patted George's shoulder. "Asherfield's barn. At ten," he reminded him. And with that, he turned and left.

George watched him go, his head spinning. Could this really be it? His heart was racing. Rebecca. This would not be received well. But if this truly was happening...

He turned, resolute and headed back to the cottage, just as the tatty net curtain that veiled his front window dropped hurriedly.

George slipped back inside the cottage and closed the door. Rebecca eyed him suspiciously. "He asked you to go tonight, didn't he?"

"Aye, he did," he said defiantly.

"Please tell me, for the love of God, that you're not going."

"I am." He avoided eye contact, but somehow he could still feel her eyes burning a hole in him. Eventually she broke the almost unbearable silence with a long sigh of disdain.

"George. You know how I feel about this. Every day men in these groups are arrested," she was clearly on the edge of exploding. "We could not survive without what you bring in. And we barely manage on that, truth be told."

"But this could change all that - " he began, but that was trigger enough.

"How will it change, George?! Tell me that!" Rebecca barked.

George decided it was now or never. "Because we're going to bring down the Government! That's how!" he snapped. Rebecca was visibly shocked. Whatever it was she thought Uncle Tommy's group was up to, it almost certainly wasn't this.

"What? No! This is ridiculous George! You'll hang for this! Think of the children!"

"I *am* thinking of the children!" he retorted. "I don't want them to spend their lives scraping a living like we do! This is our chance to change all that. This is what I believe in. Equality for all men. Distribution of wealth. An end to this miserable existence! It happened in France. It happened in the Americas and we're going to make it happen here!"

"Smashing looms is one thing, George, but

what you're talking about is treason!"

George was furious. "I should not be taking this from a woman. No man's wife should ever speak out of turn in this way! How dare you?"

"I dare because I love you, George! And if you loved me, you wouldn't do this!" Rebecca was hysterical. And clearly terrified.

George refused to engage. "I've had enough! I'm going to the White Horse," he snapped, but Rebecca was not ready to back down.

"No George! You're not to go!" she shouted, stepping in front of the door to bar his exit.

George lost his temper. "Out of my way! I am master of this house, not you!" Brutally he seized her by the shoulders. Rebecca barely had chance to gasp in pain before he angrily tossed her aside, as if she were a rag doll. She crashed into the dining table, taking the full force of its hard edge in her diaphragm. Crockery and utensils scattered everywhere as she stumbled, unable to breathe, before crumpling to the flagstones. The front door slammed. She lay awkwardly for a moment, white with shock and her lungs a vacuum. She croaked a couple of times before the air rushed back into her chest. It was only then she began to sob, silently at first, but eventually she found her voice and wailed "You'll hang for this, George! You'll hang!"

But he was gone. Gathering herself together, she was suddenly aware there was a small figure watching her from the foot of the stairs.

"There was a noise, Mama. I woke up. I'm hungry!"

It was Joseph, their two and half year old son. She steadied herself for a moment and then stood, trying to hide the pain.

"It's alright Joseph. I just tripped. A loose stone on the hearth my love. I... I didn't see it. Papa will fix it in the morning. Now, let's get you back into bed before you wake your brother and sister…"

Pentrich – England's Last Uprising

3. Comrades in Conspiracy

Still raw from his altercation with Rebecca, George flung open the door of the White Horse Inn. He made straight for the bar, cutting through the thick haze of pipe smoke like a knife through butter. The pub was his home from home. He often helped out behind the bar - his mother, whom everybody knew as Nanny Weightman, was the landlady. The comfortable surroundings immediately diluted his rage, but he was still shaking by the time his mother handed him his first mug of beer.

A well-proportioned woman in her mid-forties, Nanny Weightman could read her son like a book. If she could actually read, that is. She was also wise enough to know when to let sleeping dogs lie. She continued to serve ale and joke with the numerous patrons for a few minutes, while keeping one eye on her son, waiting for the right moment. George had gulped back almost the whole mug before she spoke to him directly.

"What's up, George, lad?" she queried quietly, wiping down the counter with an ale stained bar towel. George himself wasn't even sure. By the time he'd arrived at the pub he was angrier with himself than he was with his wife. He shrugged. He felt out of sorts. Guilty.

"Just need a bit of Dutch courage I 'spose, Nanny." He called her Nanny, even though she was his mother, just like all her customers did. It somehow seemed the natural thing to do. She raised an eyebrow.

"Going to the meeting then?" she asked, wryly.

"Aye, that I am," George said, banging his empty mug down on the bar. "Lookin' forward to it an' all."

"Big one tonight, in't it?" she smiled knowingly.

"That it is, Nanny. That it is," he said pushing the mug towards his mother. She smiled.

"How's about a bit a' summat stronger lad? You'll need hairs on your chest tonight, I reckon." She handed him a shot of whisky.

George smiled.

"How's about a chaser an' all?" he asked cheekily. Nanny rolled her eyes and poured him another mug of ale.

"You'll have to get a spurt on though, lad. They'll be startin' soon enough. Make sure you get yourself a good spot."

George nodded, knocking the shot straight back.

"Bet Becky was none too pleased, though, eh?"

George was silent. He wiped his mouth and reached for the second ale. "George?"

He shook his head "No. She weren't Nanny,

truth be told," he said. "She doesn't understand. She thinks we're foolish."

Nanny Weightman nodded. "Let's hope she's proved wrong, eh? She'll come round in time, George. She just doesn't want to lose you. So you need to be careful. And resolute. And strong. And determined. I believe in you. In all of you. And what you stand for. So will she. You need her on side." She gently touched the back of his hand.

George nodded, and raised his mug. Nanny continued serving. He sat pensively for a few moments, idly turning the mug in his hand and eyeing the dregs in the bottom. In that moment, his mind was made up.

"For England," he said, raising his tankard for one last swig - "And all who toil for her!"

Nanny smiled. "On your way, George! Before they start without you!"

"Right you are, Nanny!" he grinned. And with that he headed off into the night, his belly full of beer and his heart full of optimism.

Hoping for a good turnout, George made his way to the outskirts of the village where Asherfield's farm stood. The barn the reformists were due to meet in was at the top of a hill, hidden by an orchard of apple trees. He slipped through the gate at the bottom of the field and strode purposefully between the trees rather than following the cart track directly, just in case. He was hoping for a good turnout, but had not anticipated what lay on the other side of the weather beaten barn doors that he arrived at. Flickering lamp light from within spilled out onto the ground from underneath them, the only indication that something was afoot inside.

Gingerly he stepped inside.

It took a few moments for his eyes to adjust. The dimly lit makeshift meeting hall was crammed with the local disaffected. Men of all ages, their faces painted with anticipation, sat on hay bales arranged about the place in the style of an amphitheatre.

The ones towards the rear of the barn were stacked several bales high in order that the men at the back could view the proceedings as well as those at the front. The centre of the barn sported a roughly circular clearing with a single wooden bench table acting as the room's focal point. On it were various maps and papers. George's eyes darted excitedly around the crowd as they adjusted to the lighting. He picked out many familiar faces – Isaac Ludlam and William Turner, (local stone masons both), his older brother Bill, William's brother James, Uncle Tommy talking to his brother John. The place was alive with chatter as framework knitters, farm labourers, miners, wood workers and foundry workers mingled with one another, waiting for the meeting to start.

It seemed like every vocation of the working man was represented. Everywhere George looked, men he knew conversed with men he didn't. Clearly a lot of people had travelled a long way to be here. George felt a momentary twinge of shame that he'd actually considered abstaining when Uncle Tommy had asked him earlier. It was more than in his interest to be part of this group. As a working man, it was his duty.

Old Tommy spotted his nephew and

immediately made a beeline towards him, beaming from ear to ear.

"George! I knew you'd come. Good lad! As you can see, word has travelled far. We have men here from Wingfield, Alfreton, Swanwick, Butterley – even Heanor! You see?" He gestured round the busy barn. "We all believe in the cause! Now, if you'll excuse me, I think just about everyone is here now, so I'll make a start!"

George patted his Uncle heartily on the back. "Of course, Uncle," he grinned.

Old Tommy took his place in the centre of the barn. After a few moments composing himself, he struck his walking stick dramatically on the table several times in order to get everyone's attention. The congregation grew hushed. The atmosphere was tense with excitement. Expectation was high. Tommy Bacon deliberately waited a few seconds, drinking it all in, before he finally spoke.

"Gentlemen. Welcome, all of you, it is most encouraging to see so many new faces. Many of you know me already, but glancing round, a great deal present do not. So I will introduce myself. My name is Thomas Bacon, born and bred of Pentrich, but I have spent many years travelling the country promoting government reform and equality amongst men. A founder of the Ripley Hampden club, I have chaired reformist discussions for more years than I care to remember. Some of our long standing members are cynical about the growth of our numbers tonight, believing you have attended due to rumours of recent developments that may favour our cause. But if we are to succeed, we need as many willing men as possible and I do not care whether you join us today, or whether you were at my side when we took down looms in the name of General Ludd. I have a saying that I have carried with me for many years. The people should never fear of its government, *but the government should certainly fear of its people.*"

The room cheered. Old Tommy raised his hands to quiet his audience. "Well the time has come for me to replace the word 'should' with the word 'will'!" The cheer was even louder this time. He raised his hand once more. Again the barn fell silent, Old Tommy knew how to play a crowd. He'd been doing this for years and now his day had finally arrived.

"So, gentlemen, I will now inform you precisely why that is. As many of our members know, I've been attending reformist meetings up and down the country on your behalf for some time now. Recently, I met with our brothers in Wakefield, where they had a very special guest. A gentlemen reformer, from London, well connected in Parliament and a personal acquaintance of our champion in the House of Commons, Sir Frances Burdett," he paused, once again gazing round almost disbelieving the sheer volume of men gathered under one roof. He continued.

"His name is William Oliver. He has been travelling the land addressing our numbers wherever he can, bringing some very exciting news. And that is this; the London reformists are planning what we have all dreamed of for some time now. Yes my friends. An uprising, which they hope will be supported by reformists country wide!"

"You mean a revolution?" George looked to his left to see who had spoken. It was Charles Walters. A local labourer.

Bacon smiled. "The very same, Charles. The plan is that working men everywhere will join forces on a single night and march on London, where many more reformist supporters will be waiting to receive us. Then united as one, we will besiege Parliament and tear down the corruption that keeps the working man subservient to his wealthy masters!"

George, almost desperate to feel part of the group, spoke next, "And when might this be, Uncle?"

"Just over a month from now, if all goes to plan. I am waiting for confirmation of the exact date," Old Tommy replied.

"But that's way too soon, surely?" said another man who George did not recognise.

"From what Mr Oliver says, the south and London is all but ready, which is why he is travelling through the northern counties briefing as many groups as he can. I think we can be ready in time, if we make a decision to act tonight." Tommy responded, confidently.

"But there's no way we can be ready in that time!" It was Charles Walters again.

"Aye, it's surely impossible?" said another man.

The crowd murmured in agreement. George tensed, but his uncle seemed unperturbed.

"We need the element of surprise. The government has spies out, looking to infiltrate our numbers and stop what we're planning. I am already hearing whispers that I and other prominent reformists are on a list for arrest. If we spend too long talking in barns like this, they will gather all the intelligence they need to crush us outright. Trust me, we can organize a people's army in that time. I have

Oliver's word and we are more ready than you think. Isaac?"

He gestured to a tall man in his early fifties with grey hair stood to his right. George knew him to be Isaac Ludlam, a stone worker from nearby South Wingfield. He was often at these meetings and one of Uncle Tommy's right hand men.

"I've been collecting as many pikes together as possible," responded Ludlam, enthusiastically. "I have around thirty hidden up at 'quarry. I hope to have fifty in another few weeks."

"Pikes aren't going to stop the King's Army though, are they?" said George.

This time another Wingfield man spoke. "No, they won't. But that's why I've already started collecting firearms together." It was William Turner, a sharp, physical looking man in his mid-forties. Turner was a stone working colleague of Ludlam's and another of Tommy's inner circle. George knew him to be an ex-military man. "We already have about a dozen," he continued, "And I'm sure lots of you have summat at home you could contribute, such as an old flintlock or a rifle you use for shooting vermin." Many nodded. "And for them what's never used a gun, I'll teach you how to shoot properly – I was in Egypt fighting Napoleon, so there's not a great deal I don't know about guns – even if you've a broken one, bring it to me before the day - a bit of time in the forge an' I'll have it working. We won't all have guns, to begin with but there'll be enough to make us a threat."

This seemed to bring proceedings back on track. Old Tommy spotted this and wasted no time.

"Thanks Will, Isaac," he interjected. "Regarding weapons, I've an idea. Armed with what we've got so far, I say we take Butterley iron works en-route. They make rifles and shot. I've heard they even have a cannon left over from all that work they did for the navy." There was a further murmur of approval. "If necessary, we'll use force to take them. From there, the plan is to march on Nottingham and join their men, as well as the men of Yorkshire, Newcastle and Humberside. Our combined forces will then take Nottingham army barracks by surprise, overwhelming them with sheer numbers. The arms we seize there would then equip our army completely. London should fall in a matter of days."

George spoke up again. He was gaining confidence by the minute and feeling more like an integral member of the group. After all, Old Tommy was his Uncle.

"And you think the reformist movement can really bring change on this scale?" He was playing devil's advocate. Sensing that the room contained a large proportion of as-yet undecided fence sitters, George wanted to give his Uncle every opportunity to bring the whole barn on side.

"I do George. In fact, this sea change for direct action means that we are no longer 'reformists'. That word describes those who merely talk of change. From now on, we are 'regenerationists' – instigators of change! In years to come, the society we set out to build tonight will celebrate the day Parliament fell." Old Tommy turned and gestured round the room, theatrically. "And everyone here will be inscribed in history as a hero of working men the world over!" He paused. The audience was back in the palm of his hand.

"So. Gentlemen. Are we ready to change England forever?" There was a resounding chorus of 'yes'. Tommy Bacon shook his head. "Gentlemen, please. You're going to have to do much better than that." He looked at that floor in mock disgust. Then, winking at George he threw his hands up and bellowed "I said are we ready to change England forever?!"

The crowd went wild. Cheering, applauding. Mugs of ale clanked together. Those who were seated stood to clap. George smiled. His Uncle Tommy was nothing if not a showman. He knew how to work a crowd. Perhaps a career in politics was his destiny after all, he mused.

Already drunk on optimism, the hundred or so strong group adjourned to the White Horse, where most of them proceeded to get drunk on ale too. As they made their way into the centre of the village, George was nurturing another feeling within him. One of purpose. Of being somebody. He felt like he *belonged* with these men. Not wanting to have that feeling diluted by neither his wife nor sobriety, George joined in the revelry, well into the early hours of the following morning. The White Horse being an inn, and his mother being the landlady, meant that there was always a bunk upstairs somewhere that George could lay his head.

The newly named 'Regenerationists' met most evenings from then on. Their numbers grew steadily and Asherfield's barn became their base of operations. Word came from Oliver that the date had moved to the ninth of June. This allowed more time for the London force to get organised, but more importantly, it meant that the various groups could make use of the cover that a new moon would provide on that night.

As the days went by and the plans grew, George was swept up in the group's dreams of a nationwide political sea change. Most nights ended in the raising of a mug of ale or two, often more, in the name of the cause. As George fell deeper under the group's spell he returned to his marital bed less and less, shying away from the implications of what insurrection on that scale might actually entail for him and his comrades, should they fail. Implications that he knew all too well his wife Rebecca was very keen to remind him of. Uncle Tommy was acutely aware of this, and as one of the meetings drew to a close a week or so later, he stopped him on his way out of the barn.

"George, could you give me a hand with these maps?"

George was at the back of the now two-hundred strong exodus of men trying to leave the meeting, deep in conversation with William Turner. He turned at the sound of his name.

"Of course Uncle, I do apologise." He indicated to Will that he would join the rest of the men shortly. Will nodded and continued on his way.

The two men, uncle and nephew, rolled up the papers together in silence. After a minute or two, Tommy spoke.

"George, I just wanted to thank you for the part you've played in organising all this – getting people to come and keeping the peace when the arguments break out. You seem a natural peacekeeper and can always see both sides of the argument. That's a skill. And it requires courage too."

"Well, I believe passionately in our cause and I'm willing to listen to the opinion of any man who I think does so too, even if it's not my own," he shrugged.

"Yes. But it can't be easy for you. I know Rebecca does not approve of your involvement here. How is she?" There was an awkward silence. George sighed.

"Not good. I've been back a few times, but she won't listen. I'm staying at the inn, most nights, truth be told. She thinks we're headed for the gallows. She doesn't believe we can win. She doesn't understand what this is. It's like she can't see past the garden gate, sometimes -"

"Perhaps she fully understands what this is, George," Tommy interrupted.

"What do you mean?"

Tommy placed a hand on his nephew's shoulder. "She doesn't want to lose you. And you must not lose your family. Talk to her. Make amends. I need you, but I'll understand if you leave us now for the sake of your family. This is going to be hard. You will face unprecedented dangers on your campaign, but the rewards will be worth it." George opened his mouth to interject, but his Uncle held up his hand and shook his head. "Men will be ordered to stop you at any cost. That cost may be your life. If you cannot take the appropriate action, then you must not go. I'm talking about spilling blood in the name of freedom. Do you understand what that means, George?"

"Aye, Uncle, I do. The Lord God himself will give me the strength to do what is right," said George.

"I pray that is the case George, for all of us. If we succeed in creating the New Republic, I will see to it you are offered a key role. You might govern this parish."

George's eyes widened. "Surely that would be your place?"

"No... I'm too old to govern now, but I shall take a seat in London when we make a start. My place is there, making sure our Derbyshire folk are properly represented."

"But I'm no leader of men! Ludlam or Turner maybe –"

"You are the best judge of that. You might not be a leader, but you are an excellent adjudicator. As you so aptly point out, you always consider both sides of the argument. You must do so at home too. Listen to both sides of your quarrel. Think carefully what is the right course of action for you and your kin. Promise me you will do this George. Talk to Rebecca before you embark on your campaign."

George nodded. "I will. I promise. I admire you Uncle. More than any man I know. But why do you say *your* campaign?"

Old Tommy Bacon sighed heavily. Heaving a knapsack full of maps and papers onto his back he said bluntly, "I won't be marching with you, George."

"What? But you must -" George was shocked.

"Look at me George. I'm sixty four years old. I walk with a stick. A life of labouring has not been kind to me. I will slow you down. You need speed on your side."

"But you're easily as agile as some of the men! And you're our leader!"

Old Tommy's face looked pained. He glanced around the barn, cautiously. They were the only two men remaining now. "There is another reason," he began with a hushed tone, "I have received news that there *is* a warrant for my arrest. If they discover these gatherings, constables from Ripley will descend on Pentrich. We risk losing everything. I am a liability."

George nodded, reluctantly accepting the truth. "But what will you do?"

"I am going into hiding. Like the wily old fox to his den," he smiled, "the Curate of Saint Matthew's is a sympathiser."

"Wolstonholme?"

"Aye. He has somewhere that suits my needs. I cannot stay at home. They know where I live. But please, not a word to anyone."

George nodded. "Of course. But who will lead us? Ludlam? Turner? Turner has been a soldier -"

"Ludlam is too hot headed. He will act before he thinks. Turner has the training of a soldier, but one who follows orders, not gives them. No. I am going to Nottingham to find our captain. I know men who have led before, from our time smashing looms. He will also know the lie of Nottingham, the barracks, the canals and so forth. It will make for a smoother execution. This is why I need you in sound, decisive mind." He paused, becoming more solemn. "I need my peace keeper. It will be hard for the men to take instruction from a stranger. They will look to you for arbitration. So please settle your differences with Rebecca tomorrow, or tell me you are not going. After I've been to Nottingham, you will not see me again until London is taken. Do you understand?"

George was silent for a moment. "Are you sure this is the right course, Uncle?"

"Yes. Absolutely. So do you promise?"

"Aye. I will not let you down."

Tommy held out his hand for George. As the young sawyer went to take it, Tommy instead pulled him to his chest in a tight embrace. The two men laughed. Eventually, Tommy broke away.

"And don't forget, my brother John will be with you. He knows my mind and can speak on my behalf. Now go. Get some ale in you with the rest of the lads, stay at my sister's tonight and go to your family fresh in the morning. I am old and tired and all this plotting is wearing me out, so I'm going to get some sleep."

"Aye, Uncle. I will. Goodnight."

"Goodnight George. And good luck."

George saluted his uncle, who in turn saluted back with a grin. The newly appointed peacekeeper turned and headed out of the barn. Although he didn't know it now, the next time he would see his Uncle would be in the utmost terrible of circumstances.

4. A Spider Weaves a Web

At the very same moment some sixteen miles away in the town of Nottingham, similar events were drawing to a close in an attic room above The Three Salmons, a seedy looking tavern secreted half way up an alley off the town's main market square.

As a gathering of the town's own reformists began to discretely disperse downstairs and into the bar, their heads also now spinning with thoughts of revolution, a gentlemanly figure held back a moment. It was William Oliver and he had his eye on one particular member of the group who had not yet left the meeting.

He lit his pipe, watching the man like a hawk.

When finally his prey finished his drink, readying to leave with his few remaining colleagues, Oliver made his move.

"Sir – a word before you leave, if may?" he said, smiling, "It is Jeremiah Brandreth, is it not?"

The man turned. He was tall, unshaven and

swarthy looking with piercing green eyes and jet black hair. Like Oliver, he instantly stood out from the rest of the group, mainly due to the long, well-worn avocado coloured frock coat he was wearing. In his hands was an equally weathered matching derby hat.

"Aye that's me, alright, Mr Oliver." His voice commanded the same presence as his look. Oliver was unsure if Brandreth was eyeing him with suspicion or distaste, or both.

"Pleased to make your acquaintance," said Oliver enthusiastically, holding out his hand.

Brandreth paused just long enough to un-nerve Oliver, before grasping his hand as firmly as possible and shaking it hard. He then turned to the small group who were loitering by the door.

"Wait for me downstairs in the bar, lads. I'll not be a minute."

The men nodded and left. Brandreth waited until they had gone. "That was some speech you made tonight. Rousing, it were. Reckon it struck a chord with plenty here."

Oliver nodded. "I commend you sir - you were most vocal tonight and spoke favourably on my behalf. I wanted to thank you. I hope it has not put you at odds with Mr Stevens, your leader."

Brandreth smiled wryly. "William Stevens may speak well of taking up the fight, but he is a procrastinator of the highest order. He is also mistrusting, particularly when someone dressed as a gentleman tells us he is representing the working man".

"Mr Stevens must decide whether they are going to rise very soon. If he doesn't trust my intention, surely he trusts Bacon, and the Derbyshire men?"

"Aye, he does," said Brandreth, "but for him, they are not enough. He needs word from Sheffield, Leeds -"

"But I bring him that word -"

Brandreth cut Oliver short. "But that's all it is - your word," he was terse, on edge. "I believe what you say is true. The problem is, here, more than anywhere, the scars of Luddism are still fresh. Men were jailed or hanged for their part in it. But we failed through not enough direct action. It is the only language understood throughout history. The magistrate does not think twice about putting disaffected men in the noose. Good men, whose only crime is wanting a fair wage. If they can do that to us, then I have no qualm. They deserve the same! France did not achieve revolution with petitions. America was not liberated at the meeting table!" His eyes burned with anger.

Oliver was excited. If only he could somehow channel this. He held Jeremiah Brandreth's gaze for a moment, as if testing his resolve. Finally he spoke. "I agree sir. I got the impression you were very much a man of action – and that you have led men before."

"Aye. I've led men who smashed looms," nodded Brandreth, "and heads too! Hot tempered, Mr Stevens calls me. A loose cannon! So my word no longer carries weight in these meetings." He laughed. "Blood thirsty, they say! Yes, I want blood! But only because them in charge will happily spill ours!"

Oliver raised an eyebrow. "If Stevens is saying that Nottingham will only rise if Derbyshire lead, then perhaps you should seek out Bacon. He is often in attendance here, is he not?"

"Aye, he is. Why?"

"There's a warrant for his arrest. If he is captured beforehand, his men might be put off. And he is old – he walks with a stick, he is no man of action." Oliver paused, letting the idea germinate. "But you clearly are. Perhaps your services are better utilised within Bacon's army?"

"What, you mean as its lieutenant?"

The bait was taken. Oliver smiled slyly. "Or as its captain - they are ripe to take up arms, but need someone experienced. Someone not afraid to take direct action. Someone with resolve."

"Aye, then," Brandreth nodded keenly. "He's due here in a few days. If Nottingham won't make use of me, perhaps Derbyshire will?"

"I think," Oliver mused, "you might be just what they need. Now, if I may be excused, I must rest. I travel to Birmingham tomorrow, to see how the rising is going there."

"Where are you staying tonight?" Brandreth asked.

"The Blackamoor's Head. It is adequate for my needs."

"I know it well. If you are, shall we say, cold in the night, ask for Lizzy. She will keep you warm!"

The two men laughed.

"Good luck Sir. Now, if you'll excuse me, I promised the lads," said Brandreth, gesturing towards the stairs.

Oliver nodded. "Of course! And the same to you, my friend. Farewell!"

The two men shook hands enthusiastically. Brandreth donned his hat and was gone. Oliver smiled, surprised at just how easy that had been. He waited a moment or two, then made his way down the stairs himself. Instead of turning right and heading into the pub with the rest of the reformists, he turned left, slipping out of a side door and into adjoining alley way.

Oliver failed to notice a hooded figure was watching his exit from the cover of an archway on the opposite side of the rat run. He let Oliver get a few yards ahead of him, before peeling himself out of the shadows and hurrying after him.

"Psst!" the figure called out in a hushed tone.

Oliver whirled round defensively. "Who's there?" he hissed.

"Mr Oliver! It is I," the figure said, dropping his hood, "Lewis Allsop."

Oliver instantly recognised the slightly chubby, piggy eyed man he'd grown to despise since his arrival in Nottingham. "Mr Allsop! Are magistrates usually in the habit of lurking in the alleyways of their district at night?" Oliver was almost scolding in tone.

"No, sir we are not – in fact it makes me most uncomfortable in my role. I have been observing tonight's meeting with great interest. We must talk -"

Oliver sighed, looking visibly annoyed. "Very well, but not here. I cannot be seen with you. They are suspicious enough of me as it is. I am lodging at the Blackamoor's Head, so walk with me as I go." Oliver turned on his heel immediately, Allsop scampering to keep up.

"It is most unfortunate about Bacon. If we had known he was key to your plans then it could have been avoided," Allsop said, apologetically.

Oliver didn't even look at him. "No matter. It

is of no real consequence. If anything, it is serendipitous. I had my doubts about Bacon. He is a political leader, not an army captain. Plus, a well-respected old man who walks with a stick will garner sympathy. That I do not want. I just pray no-one is foolish enough to take him before our plans bear fruit. I expect the old weasel to take to his den after his next visit to Nottingham."

"I will do my best, Mr Oliver, but a bounty is a bounty -"

"Very well, just keep it low and hopefully the interest in him will remain the same." Oliver was terse.

"So Nottingham is still reticent?"

"They are too much like sheep – they bleat loudly in protest, but they will only move when they have someone to herd them. Derbyshire, on the other hand, are like kindling to a tinder box, so I will concentrate my 'bellows' there for now."

"But with their leader gone to ground and a mere fortnight to go, who will lead them? Have they someone with the appropriate characteristics to meet your requirement?" Allsop asked.

Oliver stopped and huffed. He turned to face the bothersome little man. "No, Mr Allsop, I believe they do not. But after tonight's proceedings, I think I have sown seeds that will provide me with the most perfectly volatile figure head I need for my mission's success. Now, if you'll excuse me, I have an early start in the morning, so I must bid you goodnight, Sir."

"Of course," Allsop fawned, "I'm sure we'll speak more on this matter soon enough, Mr Oliver. Goodnight."

But Oliver was already away into the night. He

grunted something. Allsop was unsure as to whether it was a farewell or an insult. He watched him retreating for a moment or two before turning and scurrying back towards the market square.

Pentrich Village, Derbyshire. Thursday June 5, 1817.

It was a gorgeous morning. Summer was making its first attempt at asserting itself over the hills of Derbyshire. Becky Weightman sat at the dining table, darning a child's pair of stockings. She could hear Mary and Joseph playing in the garden. Their youngest, George, a toddler of eighteen months was finally sleeping soundly upstairs after a fitful night of fever and chill. She made swift progress on the hole she was mending, knowing all too well as a mother of three that moments of tranquility were scarce and should never be wasted.

There was a squeak of hinges from the front gate and she looked up. Through the front window of the cottage, she could see George approaching in the glorious morning sun. For a split second her heart skipped. She scolded herself. It annoyed her that he still had such a hold on her. Still, she jumped up, brushed her petticoat down and tucked her loose hair behind her ear. She heard the door latch lift and George entered, looking a little sheepish. He looked at his wife silently for a moment closing the door with his back. She looked beautiful despite the fatigue in her eyes.

She felt his penetrating gaze and fought to compose herself.

"Becky -"

"You've remembered where you live, then? Though you won't be living here much longer. You'll be lodging with the scum of Derby gaol. Or worse." She wanted to run to the cottage door and embrace him, but her anger welled up and took charge.

"Please, Becky, I've come to talk." He said quietly.

She turned away from him, pretending to inspect her work.

"I'm busy, George. I have a family to keep. Your family, remember?"

"You look lovely today. A little tired but -"

"I am George. Tired of all this. I can't really take much more," her voice cracked. She paused to resolve herself. She was determined not to let him break her with just a look. "I'm not sleeping. I'm frightened. You've turned our world upside down. I don't understand you anymore. I lie awake wondering what will become of you – of us and the children. When I do fall asleep, I have nightmares of misery and destruction. Your destruction and our misery. And the misery of everyone involved in this folly."

She turned back and George was removing his already sweat drenched shirt. He reached for a clean one that hung on a nearby wooden clothes horse. He stepped forward, breaking the sunlight streaming through the window and Rebecca saw the beads of sweat on his chest glisten momentarily, like morning dew.

"He stopped, shirt in hand. Folly? This is the will of God, Rebecca. He created all men to be equal and we will not rest until Parliament recognise -"

"The will of God? How can tearing apart

families and attacking the government be the will of God? It's always been the same and always will – murder and violence is much easier when it's in the name of religion. Will of God! I suppose your Uncle told you that?" She was angry. Angry with him and with herself. Angry with how much she missed him and wanted him, despite everything. She felt bitter, frustrated. Her heart pounded as she wrestled with the confused emotions she was experiencing.

"No, it was Mr Oliver and we intend to kill no-one unless in defence," said George, firmly.

"Mr Oliver? Who is he?"

"A gentleman reformer from London. He brought us news of the rising and told us he needed us. He has travelled the country, rallying support. This is how we know we cannot fail. Over two hundred thousand men -"

"And you believe him?" she interrupted, "A complete stranger from London?"

"He is of status, but a good man. Men like him are too few in this country – he has concern for his fellow man, whatever his social standing. He is a man of truth and justice. We are fighting for your future – all our futures."

Rebecca shook her head. This infuriated George.

"You do not understand any of this, woman! I came today to help make you understand, but I was foolish to think you might - if only you could see beyond the end of the garden gate!"

Something inside her snapped. "Garden gate? You cannot see beyond yourself! Where do women figure in your New Republic, George? Are they equal to everyone in the eyes of God? Because you're treating me worse than you treat the dog and if this is how your precious Republic is going to be then I hope you fail!"

George stepped closer, tossing his shirt aside, his face like thunder. Becky instinctively took a step backwards. She felt the table press against the small of her back.

"You will regret this day!" barked George. "When we return victorious, I may govern Pentrich. Finally I'll have achieved something you can't criticise."

"Govern Pentrich?" she scoffed, "I suppose your Uncle promised you that before he disappeared down his bolt hole -"

"Enough!" exploded George, kicking her chair aside and sweeping her sewing basket off the table. Both clattered to the floor, the sewing basket spewing its contents over the flagstones. He grabbed her firmly by the wrists. Rebecca struggled, but the table, now forced back against the wall, prevented her escape. His face was inches from hers.

"Is that how you're going to bring down Parliament? With a tantrum?" she panted, patronisingly, "I might be scared of all this, but I'm not scared of you George Weightman and neither is the King, his government or his army!" She struggled again, but George tightened his grip. Her wrists burned.

"Not afraid? You should be girl. How dare you raise your voice to me! I am master in this house and don't you forget it!"

He pushed her down, pinning her against the table top.

"George! You're hurting me!" she panted. Her chest rose and fell rapidly as she struggled to breathe from the weight of his frame on top of her.

He stared at her, for a moment, like a man possessed. "I should teach you a lesson!" he hissed.

He let go of her wrists, placed one hand firmly on her shoulder and reaching down, began to hitch up her skirt with his free hand. Rebecca grabbed at his forearm, clawing desperately, but he held her fast. He was too powerful. His arm was rigid, the biceps locked taught. Impervious to her efforts, it was like the trunk of one of the trees he spent all day sawing. The very reason he was so strong in the first place.

She heard the clink of his belt buckle and then his free hand gripped the back of her thigh tightly. He pulled her down the table towards him, its rough surface grazing the soft skin of her back through her cotton under corset.

She hated him and wanted him in equal measures, it had been too long and she loved him with all her heart – but not like this. What was her husband turning into?

Blind panic set in and her survivalist instinct took over as she sank her teeth into his arm. George cried out in pain, relinquishing his grip, the gouges she had made in it already beginning to bleed. George's face swelled with renewed anger and he moved to pin her down again.

He didn't see the blow coming at all. With as much force as she could muster she brought her knees up and planted both feet squarely in his abdomen and pushed, knocking him off his feet.

George crashed to the floor, the impact finally snapping him out of his animal-like rage.

He momentarily studied his wounds before looking at her. Her chest heaved, her breathing still heavy. In that moment, George's face changed. He felt - what? He wasn't sure. Guilt? Surprise? Shock? He looked away for a moment. Silence. Rebecca just lay there, not knowing what to do.

When he spoke, there was an odd tone of something like disgust in his voice. "I must go. I'm needed. We're meeting this lunchtime. At the White Horse."

"George..." Rebecca's voice was cracked, sorrowful. "Please. I beg of you." He pretended not to hear. "For the sake of our children... For the sake of *us*, do not go through with this!" She steadied herself with her elbows. Shaking, she slid off the table.

He couldn't look at her. "It is my duty. For the working men of this country and my children."

"But what about us, George?" She went to grab his arm, but he recoiled. She tried again and this time he pushed her away.

"No!" he snapped. "Don't you understand, woman? It's my duty. We'll change England forever -"

Anger welled up inside her. What ungodly force had taken possession of the man she loved? What could be more important to him than her and their children? The anger was quickly joined by a seething jealously.

"Go then! Go on! Go! And never ever come back! Do you know how they'll punish us if you fail? You will all hang and they will tear down whole villages. The families of the men involved will be sent to the workhouse. I cannot let that happen to us George! I want this whole business out of our lives and if that means you must go too, then so be it -"

She got no further. In that instant, George's

palm exploded across the right side of her face with such force that she found herself face down on the floor. She yelped in pain, clutching her cheek. George backed away from her, a look of total horror in his eyes. Rebecca put her hand to her face, the skin of her cheek searing. She gasped in shock. There was a loud slam of the front door. She looked up, but he was gone.

Rebecca sobbed hysterically. "George! Please! You'll hang! For pity's sake, think of the children!" When at last she could stand and open the front door, her face stinging as tears ran down the rapidly swelling welt on her face, George was nowhere to be seen.

As dusk gave way to night, George made his way up the now familiar path to Asherfield's barn. It had only been a few weeks since he'd surreptitiously made his way to that first meeting alone, but things were very different now. He was part of a growing throng of local men that made the nightly pilgrimage to the place that had become a temple of hope, freedom and change. The sound of optimism filled the air as men chatted and joked all around him. A party of fellow agitators overtook him and one of his comrades recognised George, slapping him on the back. George smiled and nodded as best he could, but the events of that morning were still troubling him deeply. But Rebecca had left him no choice. These men – Uncle Tommy – the working men of England – they needed him. He had to go. She would eventually understand. When they finally triumphed over the tyranny that held court over this land and returned home as heroes - then it would be different. She would finally be proud of him. He felt sickened by what had happened, but he also burned with anger when he pictured the look of contempt on his wife's face, the sarcasm in her voice as she ridiculed him in his own home. He paused at the barn door and let out a deep sigh, desperately trying to bury his confused thoughts and feelings. It was mere days now to the uprising. He needed to be calm. Clear headed. He thought of England. Of freedom. He looked back down the hill. Dozens of men were still streaming towards the meeting from all sides of the village. This was it. He nodded to himself. He was ready for anything.

Or so he thought. He didn't know it, but he was about to meet the man who would change everything. The man he and his comrades would come to call the Nottingham Captain. The man who tonight would swear to lead them through the fires of hell to the promised land.

That man was Jeremiah Brandreth.

5. The Nottingham Captain
Asherfield's Barn, Pentrich. Thursday July 5, 9pm.

George slipped inside the barn and was astonished by the sight that greeted him. The place was packed to the rafters. Everywhere he looked he saw the faces of the disaffected, wide eyed and giddy with anticipation. He immediately identified the man he knew was arriving tonight.

He stood with his back to the ever swelling crowd, chatting to George's fellow lead conspirators, Isaac Ludlam and William Turner - but he was unmistakable. His green frock coat and derby hat made it immediately apparent that he was by far the most colourful and charismatic man in the room. George heard the three of them belly laugh as he approached.

Will caught sight of George as he approached and he held out his hand. George shook it vigorously and then patted Will on the back. He immediately did the same with Ludlam. Brandreth watched in silence. Will gestured toward the flamboyant stranger.

"George, this is Jerry Brandreth!" he exclaimed

"The new captain from Nottingham," interjected Isaac, "just as your Uncle Tommy promised."

George held out his hand to Jeremiah. The stranger turned to face him, but did not offer his back. Instead he glanced between Will and Isaac giving them both a wry smile. It was like he was gauging their reaction. George immediately felt uncomfortable. Will gave Jerry an encouraging nod.

Isaac broke the awkward silence first. "This is George Weightman. Old Tommy's nephew."

Brandreth continued to look George up and down. Then he nodded. "Then the pleasure is mine, George. Tommy is a great man. I trust you will fight our war in his name?" Without warning he suddenly gripped George's hand and shook it enthusiastically. His voice was rich, commanding and brooding. George felt his eyes were piercing his very soul. Something about Brandreth made him feel uncomfortable, but he couldn't quite decide what.

"War?" George quizzed, frowning.

"Why, yes. A war of freedom. A war of rights. But nonetheless a war, alright. We mustn't think of this as a march, or a protest, or even a rising, George. Victories are won in the mind." Brandreth tapped the side of his head with his finger and leaned in. He was a mere inch from George's face. His gaze did not flinch. "If we are of a mind that this is a war then our campaign will be much more likely successful," he whispered, "these men will only deliver what I want of them if they have this in mind. This is my experience. Do you understand, George?"

George broke his gaze to momentarily look at first Will and then Isaac. Both nodded.

"Yes. Of course," he conceded.

"Good. That's what I need. Men who have fight in them. Men I can count on. And if you're anything like your uncle, you're every bit a fighter, eh?" Brandreth's steely gaze suddenly cracked into a smile. Without warning he slapped George hard on the back. Loudly, as if he was already addressing his audience, he bellowed "Now! We have a great deal to discuss, so if you'll introduce me to my army, George, we can begin!"

The buzzing barn fell silent.

"Me?" said George, "Now?"

"Of course lad," Brandreth continued, theatrically. "Now is as good a time as any! England, our prize is waiting!" he threw his arms wide. The room cheered. Brandreth let forth a huge belly laugh. He was quickly joined by Will and Isaac. Slightly perplexed, George stepped into the natural ring that had formed in the centre of the barn.

"Gentlemen," he began awkwardly, "as some of you may know, my Uncle – 'Old Tommy' has gone into hiding due to a warrant for his arrest." The crowd murmured its disapproval at the news. George, feeling more confident they were on his side, continued. "He fears that, as a wanted man, he jeopardises our chances of success. But knowing this, he risked everything for his Derbyshire kin and fetched us a new leader – from Nottingham. He is an experienced leader of men in matters like this and we are, I'm sure, in good hands. Gentlemen, I give you our Nottingham Captain. Jeremiah Brandreth!"

The room applauded. Brandreth took centre

stage, gesturing for quiet. The darkened lamp-lit space fell silent.

"Thanks lads. It warms me to hear such a welcome. Now, I'm sure you are wondering, why did Old Tommy pick me? Why not one of you Derbyshire men? Well he didn't. I picked him! Tommy came to Nottingham looking for someone who had led men before, but more importantly, knew the lie of the land – especially the canals and army barracks. Taking the barracks is key to our success. And I can make that happen. I have led many battles smashing looms - and their rich owners! When Old Tommy learned this, he knew I was the man for the job. Because I will show no mercy." He paused, looking directly into the eyes of as many men as he could. "Harsh words you think? Well ask yourself this - do they show us mercy? No! Because when we shout for a fair wage and working conditions we are shown the noose! Many of my comrades from those days – good honest working men - went to the gallows. But this time brothers, the tables will be turned and *we* will be doing the hanging!"

The room erupted with applause. Once again, Brandreth gestured for quiet. He quickly had it. "Because this is a war gentlemen. Of the rich against the poor. The haves against the have-nots. The workshy against the workers. They seek to control us - with machines in their mills and fear for our jobs. But the time has come, when we will control *them*. With fear of this!"

With that, Jeremiah Brandreth threw open the tails of his long flowing coat, as if he was the ringmaster of some circus, revealing two flintlock pistols jammed into each side of his waistband. The audience cheered wildly.

"And we have more where these came from, lads!" he cried above the din, "plus we'll be collecting plenty along the way! I have a list, from Mr Turner here, of who owns firearms in this area and we shall be collecting them in the name of freedom. In fact, any man who is not here that lives in this district will be asked to join us. It is his duty to do so. We will knock on every man's door and if he will not come, we will take what weapons he has, in the name of the cause!"

George watched in astonished silence. The crowd was frenzied. Almost baying for blood. Brandreth was truly a leader and a man of action. He had been speaking for only a few minutes and he had something close to three hundred men eating out the palm of his hand. He continued, with a beaming grin on his face, clearly loving the attention. "And Mr Ludlam here has some sixty pikes made for the job, hidden in his quarry. But this is only the beginning. Bring what you can find – forks, scythes – anything. We will be trading these for real weapons - first when we take the iron works at Butterley and second when we take the real prize - the army barracks in Nottingham. They will not know what's coming, brothers, when we take every rifle, pistol and sword they have, making us a true army of the working man!" Shouts of approval echoed around the barn. "And you can believe me when I say London will be next! So let us raise our pitchers and toast our victory!" The gathering duly obliged. Brandreth grabbed a tankard from the nearby table and raised it aloft, commandingly. He then upended the vessel at arm's height, pouring the remaining contents into his wide open mouth. Most of it seemed to find its way down the front of his shirt rather than into his stomach, but it mattered not. The rebels gathered around him, hoisting him into the air. He tossed the cup aside. The atmosphere was electric. George looked at Will, who nodded enthusiastically. He smiled back and then took his place in the revelry. Yes. They had found their leader. How could they possibly fail with this man at the helm?

The celebrations ran on into the early hours. When the men had drained the last drop of ale in the barn, they made for the White Horse. Invigorated with new found passion, they rowdily downed more ale and sang songs of the new British Republic. The Pentrich Regenerators really were baying for their government's blood now. Exactly how Brandreth needed them to be. In fact, most were sure they could already smell it. How could they possibly lose now? In just a few days they were to join forces with thousands of like-minded men marching towards London. Soon England would be theirs.

George, Isaac, Will and their new captain met every day from then on, procuring a room at the White Horse. They made it their war room. Brandreth organised daily reconnaissance, sending men on horseback to neighbouring towns. They returned with information from their markets and taverns – he was interested in what the local gossip grapevine and rumour mongers knew of the Regenerationist's plans and more importantly, whether the local authorities knew about them too. Idle chatter in the wrong ears could prove fatal to the group's plans. They quickly learned that nearby Ripley's magistrate had heard talk of rioting and was swearing in dozens of extra 'constables' for the weekend – hired hands paid to hit first and ask questions later. The four conspirators adjusted their planned route accordingly – a large altercation so early in the campaign could seriously slow their progress as well as affect the men's spirits if it didn't go well.

Their last planning session was scheduled for Sunday afternoon – the eve before the campaign. This would allow time for a messenger to be dispatched to, and return from, Nottingham. It would be the last check that their Nottinghamshire comrades were ready and would rise when the men of Pentrich did. Throughout the day, members of their organisation were summoned in groups. Brandreth addressed them, campaign map spread out on the table. He painstakingly walked them through the route and what resistance they were likely to meet along the way and how they would tackle it. Spoken with an almost steely authority, he explained precisely what he expected from each member of *his* army.

He was clearly assessing each man's commitment and understanding of the plan. Calculating throughout, he seemed to stare into each individual man's soul with his piercing eyes. It was an exhausting process for the four ringleaders that took up most of the afternoon and evening. Finally, as the last group left, he rolled up his map and papers, lit his clay pipe and sank into a chair. Blowing out a large cloud of smoke he turned to George and said "We are ready. Fetch me an ale, lad."

George obliged. A minute or two later, he returned from the bar room with a full tankard.

Brandreth began to sink its frothy contents eagerly.

"Thank the Lord that's over. Damn near took all day, Jerry" said George. Brandreth remained silent.

"George is right. Was it absolutely necessary to speak to every man who has sworn allegiance individually?" queried Will.

Still Jeremiah remained silent. When he eventually finished his beer, he raised his eyebrows at his three cohorts, almost in exasperation.

"Well?" it was Isaac's turn to voice his doubts about the necessity of the afternoon's exercise.

"It was essential," snapped Brandreth, almost cutting him off. "I must know the resolve of every man in our group and be sure that when action is required I can deploy the appropriate soldier knowing he is capable of carrying out the orders of his captain. One man's hesitation could cost us the success of the campaign."

"Really?" George sat down opposite Brandreth, who now had his feet up on the table. "It seemed like you were trying to frighten them into following you from where I was sitting. They're all good men, Jerry. Otherwise they wouldn't be here -"

Brandreth leant forward, his face uncomfortably close to George's. George got the distinct impression that he liked nothing more than to make those around him feel uncomfortable.

"That's as may be, but I need strength of character and there's nothing wrong with testing that with a stare and some strong words." As if to demonstrate this, he paused holding George's gaze. Then he laughed one of his now familiar belly laughs, which made George feel patronised, somehow. "Besides," he continued, "a garrison *should* fear its captain, not question him. A healthy fear will breed respect and obedience, isn't that how it works in the army, Will?"

"Aye Jerry, it is," concurred Will.

"Puts a bit of wind in their sails, is all." Brandreth said, still fixing his gaze firmly on George.

"As long as it doesn't put the 'wind' up them," George said, calmly. Brandreth's face switched. He looked broody, predatory somehow.

"Perhaps I should have interviewed you, George? You seem to be the only one here who continuously questions my methods. Do you doubt me?" George remained stony faced. "Well? We can't tolerate descent in the ranks at this stage in the proceedings." Brandreth suddenly turned towards Ludlam and Turner. "Isn't that right, lads?" he beamed. The two men nodded.

"I agree, Jerry. But it's just that my Uncle Tommy said -" began George, but Brandreth held up his hand.

"Yes, yes. We know. Listen. Old Tommy needn't worry and neither should you. I promise you. All three of you. You can trust in Jerry Brandreth to lead us to victory. Isn't that so?" he looked again to Will and Isaac. They both nodded once again.

"Yes," said George, "I have every faith in you. I'm just concerned for the men, that's all."

"Quite right, lad, quite right. Now, we've worked hard all afternoon. What say we all have a drink? A toast to victory."

All three men nodded at Jeremiah's suggestion.

George rose to fetch more ale. At the door he turned round.

"So what happens now?" he asked.

"We enjoy our last evening as ordinary men. Savour it George," he gestured grandly, spreading his arms, "because come the morrow, our meagre lives will be changed forever!" All four men laughed.

"A toast it is, then!" proclaimed George, disappearing from the room.

Jeremiah Brandreth had never been more right. The four men's lives were about to change forever. But not one of them could have predicted just how catastrophic that change would truly be.

6. The Night of the Rising
Hunt's Barn. South Wingfield. Monday, June 9, 1817. 10pm.

The night of the rising had finally arrived. By now, the volume of rebels that represented Derbyshire had swollen to such numbers that they could no longer meet in Asherfield's barn in Pentrich. So they had chosen instead to commence proceedings from much larger premises, a barn belonging to a farmer named Sam Hunt in the neighbouring village of South Wingfield.

As the sun had set an hour and a half earlier, a foreboding looking blanket of storm clouds had drawn a veil over what ought to have been a warm, starry, moonless summer night. An agitated wind tugged at the trees that shrouded the rebel's hilltop rendezvous site.

As several hundred men filed inside, each one was handed a large wooden pike from a pile at the door by either Will or Isaac. George stood just inside, greeting each one and thanking them for turning out, while trying to keep a mental note of their numbers. Outwardly he appeared jovial, excited even, but inside he was tired and oddly fearful. He had not slept well the night before. A combination of trepidation and arguably too much ale at the hands of Will Turner, Isaac Ludlam and Jeremiah Brandreth. On top of that, he had found yesterday's 'interrogations' led by Brandreth a draining exercise. Furthermore, something about Brandreth's demeanour that afternoon had left him feeling disturbed. It had bothered him all day, while he'd been helping his mother out with bar duties at the White Horse. It was almost like, as the day of the rising drew nearer, Jeremiah had become more frenzied. Volatile. Unpredictable even.

"You alright, George?" Isaac asked, catching George off-guard.

"Mmm?" George was suddenly aware he was staring into space again.

"I said are you alright?"

"Yes. Yes, I'm fine, Isaac. Just a bit worried about these clouds we've got coming over. I fear it might rain."

"Yes. But we should also be grateful of the extra cover. Wi' no stars out we'll be even harder to see. Perfect for when we take the ironworks at Butterley. Or the barracks in Nottingham, for that matter."

"Isaac's right," interjected Will. "The cover from the cloud will make both our attacks much more likely to succeed. Hopefully, neither of those places will know what's hit 'em. Black as coal, it'll be."

"I suppose. I think it's already started to drizzle over Belper way, judging by the sky. 'Spect it's coming this way an' all," George nodded in the direction of the town, which lay some six miles to the south.

Barely had he finished his sentence, when he felt a spot of rain hit the back of his hand. He glanced skywards. The clouds that shrouded what should have been a beautiful summer firmament looked inky black and angry. Another spot fell this time on George's head. "Please God, no," he mumbled.

"Right you two!" It was Will. "Looks like most of who's coming are here now. Jerry's keen to get cracking and it's after ten now, so any latecomers can let themselves in. Let's get these doors shut so we can make a start."

Isaac and George nodded. They heaved the large double doors closed between them and weaved their way through the crowd to the centre of the makeshift theatre.

The far end of the barn had a wooden stair case that led to an upstairs grain store. As instructed George and Isaac took their places at the bottom of it. Will made his way up the stairs. Jeremiah was nowhere to be seen – he wanted his entrance to make maximum impact on the rebels and had therefore secreted himself at the back of the upstairs section, preparing the speech that would begin the campaign.

George looked round the audience. Easily over two hundred, most of them had pikes or failing that, farming utensils that could act as a makeshift weapon in the hands of someone with the right inclination. Around twenty of the men had firearms – a mixture of old pistols and farmer's shotguns. He prayed it was enough of a show of strength to see off any opposition they might encounter on the way to Butterley. At least once there they would hopefully be able to swap their sticks and tools for something more substantial. There was a definite buzz of anticipation. The room's atmosphere was further thickened by pipe smoke now the doors were closed.

Suddenly, without any announcement, the door to the upstairs store room was flung open noisily. Jeremiah Brandreth stood at the top of the stairs. The sound of the door banging loudly had the desired effect. The room fell silent. He surveyed his army silently for a moment or two. Along with his signature green frock coat, he wore his framework knitter's apron about his waist – no doubt a symbol of his working man status.

Theatrically, Brandreth threw his coat tails behind him to reveal the second purpose of his apron – it was a makeshift gun belt. Stuffed into the apron's waistband were two hand pistols. He drew both weapons and held them defiantly aloft as he slowly made his way down the wooden staircase.

All eyes were on him. He stopped again, about five or six steps from ground level and began to address his men, as if from a podium.

"Working men of Derbyshire! Are we ready?"

A resounding cry of "Yes!" went up from the barn floor.

"To take on the King's government?"

"*Yes!*"

"And stop at nothing until Parliament is in our hands?"

"*Yes!*"

Brandreth paused just long enough to ratchet up the tension one notch higher. "I have long awaited this day," he said nodding purposefully, "I expect every man to do his duty and stop at nothing 'til we achieve our objective. So are you with me lads?"

"*Yes!*" the cry came again.

"Because you are either with us, or against us! And if any man shows he is against us, then I for one have no problem with blowing his bloody brains out!"

The crowd roared with excitement. Those who had weapons held them aloft.

"Excellent! Then cry havoc and let slip the dogs of war!" he bellowed and marched down the rest of the stairs towards the main doors, the crowd parting for him as he went. He stopped by the barn's entrance and turned back towards his audience, waiting for Isaac and Will to catch up and swing the barn doors open in the pre-planned manner.

"To Pentrich!" he shouted, wielding his pistols aloft once more. The audience cheered raucously. "Then Butterley!" An even louder cheer this time. "And on to Nottingham! Where we will change the history of England forever!" The sound of approval from his ragtag battalion was almost rapturous. At that moment, Isaac and Will threw the barn doors as wide as they would go. The crowd surged, but Brandreth shoved his pistols back into his waistband and held up both hands, gesturing for them to stop.

"Wait!" The congregation instantly did as they were told. "I need every last one of you to follow my orders to the letter. I need each and every last one of you to do your duty to your fellow working man and to England. Is that clear?"

Once again, the crowd affirmed their allegiance. Brandreth grinned. "Good. Because out there is a battlefield. This is a war. There will be casualties. On both sides. But through your strength, your resolve and your dedication we *will* win. You must be strong. You must be courageous. This is the most important thing you will ever do in your lives. You will go down in history. Your children and your children's children will talk about the events of the coming days with pride in their heart because you gave them *this*!" Brandreth gestured to the countryside that lay outside the barn doors. "England awaits!"

His troops cheered loudly as he turned and began striding down the hill, his army spilling out of the barn in his wake.

Will and Isaac flanked the barn doors, holding them ajar as several hundred men filed out. George eventually appeared, somewhere near the back of throng. Will caught his eye.

"How about this, George? We are finally making history my friend!" George stopped and nodded. He seemed a little distant somehow – pensive.

"Uncle Tommy says history is written by the winners," he said calmly. Isaac suddenly slapped him squarely on the back.

"Well, we'd better win then, eh? I for one am ready for victory!" he cried over the noise of two hundred cheering men.

George nodded. "Well we can definitely expect an engagement at some point tonight if Jeremiah Brandreth has his way -"

"Aye, and we shall give them hell!" cried Will, hoisting his old army pistol aloft. Both he and Isaac bellowed with laughter as they took their place in the surging mass heading towards the centre of South Wingfield village.

George collected up the last remaining pike. He paused a moment, gauging the weight of it in his hand. It felt... unfamiliar somehow. He was a well-built man. He wielded a woodman's axe and used large bow saws daily without a second thought. Both of those tools equally deadly if used with such intent. But now it was dawning on him that he was *armed*. With a weapon. A weapon that he would, should the situation arise, be required to use in order to defend himself. Possibly even take someone's life. He hadn't really thought about that possibility becoming a reality until now. And judging by the way his colleagues were already half frenzied before they'd even started their campaign, that would likely be sooner rather than later. Jeremiah Brandreth's words echoed around his head. "Out there is a battlefield. This is a war. There will be casualties. On both sides..."

"George!" His brooding was broken by a cry from Will Turner. He looked up. Will had stopped and was beckoning at George to catch the rest of the men up. "Come on, man! It'll have to do for now! I'm sure we'll get you something with a lot more *'oomph'* once we get to Butterley!" he mocked. George nodded and smiled, albeit somewhat hollowly. With a deep breath, he strode off after his colleagues.

It wasn't long before the Nottingham Captain called his rebel garrison to a halt. They'd arrived at the small square that was the centre of South Wingfield village. It was now spotting with rain.

"Hold here, lads!" he commanded. Will appeared immediately by his side. The two exchanged a brief whispered conversation. George observed that Turner seemed to be gesturing towards certain houses, using his pistol as a pointer. Brandreth nodded his agreement. As the last of the rebels arrived, the tiny village square seemed almost ready to burst. Some of the residents came out of their cottages, mouths agape, realising that the rumours they'd been hearing of an impending revolt were actually true. Others peered fearfully from behind tiny panes of glass.

The men formed a natural arc around Brandreth, who stood on a slight rise to the rear of the square. He raised his hands for quiet.

"Right Lads!" he commanded, "The plan is to knock the doors of men you know who have not yet joined us and also where you know there are arms we can take for the cause. If anyone does not want to join us we persuade them it is their duty to help free their country. Is that clear?" The band of men indicated their understanding with cries of 'aye' and 'yes'. Some waved their pikes aloft.

"Right," he continued, "Isaac, Will, with me, Charles, James!" Brandreth waved at Charles Walters and James Turner, Will's younger brother, both of whom were stood right in front of him. "Try - Hardwick's cottage?" he looked towards Will for approval, who nodded. "Hardwick's cottage. Over yonder," he gestured in the direction of a modest dwelling set back from the road. "He's too old to come with us, but I'm told he has a gun – don't come back without it. We'll take the farmhouse behind. Anyone here from Wingfield, I want you to go to your own neighbours if they are not already here. Let's move!" Men began to disperse hurriedly. Brandreth scanned the crowd until his eyes fell upon who he was looking for. "George! I need you to wait here with the rest."

George nodded his compliance. With that, Brandreth, Will and Isaac headed off to the previously indicated farmhouse a few hundred yards behind the cottage belonging to old man Hardwick.

The village echoed with the sound of knocking doors. George stood at the epicentre of the whole operation, watching with interest. Perhaps he was worrying about nothing? Perhaps Jeremiah was nothing more than a strong and determined leader? The kind of leader they needed?

Moments later Charles and James returned to the group, coveting a pistol.

"Jeremiah was right," mused Charles, "we got this off old Hardwick no problem. All he asked was that we bring it back when we're done." It took a moment for George to realise they were addressing him, as if he were the commanding officer in Jeremiah's absence. He nodded.

"Aye," added young James, a lad barely in his twenties. "I said that'll be Monday at the latest!" he laughed. Charles held the pistol out to George, which took him by surprise.

"No. It's yours. You fetched it. You keep it." George felt immediately uncomfortable with the idea of having a firearm in his possession.

"If you're sure?" said Charles, "Perhaps I should give it to -"

His question was cut short by the sound of a commotion coming from the farmhouse.

George turned and was immediately shocked by what he saw. At a nod from Brandreth, Isaac and Will grabbed a loudly protesting man stood in the farmhouse doorway. George instantly recognised him as Henry Tomlinson. They held him firmly, one on each arm, while Brandreth stepped past him into the house itself. He reappeared moments later brandishing a large shotgun. George could vaguely hear a female voice shouting from within. Brandreth slammed the farmhouse door, cutting her off mid outcry. He indicated to Will and Isaac to bring their captor. The two men began to drag him down the lane back to the rest of the men. George could barely contain the horror on his face.

"I'll not go wi' yer, I tell thee! Now get your bloody hands off me!" he heard Tomlinson shout.

Brandreth turned on the struggling man. "Oh, really? Well perhaps this will change your mind?" Suddenly Brandreth delivered a firm punch to the farmer's sternum, who immediately collapsed to his knees, winded. Brandreth nodded to his two henchmen to let go of the man. They did so and Tomlinson was immediately face down in the dirt. George bolted from his vantage point, pushing his way through the crowd. The men parted, but by the time he reached the farmyard gateposts, Brandreth barred his way, brandishing the newly acquired shotgun.

"You've hurt him!" said George. Brandreth held up his hand.

"He threatened to report us, George. I can't have that!"

But George wasn't interested. He pushed the weapon aside and ran over to the crippled farmer.

"You alright, Mr Tomlinson?" he asked, kneeling beside him.

"Yes," Tomlinson wheezed, "I think so, George."

"You best help the man to his feet George. He said he weren't comin' wi' us, but I think we've managed to change his mind now, ain't that right Will?" he laughed.

"Aye Captain, I think we have," laughed Will.

"And it was nice of him to let us have this beauty," Brandreth added, inspecting the shotgun. "Though we had to use a little persuasion with that an' all."

Some of the nearest men laughed. Without a single glance back, he made his way to the centre of the crowd. By now, a number of men were leaving their homes to join the rebels. "Well done lads!" he bellowed, "Keep getting them numbers up! You know it makes sense. It's every man's duty to turn out and fight for your rights!" He turned back to Will and Isaac and gestured that they join him. "Right everyone! Onwards! Come on!" Brandreth gestured in the direction of Pentrich. "Here you go, Isaac, this is yours now," he said, handing the shotgun to him.

"If you're sure Jerry?"

"Aye, I'm sure. You've earned it! Give your pike to someone who ain't got one"

"Thanks," Isaac took the weapon.

"Come on Lads! Pentrich is waiting!" shouted Brandreth, and he began to lead the crowd out of the square.

Tomlinson was getting his breath back. As George helped him to his feet, the farmer turned to him.

"I would have thought better of you than to get mixed up in something like this rabble," he spluttered.

"We're fighting for our rights and our freedom -"

"By dragging men from their homes and

beating them?"

George shrugged awkwardly. "You're either with us or against us. That's what Jerry says. I think he got angry because you weren't prepared to listen. This is important, it affects all of us. All our futures. Come on. We'd better get moving. He keeps looking back. You have to come with us now."

George shivered. It was spitting with rain now, but it was nothing to do with that. He turned to leave.

"George, listen to me," Tomlinson implored, halting the sawyer in his tracks. "I'm sure what you stand for is right and just, but think about what you're doing -"

"It is every man's duty to join us," George repeated, but it felt like somebody else's words.

"Really? Only you don't sound so convinced yourself, lad. I know you plan to march to London. But what can a few hundred men do? George, listen to me!"

George shook his head. "A few hundred of us now, but by Nottingham it will be much more. Tens of hundreds. This is much bigger than you know about. We are going to change England forever. Finally the country will belong to the working man! Now let's get going!"

"You know my wife and my baby are sick, George. I can't come with you. Even if I wanted to. They can't manage on their own. They need me. The farm needs me. You already have my gun, please! Let me go home."

Silence. George peered into the night at the rest of the men, now about a quarter of a mile down the road that led out of Wingfield towards Pentrich. The wind carried vague sounds of a chant that they had started. He looked back at the injured farmer, torn. Finally he spoke. "They're probably far enough away not to notice now. Go. Go Now. But remember, we're doing this for people like us."

Tomlinson nodded. "Of course. What will you tell them?"

George shrugged. "I don't know. You gave me the slip. Let me worry about that."

"Thank you. Whatever the outcome of your efforts, I promise you I will not forget this George. Good luck, lad. You're going to need it." Tomlinson held out his hand. George glanced back towards the now distant rebels nervously, then placed his palm in Tomlinson's and shook it vigorously. The farmer smiled with relief, then turned and headed back to his home. George watched him go thoughtfully, then sprinted to catch up with the march.

7. Death in Pentrich

By the time George caught up with the march, his heart was hammering in his chest. He slowed to a jog and slipped into the back few ranks as furtively as possible. His pike firmly over his shoulder he fell into step once more. Fortunately, the rebels were now focused on their chanting and his temporary absence had apparently gone unnoticed. He could hear Brandreth leading the chorus from somewhere at the front of the crowd, shouting each line and then allowing them to repeat it:

"Every Man his skill must try!
He must turn out and not deny!
No bloody soldier must he dread!
He must turn out and fight, for his bread!
The Time has come, you plainly see!
The government opposed must be!"

The sound of two hundred plus pairs of boots

beat out a rhythm to accompany their rousing working man's shanty as they entered Pentrich village. George finally caught sight of Brandreth as he broke rank, dashing up some stone steps that led up to the village church. Using them as a makeshift podium, he called a halt to his army. The men obeyed unquestioningly. There was a real buzz to the air – an atmosphere. George could feel it, a kind of excited anticipation. He himself had butterflies – this was actually it, they were finally doing what they'd been carefully planning for the last month. But he also had this gnawing feeling that the whole campaign was somehow dangerously teetering on the brink of chaos – that rebels could become rabble. And that he was staring right at the man who held the outcome to this fragile state of affairs in the palm of his hand – Jeremiah Brandreth.

"Right men," he bellowed from his podium, "into groups! You lot, from Mr Brassington onwards – over there. Everyone stood behind Mr Buxton, move to this side. The rest, stay in the middle!"

The men separated into their ordered groups. Brandreth smiled wryly. He seemed to be really enjoying the fact that he was holding unquestioned command over such a substantial amount of men. "Right. Myself, Will and Isaac will take you lot -" he gestured to the first group, "- and cover this side of the village. Second group will cover all the houses south of the church. George?"

George raised his hand, stepping forward. Brandreth made eye contact. "George. Take the rest down the main road to meet the men who are waiting to join us at the White Horse. Don't miss any houses on the way! Knock on every door where you know there's men folk who aren't with us yet.

Do you understand?"

"Aye Jerry. I do" said George.

Turner stepped forward. "Widow Hepworth's house is covered by our group, Jerry. I know for a fact she has a shotgun."

"Aye, an' a manservant an' all. A burly fellow. He'll come in very useful. She's a right cow though – she'll not give anything up unless forced," Isaac added.

"Right. Leave that to me," said Brandreth, grinning. Then he addressed his troops again. "Right lads! You know what to do! Let's move!" He clapped his hands together and the groups began to disperse.

George took his cue. This was his chance to express some authority and hopefully help keep things on an even keel. "Right, everyone who is with me, this way!" he ordered sternly, surprising himself in the process.

Once again their numbers swelled, as rebels knocked doors and persuaded the village's men folk that it was their duty to join them. Some took a leaf from Brandreth's book, favouring less savoury canvassing tactics than just persuasive rhetoric. A protesting woman was thrown to the ground in an attempt to silence her. No one seemed to notice in the growing melee.

George's group arrived at the White Horse, where another enthusiastic group of rebels spilled out to greet them, Dutch courage in their bellies. George shook hands with the ones he knew and greeted the rest with an enthusiastic nod. The mood they brought with them was one of rowdy enthusiasm and once again George felt he had a sense of belonging. Some of them were perhaps a little more worse for wear than he'd like, but did it matter? They were brothers in arms, united in a common cause. Tonight they were going to strike a blow for the working man and soon they would be reclaiming England for their own kind. At least Jerry had been too preoccupied with his own self-importance to notice that he'd let farmer Tomlinson go.

"How many are we?" asked one of the pub-goers.

"Dunno, maybe two hundred and fifty? I'll try and count us all when we regroup," said George. A man called Buxton appeared, offering George a pistol. "Jerry said you should have this, seeing as you're one of the leaders." George looked at the weapon. Perhaps Jerry was right. He was a leader after all. He should be seen to be resolute. Strong. Such a weapon might give him the courage he felt he lacked. He held out his hand.

"I took it off -" Buxton continued, but he never got to finish his sentence. Suddenly he was cut short by a terrified scream coming from down the hill. The voice was female and one George recognised only too well.

"Mrs Hepworth!" he shouted, pushing Buxton aside and sprinting in the direction of her cottage.

As the house in question came into view, in the distance, he could see Brandreth hammering on the front door, flanked by Isaac and Will.

"Come on you old Banshee!" he bellowed, "Open up and let us in! We know you have weapons! And a man! Open the door or we'll smash it down!"

"Go away!" cried a voice from within,

hysterically, "I'm a widow! For the love of God, leave me alone!"

"She needs to pipe down, Jerry. Screaming like that, someone will think we're trying to kill her!" said Will.

"You two keep trying here. I'll see if there's another way in," said Brandreth. He moved round the side of the house where a small ground floor window caught his attention. Drawing one of his pistols, he used the weapon's handle to smash it.

"Get out!" the old lady screamed from somewhere within.

Brandreth peered through the small opening and saw the dark figure of a sizable man moving rapidly towards him. He looked to be brandishing the very shotgun he'd come to take.

"Don't worry, Mrs Hepworth, I'll deal with these bastards," Brandreth heard the man cry. He reacted instantly. Pointing his pistol through the jagged remnants of the window he'd just smashed, he pulled his trigger.

George was just shy of a hundred yards from the cottage when he heard a deafening crack. The sound was unmistakable. Gunfire. His heart hammered in his chest.

Brandreth instantly recoiled, his ears ringing. Smoke from the discharge billowed from the window, instantly filling his lungs and causing his eyes to water. The taste was acrid and the heat in his chest was searing. He steadied himself as the cloud dispersed. Coughing loudly, he peered into the interior.

He saw his target crumple slowly to his knees, his face contorted in a mixture of agony and horror. Dropping the shotgun he was carrying, the figure clutched his abdomen as a crimson stain spread rapidly across his shirt. He tried to stop himself, fumbling at a nearby wall but it was no good. The man let out a curdled growl and a fountain of blood and vomit issued from his mouth, splashing noisily on to the flagstone floor beneath him. He was dead before he hit the ground, having taken the full impact of the explosion square in the heart. The momentum from his fall caused him to roll awkwardly onto his side, his eyes wide and his tongue lolling from the side his mouth, like some macabre gargoyle. The impact forced the remains of his last breath from his lungs, along with a mixture of spit and blood. And then he was still.

Brandreth thought he looked not unlike a recently stuck pig on a butcher's slab. As he looked on, another figure appeared – that of a woman. She knelt beside the dead man and immediately began to wail uncontrollably. Calmly Brandreth reloaded his gun and then turned and began to walk away from the house.

"You've killed him Jerry!" exclaimed Isaac, now at the broken window. "You've killed the man!"

"Well, if the howling old banshee had opened the door, I wouldn't have had to teach her a lesson, would I?"

George arrived on the scene, his lungs seemingly on the brink of bursting. "I heard a shot," he gasped, "What in God's name is going on here?" Brandreth ignored him. George went over to the window and peered in. His blood ran cold as he was greeted by the grim scene he had feared the most. Mrs Hepworth was cradling the body of her manservant, her shoulders shaking as she sobbed.

The flagstones about them were wet and crimson. It took George a moment to take it all in. Finally he spoke. "Mrs Hepworth! Please, let me in. It's George Weightman. I can help -"

"How on God's earth can you help? Can't you see he's dead, George? Leave us alone," she looked up, tears streaming down her face. George looked at the window frame. If he was careful, he might just be able to squeeze through. He used his boot to break off some of the larger remaining shards of glass and then leaned in, covering his hands with the sleeves of his coat. Mrs Hepworth immediately grabbed for her manservant's dropped weapon and pointed it at George, shakily.

"I said stay away!" she shrieked, cocking the weapon. Suddenly, George felt a hand on his shoulder. It was Will.

"George! There's nothing you can do. We must get moving!"

George turned, angrily. "This shouldn't have happened!"

"Jerry says he had his gun. He would have shot our captain. If that had happened, our campaign would be over," Will said, firmly. "You didn't see, you were too far back. I saw him through the window. We must go before she fetches a physician!"

"Physician?" barked George, incredulously. "What use would a physician be? The man is dead! Magistrate, more like. And that's what you're really bothered about, isn't it Will?"

"We have to show strength through action. If we can't do that, we will fail."

George was incensed. "By shooting the very people we march for?" he turned back towards the smashed window.

"George, come away! Before she takes your head off with that thing. There's nothing you can do now. We need to leave. Nottingham is waiting!" Will grabbed the sawyer's arm, but George shook him off, exploding with rage.

"No more killing! This stops now! Look at her. She is an innocent woman. As he was an innocent man. This should not have happened! The next person I see who so much as points a gun at one of our own, or anyone who is unarmed and not a threat, I will shoot them myself. Is that clear?"

He turned. Will, Isaac and Brandreth stood in silence. "I said is that clear?" Will and Isaac nodded in agreement. Brandreth responded by shoving his pistol back into his waistband, turning on his heel and heading back towards the road. Will and Isaac turned to follow him.

George tentatively put his head back through the window, his hands held up in front of him. "Mrs Hepworth," he began.

She raised the shotgun in his direction, but could barely see him through the tears streaming down her face. "Please! I am unarmed. Listen to me. Please, I'm begging you. I'm so sorry. This should not have happened. I have to go. There's nothing we can do for him now. But I promise you, when our campaign is over I will personally see to it that this incident is dealt with. There will be justice. You have my word."

She lowered the weapon. "Just go, George. Before I change my mind and take your head off. Actually, no, take it. I'm not lowering myself to the level of scum that your friend is." Mrs Hepworth threw the gun across the hallway towards him. It clattered to a halt in front of the window.

"Nor am I," he said, "ever". Lowering his hands, he turned. "I made you a promise. I will not let you down," he called back through the window, before heading back towards the rest of the men who were now all assembled on the road. Disgust and despair gave way to hatred as he caught sight of Brandreth leading the men in another rendition of their anthem as he approached. In that moment, George vowed that when all this was over and the government was deposed, Jeremiah Brandreth would pay for this. Of that he was sure.

8. The Siege of Butterley Ironworks

"Right men! Butterley ironworks is ours for the taking!" Brandreth announced. Once more it was met with a rowdy cheer. As the men began to move out, he caught George's eye. He smiled. "Ah, George. Got a little job specially for you," he said gesturing back up the hill towards the centre of the village. George opened his mouth to protest, but was silenced by the sound of a horse whinnying. He turned in the direction that Brandreth had indicated and saw his brother, Bill walking a horse towards them.

"What's this for?" asked George, bemused.

"Let's just say we borrowed it for the cause," quipped Brandreth.

"Stole it you mean," snarled George.

"It shall be returned once it's served the cause. Now, be a good citizen and ride to Nottingham by the Nuthall Road, if you please."

"Why me?"

Brandreth shrugged "Bill tells me you're a good rider. We can't have someone inexperienced taking on such an important task. So – the Nuthall Road. Do you know that route?"

"Aye, I do."

"Excellent. You will meet a man by the road before you reach Nuthall. He has been told to look for a messenger on horseback from the Derbyshire men. He will speak a sentence that ends with the word 'love'. You must reply with a sentence ending with the word 'well'. Thus he will know who you are. He will tell you the status of the Nottingham contingent and then return to them with news that we are on our way. I cannot emphasise the importance of this task, George. It is vital for the success of our campaign. Is that clear?"

George was tense. He eyed Brandreth suspiciously. There was a rumble of thunder. The rain was picking up. The persistent drizzle that had been coming down since they entered Pentrich was becoming a storm that looked it might settle in for the night.

"George. We don't have time to bicker. The weather is conspiring against us. We need to move fast," said Brandreth sternly.

George pondered the situation. Nottingham was vital. The sooner they met up with the men of Nottingham the better. That would bring stability to the proceedings and hopefully much needed order. Brandreth would then have to answer to a higher commander. He nodded. "Aye. It's clear Jerry. As day," he took the reins of the horse, nodding to his brother.

"Excellent!" exclaimed Brandreth. "Meantime,

me and the lads will take down the ironworks. Now go!"

In one resolute swift movement, George placed his foot into one of the stirrups and mounted the steed. Kicking his heels he let out an aggressive shout and the horse instantly took flight.

Brandreth watched him go, his eyes narrowed. "That's the fly out of the ointment then," he muttered under his breath. With that, he sprinted to the front of the march. "Right lads!" he bellowed, "Looks like this rain is settling in for a while so let's make good haste to Butterley if you please, gentlemen! With a bit of luck, we can shelter in there until this passes over!"

The men cheered. Brandreth grinned, taking his place at the front of the group. Will to his left, Isaac to his right. Once again they took up the chant, as the now three hundred strong group made their way out of Pentrich towards their first key target: Butterley ironworks.

George gripped the reins of his mount as if his life depended on it. Bent low in order to stay off the worst of the bitter wind and now torrential rain, he kicked his heels as hard as he could, channelling his anger, he drove the beast onwards and ever faster with a rage that was unforgiving. It was a hellish journey. The hill up into the nearby village of Codnor made both of their legs burn. Ditches and shrubs were jumped rather than circumnavigated. Nothing was going to stand in the way of delivering the message as quickly as possible. The sound of horse hooves pounded in George's ears, occasionally being drowned out by the ever increasing peels of thunder that the overhead storm had brought with it. Lightening preceded each deafening rumble by only a fraction of a second, momentarily illuminating the nightmare path ahead. But George was grateful for the ephemeral snapshots of the terrain it provided – without them, the lack of moonlight combined with the cloaking black of the clouds meant that both he and horse were almost blind. He knew exactly what Brandreth was doing. He'd seen George's reaction to the murder of Widow Hepworth's manservant and this made him a threat to his dictatorship of the rebels. The man Old Tommy had deemed the peacekeeper of the group needed separating from *his* army. They were being moulded in his image, whipped up into a blood lust driven frenzy. Did he really want the same as what the others wanted? They hardly knew the man that they had instilled as Captain and in George's mind, something about him just did not ring true when it came to the cause. The words of his mantra now haunted him. "You're either with us or against us". They weren't a statement. They were a threat.

George tried to put it out of his mind and concentrate on the mission in hand – getting a message to Nottingham. Things would be better once they reached there. They would rein Brandreth in. Bring things back under control. Give the men focus before things spiralled any further into anarchy. He bore down towards Langley Mill. The elements were almost overwhelming, but George was determined that nothing would stop him. He had to get that message delivered as soon as possible. Hopefully he would be back with the lads in good time and thus prevent any further escalations that might turn rebels into rabble.

The wind bit hard and almost unseated him as he wrestled the horse into changing course at a junction in the path. Blinking the rain out of eyes he caught sight of a signpost. Eastwood. He was almost half way now...

Butterley ironworks was situated near the foot of the settlement at the junction of a wide road to Ripley and the tree lined lane that led back to Pentrich. It was a tall foreboding red brick fortress with high walls and a circular towered gate house. The gates themselves were of a heavy oak beam construction some eight feet high. Apart from a small hatch in the right hand gate, the forge looked ominously impervious to any kind of attack. The sound of hammering echoed off the walls of its great yard. Smoke bathed in the red glow given off by the fires below rose from the furnace chimneys giving the place a hellish feel.

The entrance was illuminated by a number of posted gas lights that added to the eeriness, their light reflecting off shiny wet cobblestoned carriageway that led downhill to the gates. Two dark cloaked figures approached the building. They stepped into the misty pool of light, revealing that they were armed town constables, rifles slung over their shoulders, their signature top hats and dark brown cloaks heavy with rain. One of them took up a guarding position at the end of the cobbled approach, while a second knocked loudly on the thick oak of the stone gatehouse door.

"Mr Goodwin!" he barked, trying to make himself heard over the sound of rain lashing the flagstones around his feet. "Mr Goodwin! Constabulary reporting back sir!" he rapped again.

"It's definitely them, sir," barked the other, peering into the darkness at the groved lane that led back to Pentrich, "I can hear 'em chanting. They're definitely on their way".

Suddenly the gatehouse door creaked open. A smartly dressed bearded man stood before them, peering at his pocket watch. It was George Goodwin, the forge's duty manager.

"Mmm. It's definitely them is it? A little later than we expected. I imagine this damnable rain is slowing them down. Cartwright, isn't it?"

"Aye. Mr Bennett here says he can hear 'em chanting like," he said, nodding to his companion, "Can't hear it m'self what with this bloody rain. But then his young ears are a bit keener than mine I shouldn't wonder. Is everything in place?"

"Oh yes," he smiled, "We've used the biggest bags of sand we could for the main gates. The men behind them all have firearms and have been instructed in their proper use. As for the gatehouse," he continued, gesturing behind him, "We've blocked out the windows with sand bags, but we've left gaps wide enough for our rifle tips. There are enough pistols for everyone in the gatehouse. On the top floor, we've stockpiled cannon shot to drop on their heads if they get close enough to make an attempt on the gates." He laughed. "One of those on your head from ten feet and you won't be getting up, so I'd say yes constable, everything is in place. I think we've done Mr Outram and Mr Jessop proud."

The Constable nodded. "I'm sure you have, Mr Goodwin. Right, if you want to get inside, we'll meet 'em face to face and I'll shout you if we need you."

"Thank you constable. But I really don't think

that will be necessary. I haven't been manager of this ironworks all these years without learning how to control a bunch of disgruntled labourers. I'll address them personally. Without a gun, thank you. I'd like to think we can resolve this without spilling blood if possible."

Cartwright shook his head, scattering water from the brim of his hat. "With respect sir, I must insist we stay. We've orders too, from the magistrate himself - that we must accompany you. That way, if there is the slightest sign of trouble, we'll be ready to defend you personally sir."

Goodwin sighed. "Very well. But remember, all my men are armed and ready too. And they'd need a cannon to get through these gates. Which, ironically, is one of the things that is bringing them here in the first place, I suspect."

"Sir!" cried Bennet, peering through the lashing rain, "They're approaching the junction!"

Goodwin clapped his hands together. "Right then, gentlemen. Everyone inside the gatehouse please."

The two constables stepped inside, grateful for the respite from the downpour. Goodwin slammed the door shut.

"Look lads, our first prize!" exclaimed Brandreth, gesturing the men to cease their chant as they neared the end of the lane that joined the Ripley road. He indicated the edifice some two hundred yards ahead of them. "Time to swap them pikes for some proper weapons!" He was about to break cover from the tree-lined lane when Will barred his way with an arm. The entire group halted.

"What is it?" Brandreth asked.

"Wait, Jerry. This don't look right somehow," said Will.

"Why?"

"He's right, Jerry," Isaac added, "this place is usually much busier than this, even at this hour. The furnaces burn through the night with men coming and going all the time. Deliveries and dispatches an' all."

Brandreth paused. Thoughtfully he filled his pipe and lit it, using one of the trees as cover. "As if they knew we were coming," he mused. He took a few thoughtful draws on his pipe. Then he spoke again: "Right. Isaac, Will, er..." he looked round at the men at the front of the group. "James, Bill... and anyone with a gun actually, follow me. The rest of you, wait here. Where's John Bacon?"

A man stepped forward. "John, you're in charge here. Get under these trees at the sides. Use them as cover. Don't move until one of us three gives you the signal. We'll do that when and only when we've gained access. Is that clear?" Bacon nodded. "Good man," he said, patting him on the shoulder. "Right, as I said, everyone with a firearm, follow me."

A group of about twenty men followed Brandreth, Ludlam and Turner across the road as they tentatively made their way toward the cobbled carriageway that led down to the gates.

"Be ready, lads!" he hissed, drawing one of his pistols. The entire group followed suit.

They arrived at the gates a few moments later, their senses bristling and their weapons at the ready. Brandreth used the butt of his pistol to rap loudly on the main gates.

"Who's there? What do you want?" came a

voice from inside the gatehouse, causing them all to spin round. Turner immediately trained his gun on the gatehouse door. The rest of the men eyed the walls of the ironworks suspiciously.

"We want your men and your arms! Open up! We are a working men's army, leading a revolution against our corrupt government! It is your duty to join us!" Brandreth commanded, loudly.

The door to the gatehouse opened a crack and Goodwin slipped out, pulling the door to behind him. He raised his hands to indicate he was unarmed. Immediately, Brandreth cocked his pistol and pointed it in Goodwin's direction. A number of the other rebels immediately did the same. There was a tense silence.

Eventually Goodwin spoke. "Well I'm sorry, but you shall have neither. In fact, looking at your numbers here and the ones hiding across the road, I'd say you have far too many of both already."

Brandreth looked puzzled. "What's that supposed to mean?"

"It means you won't get away with a simple charge of rioting and a spell in Derby gaol. Your numbers show serious intent. When caught, you'll hang for this, so you ought to abandon this folly immediately, sir."

Brandreth stared at Goodwin for a moment. Then he broke a wry smile. "Ha! There'll be no-one left to hang us when we're done my friend! From tomorrow, England will belong to the working man and you're either with us, or against us. And if you're against us, well I must warn you, we are armed!" he said, waggling his pistol and then aiming it squarely at Goodwin's chest.

"Yes, I have noticed. And so are we."

The door to the gatehouse opened once again and the two constables stepped out, their rifles aimed at the rebels.

Brandreth scoffed. "Just the two? I think you are outnumbered my friend. Shoot me and you'll all die for sure. So if you'll just open up, you can keep your heads on your shoulders, eh lads?" The men jeered. "Now. Come on – we want your weapons and your munitions if you please, sir."

Goodwin remained stony faced. "Well, I'm afraid you can't have them, because, you see, they're all in use right now. If you'd like to look at those windows up there – you'll see we have rifles ready in every one of them," he said, gesturing to a row of small windows high up in the forge wall, overlooking the men. On cue, the hopper style windows, tipped open to reveal around a dozen rifle tips. They all clicked ominously, as the forge workers manning them cocked their weapons. Many of the rebels looked up and then around at each other. A mixture of panic and terror swept across their faces.

"Same goes for this gatehouse," he continued, gesturing above. Again, windows opened to reveal gun barrels trained on the insurgents. "We've been expecting you for some time you see... so it is actually you who are outnumbered, Mr... I'm sorry, I don't know your name. Which is interesting, as you seem to captain local men, most of which I do know..."

Goodwin stepped forward. Brandreth took aim. Immediately the two constables trained their weapons on Brandreth's head. Despite the fact that the situation was now at flashpoint, Goodwin seemed to ignore Brandreth and stepped past him to get a closer look at the rebels themselves.

"Interesting. I see a Weightman there... Bill I think? We watched your brother George ride past on a horse not half an hour since. And Isaac Ludlam... I was very surprised to hear you were mixed up in this, Isaac. Very surprised. What are you thinking, man? You, of all people, a man of God."

Isaac stood firm. "I represent the working man, Mr Goodwin. We're just standing up for our rights. Something I expect you don't care too much for here, as you serve those who seek to enslave us."

"Don't care for? Don't care for?" Goodwin's face changed. "I sweat blood for these men what work for me, Mr Ludlam. I fight for fair pay and good working conditions but I do it because these men want to work! They want to make a better society, not smash it apart like you lot!" Goodwin suddenly shoved Isaac by the shoulder. Brandreth raised his pistol once again, but Will suddenly grabbed the end of the weapon, pointing it away.

"Too close Jerry! You could hit anyone," he hissed. The two constable's rifles meanwhile remained pointed at Brandreth's head.

"Look at me, Isaac Ludlam," continued Goodwin, "look at me and tell me your heart is truly in this. You're not even carrying a bloody gun – all you've got is a sharp stick! You're going to bring down the government with a sharp stick, eh Isaac?" he shoved him in the shoulder again. Isaac refused to respond, looking for all the world like a scolded child. Goodwin continued his attack. "Go' on wi' yer – go on home, before you're caught and hanged... Can't you see what's going on? There are constables here, and a lot more in Ripley, sent by the magistrate. They know what you're doing and they're ready for you. Listen to me, Isaac. You will go to the gallows for this – do you understand that? Unless you bugger off home now and forget this night ever happened!"

"He's lying, Isaac!" interjected Brandreth, "So some local wig has got big ears and happens to drink in the right pub... so what? They can't stop us. He's frightened of us, Isaac, that's why he's trying to talk you out of it."

Isaac was visibly trembling now. Eventually, he found it in himself to look Goodwin in the eye. "Mr Goodwin... if you think what we're doing is bad... well... then I am as bad as I can be. So, I owe it to these men. I must go on. I cannot go back."

Behind Goodwin's back, Brandreth gestured to the men, throwing his hands in the air. They responded with a cheer.

Brandreth grinned. Goodwin hadn't quite got the better of him just yet. "Now, you heard what Mr Ludlam has to say on the matter, so perhaps you'll do us a favour and bugger off back to the hole you crawled out of, along with your two monkeys over there and we'll be on our way."

Goodwin span round. "I'd be delighted, Mr?"

"Brandreth. Jeremiah Brandreth," he said, squaring up to Goodwin, just inches from his face. Their eyes met. Goodwin was unfaltering. He'd met men like him before. He wasn't scared of him. Brandreth continued, without even blinking, "A name all England will come to know very soon. Mark my words."

Neither man wanted to be the first to falter. They stared at each other for what seemed like an age. Rain dripped from the end of Brandreth's nose. He stood fast. All the time painfully aware that at least twenty weapons, maybe more, were trained on him and his men. Suddenly, he lowered his gun. "Right lads!" he announced, "March on!" He waved, indicating to the others that they move on. With that, he turned to face twenty somewhat confused rebels.

Goodwin glanced at Isaac and shook his head. Isaac just looked away in what Goodwin could only think was shame. Brandreth moved as if to leave. Will, shocked at what had just happened, grabbed Brandreth by the arm, but the Nottingham Captain shook him off, refusing to engage him.

"So that's it - we're leaving?" said Will, astonished. "But what about the arms, the shot we desperately need?"

It was Isaac who spoke. "Are you blind Will? They are armed to the teeth and all on higher ground, we'd be cut down in seconds, man!"

"We haven't even tried!" Will protested. "He could be bluffing! I say we rush them! If we get Goodwin as hostage they'd have to let us in!"

Isaac shook his head vehemently. "It'd be a waste of good men for us to engage such a strong enemy this early!" We don't have enough arms! We might never make Nottingham at this rate! That's where our real strength lies."

Will was uncomfortable. Brandreth just didn't seem to want to acknowledge him.

"Jerry?"

"I said march on," Brandreth snapped. He waved his arm in the direction of the rest of the men. "Come on, lads!" he added.

The men turned to leave. Will shrugged and began to follow the rest of the men. Brandreth took a last look round Butterley ironworks and began to follow his comrades. Goodwin smiled. The two constables lowered their rifles, watching the rebels trudge off into the rainy night. After a long pause, constable Bennet turned to his superior.

"So we're just going to let them go?" he asked, confused.

Goodwin smiled. "Yes. I have had strict orders from the magistrate. Our job was just to make sure the ironworks were secure."

"They're to be taken in Ripley then?" asked Cartwright. Goodwin chuckled. "Oh no. They know about the extra constables in Ripley, so they'll be avoiding the town like the plague. No, I expect they'll go via Codnor and head for the Nottingham road that way."

"Then, what a waste of men, surely?" said Bennet.

"What, the extra constables?" said Goodwin, "They'll be sent home now. They were just needed to act as beaters - flush the quarry down a different route as it were. No, there are much bigger plans afoot for Mr Jeremiah Brandreth and friends, of that I'm sure. Tell you what. How about a drop of something warming for you gentlemen?" He turned back towards the gatehouse. "After all, you've earned it."

"That, Mr Goodwin sir, is a capital idea!" grinned Cartwright. He slapped Bennet on the back and the two constables followed him inside.

9. Flashpoint

On the Nuthall road to Nottingham, the rain was now coming down in sheets. His skin soaked to the bone, George pulled hard on the reins of his horse, until she slowed first to a trot and finally to a steady walk. He brought her to a halt by a water trough. Steam rising from her hide, she bent her head forward to drink eagerly.

George dismounted and peered out into the darkness. He figured that if he was the one given the task of hiding on this road waiting for a messenger on horseback, he'd hide somewhere along this stretch – there was good cover from the hills and trees either side. Especially considering the current inclement weather. He was not disappointed. Within a minute or two of his arrival, a cloaked figure peeled himself out from the shadow of one of the larger oak trees by the side of the road. George eyed the figure with caution as he approached him and his steed gingerly. What if this was not the messenger?

What if this was a constable or even worse, a magistrate? He tensed, preparing to leap back into the saddle at the last moment and possibly steer his steed right at the figure if he seemed hostile. He had to deliver his message at any cost. The success of the campaign depended on it. At that moment, now some ten yards distant, the figure spoke. The tone of his voice was tentative.

"I mean you no harm sir. Your horse seems a fine specimen, though she looks thirsty and tired. You have worked her hard. She will serve you better if you show her some *love*."

George nodded. The code word. This had to be him. His heart pounded, partly from the exhaustion of the breakneck ride so far, partly with adrenalin. He struggled to remain calm. "Aye. She's a good 'un, aren't you girl?" he said, patting her flank affectionately. Then he caught the man's eye and added "Don't worry, I treat her *well*."

Instantly, the figure dropped his hood. He was a clean shaven ruddy faced man, slightly chubby, with beady eyes. He looked about nervously for a moment than whispered furtively "Has it begun? Are Derbyshire on their way?"

George exhaled with relief. "Aye! Nigh on four hundred men by now I expect. When I left, we were on our way to take the ironworks at Butterley, so there'll be more men and firearms from there. What of Nottingham?"

"Tell Jeremiah Nottingham is taken."

George was visibly shocked. "Taken? That's incredible news, my friend! Are you sure?"

"I'm certain, sir. They await you and your colleagues so that you may storm the army barracks together."

"Excellent! This will surely spur my comrades on. We will be with you as soon as God permits it."

"Then you must hurry back! I will tell our group to make ready for your arrival."

"I will sir, I will," said George. "We will be with you soon, brother!" He held out his hand. The messenger shook it vigorously. "I wish you well. Take care! And don't go too hard on that horse of yours, or she might not make it back!"

The two men embraced. George then took to his mount once more, his enthusiasm reignited. As he turned the horse on its heels, the messenger cried "God speed you!" and saluted.

"And you sir, and you!" George responded. Digging his heels in to her ribs, he leaned forward as the horse took off back the way they had come, his renewed vigour allowing him to ignore the now torrential rain. However George's new found enthusiasm was short lived...

Langley Mill, 3am.

As the rain had transmogrified into an angry storm, so had the mood of the Derbyshire rebels. As George approached the village, his heart sank. Even from a distance he could tell something had gone very wrong with the march. The savage wind carried snippets of sound that made his blood run cold – drunken shouting mixed with the sporadic cracking of firearms and screaming. He slowed his horse to a trot, astonished at the anarchy he was riding into.

It was total and utter chaos. Intoxicated men ran about haphazardly. Guns were discharged skyward randomly, accompanied with loud jeers of delight. The sound of bottles smashing startled his mount. She reared on her hind legs and gave a loud whinny and George had all on to prevent himself from being thrown into a ditch. He decided to dismount for his own safety, tethering her to a nearby fence. To his left, a group of men he didn't recognise set about smashing the lock off a large barn using rifle butts. The padlock showed little resistance and gave way almost immediately. The group cheered and began to help themselves to the barn's contents.

A beer bottle whizzed past his head. As he strode to the centre of the village he was horrified to see a stack of hay bales actually ablaze, surrounded by men with ale tankards desperately trying to dry themselves out. The rebels no longer resembled any kind of army. They were a frenzied rioting rabble.

Some local men ran into the village square, loudly challenging the drunken rebels. Immediately a brawl ensued. George caught sight of his brother Bill sat sheltering from the rain under a tree, several bottles scattered roundabout. He immediately made a beeline for him, dodging brawlers and some terrified newly liberated chickens.

"Bill! What is going on here? What happened at the ironworks?" he asked, tersely.

Bill looked up, clearly the worse for wear. "George! You're back. Did you deliver the message? What news from Nottingham?"

"Never mind that. What the bloody hell has happened?"

Bill shrugged and took another swig of ale. "They were ready for us, George. They were barricaded in, with constables from Ripley. They knew we were coming."

"But how? Did we get any weapons?"

"We got nothing, George. They told us more constables were on the way, from Alfreton and Ripley. We left empty handed. They were ready for us! The men were pretty down, so Jeremiah decided we needed our spirits raising -"

"By raiding the ale houses and getting everyone drunk? Is that how he thinks we should face the King's troops? For the love of god! I need to speak with him. Where is he?" George exploded, cutting his brother off mid-sentence.

Bill pointed the tip of his bottle towards an inn called The Navigation across the road, by the canal. "In the pub."

George turned on his heel and made the straight for the building his brother had indicated. Isaac stood in front of the door, pistol in hand, as if standing guard.

"George! You're back! What news of Nottingham?" he asked.

George ignored the question. "How many pubs have you done this in?"

"This is the fourth. A lot of men need a lot of ale!" he laughed. He was clearly intoxicated too. "Don't worry, they'll sober up soon enough! We just needed a break from this God awful weather."

But George wasn't listening. Rolling his eyes, he barged past his comrade and went inside.

The ale house was packed with revellers. They all seemed to be cheering and looking towards some spectacle taking place at the bar. George forced his way through the crowd, just in time to see Will, grappling a man he presumed to be the inn keeper into a headlock on the bar. Brandreth held a tankard of ale in one hand and a pistol in the other. He cocked the weapon casually as he sipped the last dregs of his beer and placed it squarely against the Inn Keeper's temple. He then dramatically cast the mug aside. The lads jeered encouragingly.

"You see, there's no point in offering you any money my friend," he scoffed, "because by the morrow, any bank note with the King's face on it will be worthless. Ain't that right lads?"

The crowd cheered. George was outraged.

"What the hell is this? Brandreth? Will?"

Brandreth smiled. "Ah, you're back. Just getting the fire back into our bellies, George, that's all. And a little respite from the rain, eh lads?"

There was a resounding "Yes" from the group.

"And that includes terrorising the landlord?" snapped George.

"Let's just say he was a little rude about our intentions, right, Will?"

Will nodded. "Aye, that he was, Jerry. Said we'd outstayed our welcome."

"In fact, he said it was time to 'pay up and push off', didn't he Will? Which personally, I thought was a bit rude. So we thought we'd teach him some manners, right lads?" said Brandreth. He was clearly loving the spectacle of the whole thing. The men laughed.

"Let him go, Will." George commanded. He turned to the crowd. "Everyone, listen to me. Put your drinks down. We need to move out now!"

Brandreth sighed. "Mr Weightman. It must be catching. Now you seem to have mislaid your manners while out on your errand. In case you have forgotten, I give the orders round here. Isn't that right, Will?"

"Aye, that it is, Jerry."

George had had enough. He crossed the bar

and squared up to Brandreth. His eyes burned with rage as he stood nose to nose with the Nottingham Captain. Brandreth stared back, refusing to budge. George realised he wasn't drunk, at least not on alcohol. He was clearly intoxicated, but it was by the power and the chaos he was wielding. Suddenly George felt something hard against his ribs. He looked down. It was the barrel of Jeremiah's gun. He looked back into Brandreth's eyes once more.

Without blinking, he said calmly "Let him go. He's done nothing."

"Give me one good reason why," Brandreth whispered.

"Because we need to move out of here right now."

"And why might that be, George?"

His heart pounded, but he kept his resolve. Finally, through gritted teeth he said loudly "Because Nottingham is taken!"

"Well, that's excellent news!" said Brandreth, breaking into a broad grin. He put his arm round George, patting him firmly on the back. "That's most excellent news indeed!" He gripped George by the shoulder and turned him to face the crowd. "Did you hear that lads? Nottingham is taken!"

The men let out a rowdy cheer and clanked their tankards in celebration. George could still feel the pistol, now pushing into his back. As the men celebrated, Brandreth pressed his lips to George's ear and whispered "Challenge me like that again in front of the men and I will not hesitate to kill you. Do you understand?" he then shoved George towards the crowd who in turn embraced him noisily. Brandreth nodded to Will to release the inn keeper with a wry smile on his face. Surreptitiously he lowered the gun and placed it back into his waistband. Will did as he was commanded and the man slid off the bar and collapsed in a heap on the floor. Brandreth punched the air, bellowing "Onward to victory, then lads!" The mob began to vacate the tavern, Will included. Brandreth began pushing his way through the crowd to the front, eager to resume his position as leader. George stood fast, watching them leave.

Finally, when the pub was empty, he looked round, taking in the full extent of the devastation. Beer bottles littered the floor. Stools lay broken. The flagstones were wet with spilled ale. George felt ashamed. A noise startled him. He turned to see the inn keeper's wife had appeared from somewhere and was helping her gasping husband off the floor.

"I'm sorry. We're just standing up for our rights -" George began.

She didn't look up. "By ransacking our village, hammering down our door in the early hours and stealing all our ale? Your men are out of control!"

George nodded. "I think you're right. I wasn't here. Hopefully when we get to Nottingham -"

"Just leave will you?" she blurted out, sobbing.

"This man," her husband gasped, feeling at the bruises round his throat as he stood up, "He saved my life."

George turned to leave. Then he paused, took out the purse he had in his pocket and emptied all the money he had onto the bar. "It's all I have. I'm so very sorry."

As he made for the door, he heard the woman say "I don't care. He's still one of them. I hope they all bloody hang, I really do. We need to get you cleaned up..."

He stood in the doorway for a moment, unsure what to do. Dawn was rapidly approaching. It was still raining, but the clouds were now bathed in an eerie shade of pale yellow, that peculiar illumination that precedes sunrise. He peered into the distance and could see the last of the rebel stragglers heading in the direction of Nottingham. Not only were they now a drunken rabble, he was pretty sure that their numbers had dwindled to half the original amount during his absence. No doubt the storm had proved too much for their resolve. He shook his head.

"So much for an army of the people," he muttered. The fate of the revolution lay in Nottingham's hands now. He had to get there no matter what. His colleagues might have failed him and the cause, but he had made a promise to his Uncle Tommy. If only he were here now. If he ever needed some support, it was at this precise moment. Never had he felt such a feeling of complete and utter despair. Perhaps he should just go home? He thought of Rebecca and the children. Perhaps his wife had been right all along. No. He would look even more of a failure than he did before he left. He had to see this through, no matter what lay ahead. By the sounds of it, the revolution was well under way, just a handful of miles down the road. Everything he'd dreamed of these past weeks was still happening, just a couple of hours from here. He looked up at the sky once more. Chances are, the Nottingham group would already be midway through the assault on the army barracks, making full use of what little night time cover remained. Before he knew it, they'd be on the canals and heading for London. He made up his mind. He would make one of those boats no matter what. Stepping out into the rain once more, he ran to catch up with his colleagues.

"Not long now! Nottingham by dawn!" shouted Brandreth from the front of the marchers, "And if we do run into any of the King's men, they'll be getting some of this, eh lads?" he fired one of his pistols into the air. Many of the men with guns followed suit and the sound of weapons discharging filled the air.

Sprinting towards the group, George was but a couple of hundred yards away from the rebels when he heard a blood curdling scream. Peering into the haze ahead of him he saw the figure of a man collapse. He recognised him as Charles Walters. By the time he arrived, his worst fears were confirmed. Walters lay in the middle of the road. Blood poured from his hip, diluting in the muddy puddles around him.

Isaac and Will were first on the scene.

"In the name of God! Charles!" cried Ludlam.

"What happened?" barked Turner.

Isaac looked panicked. "I don't know. He's been shot!"

"Oh God! Help me! The pain! I'm going to die!" Shrieked Walters, his voice cracking in a mixture of terror and agony.

George ran over to the fallen man and immediately assessed the wound. Blood was seeping through a hole in the top of his trousers at a rapid rate.

"We need to get this man to a doctor and fast!" he ordered.

"But we don't know any round here!" said Ludlam, almost hysterical.

Brandreth appeared. "I can't let you do that, George. A physician will alert the authorities. We will have to tend the man as best we can here."

"He will die, Jeremiah. Unless we get him to a doctor as soon as we can, he will die. What is wrong with you? Do you have no remorse? Not even for one of your own loyal followers?" George grabbed Isaac's arm. "We'll take him to the inn. They will know the local surgeon. Isaac, you must help me."

"But Jeremiah said -"

"Fuck what Jerry said! He is going to die unless we help him now!" Isaac pulled himself free of George's grip, his eyes wide with panic. Suddenly another man knelt beside George.

"I'll help. What do I do?" It was James Turner, Will's younger brother and Walters' friend.

"Put your hand over the wound. Stem the bleeding," George barked. Walters cried out in agony.

"Good man," George continued, "get your arms round the tops of his legs. I'll lift him from the chest. We need to get him there as quickly as possible. Can you run?"

James nodded. "Good. Lift on three. Ready? One, two, three!" The two men stood, shakily, Walters' now limp body hoisted aloft between them. His face was pale and his eyes rolled into the back of his head. He groaned. "It's the shock," said George, "we need to run, now!" the two men tore off, crab-like, in the direction of the inn. George was vaguely aware that some of the others were following them. They soon arrived at the entrance of the Navigation. Holding Walters as best he could with one arm, George banged as hard as possible on the door.

A muffled shout came from within. "I told you to be on your way!" It was the inn keeper's wife.

"Please! In God's name we need help – you must open up, a man is wounded. Unless we get help he will die!" George shouted.

The door swung open. The inn keeper's wife stared in horror at the scene. "Oh my Lord. I'll not see a man die outside my tavern. Bring him in! Quick as you can. But that lot can clear off!" she motioned in the direction of the others that had followed George and James back to the pub. As they stepped inside, George caught sight of Isaac, Will and a few of the others that had followed them. In this distance he could see Brandreth, reloading one of his pistols. Then the door slammed shut behind them.

10. Ambushed!

"Let's get him on the bar," panted George, breathless. The two men staggered with Walters' limp body across the pub. The inn keeper's wife hurriedly swept everything that littered the broad wooden counter to one side. George and James lowered Charles' blood soaked body carefully onto the surface. He groaned again.

"Stay with us, Charlie," said George, "we need to look at the wound. Sorry, but this might hurt." He tore open his trouser leg from the bottom up. Walters suddenly writhed in pain. George indicated to James to hold the man steady. "Right. Mrs, er, I'm sorry, I don't know your name."

"It's Goodman. Mrs Goodman."

George nodded in acknowledgement. "Mrs Goodman, we need to know where your local physician lives. The shot is in the thigh. It needs to be removed and the wound stitched, otherwise he will bleed to death." He reached over the counter and picked out a couple of clean bar towels. "In the meantime, James, tear this cloth to strips and tie it round his leg here - It will stem the blood flow." James produced a pocket knife and set to work.

"Mrs Goodman. Where is your husband?"

Mrs Goodman looked sheepish. "He's gone somewhere."

"To alert the authorities?" queried George. She nodded. "Fear not. Just tell me the house of your local physician. I could not care less about this uprising right now. I will not allow another life to be lost in vain this night!"

"He lives across the road. The white cottage with the ivy and the iron fence. You can't miss it. His name is Davenport," she replied.

"Thank you. James, please keep this towel pressed firmly over the wound with both hands. I shall return momentarily." George ran from the tavern. He immediately saw the cottage Mrs Goodman had described. Ignoring the group of rebels still lurking outside, he dashed across the road and hammered on the door. After a few moments, the door opened. A balding middle aged man peered out in his night shirt.

"Are you the local physician?" asked George, hurriedly.

The man looked bemused. "I am. What on earth is going on at this objectionable hour?"

"Your skills are required. A man is severely wounded, perhaps fatally. You must come at once and bring your bag please, sir!" George pleaded.

"Wounded? How?"

"He took a bullet to the thigh. Please come right away, I beg you. He's over at the inn."

"Very well," he tutted, "I'm coming." He

ducked back inside the house and reappeared moments later with a doctor's bag. He closed the front door of his cottage and the two men dashed across the road. Davenport, still in his night shirt, eyed the group of loitering rebels with suspicion. George opened the door of the inn and beckoned him inside.

Doctor Davenport was not ready for the sight that greeted him.

"Dear lord. Mrs Goodman! Who are these men? What is happening here? What are you doing with firearms at this hour in the morning?"

George and James looked at each other blankly. James shrugged his shoulders. It was George who eventually spoke, trying desperately to not frighten the doctor off. "There's been a riot. Men from Wingfield and Butterley have been here rioting."

"Is this true Mrs Goodman?" the doctor asked.

"Aye, it is," she replied.

"And to what end? Why are they here in Langley Mill?"

"Please," implored George, "if you could look at the patient? I will see you are paid, I promise. My name is George Weightman. I live at the White Horse in Pentrich, please!"

Davenport looked at the destruction around him and then glanced nervously out of the window. More of the rebels had now come back to the inn to see what was happening.

"No. It is obvious to me what is going on here. You three men - and the rest of you out there," he gestured to the window. "You are the scallywags causing the trouble and I shall not be part of it! Neither will you Mrs Goodman if you have any sense. You clearly have no intention of paying me, judging by what's been happening here. In fact I expect I'll end up in a similar state to your friend here if I remain in your company too long!" Davenport was visibly shaking. "No - I'm sorry, I will not help you. Mrs Goodman – where is your husband?"

"He's gone to fetch the local magistrate," she replied.

"Excellent, then hopefully he'll be on his way with a few constables to sort this rabble out!" He snapped his bag shut. "Good night to you," he said brusquely and turned to leave.

"Please sir, I'm begging you on this man's life! Do not leave!"

But it was too late. Davenport was already opening the front door - but his exit was momentarily blocked by a tall swarthy looking man in a derby hat and long frock coat. Before the figure had time to realise what was happening, Davenport slipped past him and was gone.

"So much for the Hippocratic Oath," exclaimed George.

"Is the physician not going to treat the man? Nottingham waits!" It was Brandreth.

George had had his fill. "Don't you care about anything else? Unless we do something now, Charles may die!"

Brandreth shrugged coldly. "Every war has casualties... So is he treating him or not? He should look at young James Hill while he's here – he says it was him that shot him accidentally and now he feels faint," he laughed. "Do any of you men have the stomach for this job?"

"The doctor has gone, Jerry. Between us we've

managed to scare the man witless, I expect," said George, moving back towards Charles. He took his coat off and threw it on a nearby table.

"Right. Mrs Goodman, fetch a bottle of the strongest spirit in your bar and be ready to pour some in the wound before we dress it. It will help clean the wound and stop infection. What I'm about to do will hurt, so I need you to hold Charles down while I do this."

"Perhaps I can persuade him to change his position!" Brandreth said, pulling out a pistol and turning back towards the door.

George leapt to bar his way. "No! Haven't you caused enough misery for one night? Why don't you just go? I will tend the wound. Now please leave so that I can save this man's life. Or so help me God I will strangle you with my own bare hands, gun or no gun!"

Brandreth let out one of his belly laughs and shoved the pistol back in his waistband. "Fine. Just as well I need to save my ammunition George. You stay here and play nursemaid if you like. I've had my fill of you and your gutless moralising. I said I needed men who had guts and you clearly do not. You couldn't even strangle a lame cat, let alone me. Shame to let your Uncle Tommy down. Never mind. Goodbye George! Nottingham and Parliament awaits!" And with that, he swept out of the pub and was gone.

George watched him from the window for a moment. He strode off in the direction of the Nottingham road. The rest of the remaining rebels went with him as he cried "Right lads! Onwards to victory!"

"Do you want to go with them?" said Mrs

Goodman.

George turned his back on the window. "Not any more. I am done with this business. My dream has died. But this man is not going to. Now, will you help me?"

"Aye, I will. You are a good man George. What do I do?"

"I need that strong liquor, a sharp knife, a candle, a needle and strong thread, a clean towel or two and as much light as you can give me."

"Is this sharp enough?" asked James, holding up his pocket knife.

"Yes," said George, "good start!" He took the knife.

Mrs Goodman sprang into action. She threw clean towels at George from behind the counter, handed him a bottle of gin and hurried off up the stairs behind the bar. George rolled up one of the towels and shoved it in Charles' mouth. "You'll need to bite down on this Charlie. I'm going to take the shot from out of your leg. Do you understand?" Walters nodded. He was becoming feverish.

Mrs Goodman returned with a couple of lanterns, a sewing basket and a candle. She lit the lanterns and the candle and placed the sewing basket on a nearby table.

"Where do you want these?" she asked, indicating the lamps.

"I will need you to hold the lamps as close to the wound as possible. I need to see as clearly as I can. Put the candle there, on the end of the bar, please," ordered George.

Mrs Goodman complied. George moved to the candle and held the blade of James' knife in the flame for a few moments. "James, I need you to hold

Charlie as still as possible. All your weight on his legs please. If he moves suddenly from the pain, I could injure him quite badly. I might even cut an artery and he will certainly bleed to death. Understand?"

James nodded. "Aye, George."

"Right. You can take your hands off the wound. Mrs Goodman, the lamps – as close as you can if you please and keep them steady."

He turned to Charles. "Ready?" The man nodded. George nodded to James, who leant with all his weight on Charles' legs.

George knelt by Walters' side and slowly inserted the sterilised knife into the wound. Charles let out a stifled wail. James braced himself - holding Charles still took all his effort. George carefully manipulated the knife, which was rapidly becoming coated in blood, as he felt carefully for the shot embedded in the Charles' thigh.

"Damn it. I can't find it. No! Wait. Yes. I have it! Bite hard Charles. It's coming out… now!" With a single swift gouging movement George first manipulated the lead marble like object to the surface and then flicked it out on the wooden counter top. Charles let out a stifled scream that almost masked the noise the shot made as it clattered onto the flagstone floor.

"Good man," he said, grabbing the bottle of gin. He pulled the cork out with his mouth and spat it across the room. He then poured almost half the bottle into the wound. Walters writhed in agony. George took a large swig from the open bottle himself, then slammed it down next to the sewing basket. He threw the lid open, selected the thickest needle he could find and skilfully threaded a length of the toughest looking darning thread he could through its eye. He cut it free of the reel with James' knife and began to sew up the wound.

He worked quickly and skilfully. The whole operation probably took only a few minutes, but to all present it seemed to take a life time. Walters let out stifled howls throughout the process. Tears streamed down the side of his face and with each suppressed scream, foamy mucus was ejected from his nostrils on to the rolled up towel in his mouth.

Suddenly it was over. George stood up and let out a long sigh. "All done," he said, almost as if he'd mended a sock rather than undertake a life threatening operation.

Eventually, Mrs Goodman spoke. "How did you know what to do?"

"I'm a sawyer by trade, madam," said George. "Let's just say I've had more than one run in with a sharp wood saw over the years!" He grabbed the bottle of gin once more, glancing at Mrs Goodman. She nodded. He took another slug. "And when you're in the middle of the woods with your leg hanging open, you soon learn it's best to go to work prepared."

Suddenly Walters seemed to come to. "Is it done? Will I live?" he spluttered, spitting the towel out.

George grinned "Aye. You should be fine, Charles. You need to keep it clean though. James, take my horse tethered out by the barn across the road back to Pentrich and fetch the cart from the side of my house. It will be the safest way for Charles to travel and keep the wound together. Mrs Goodman will you make him comfortable until James returns?"

Mrs Goodman nodded. "I will, of course."

"Right, I'll get going," said James. He shook George's hand. "That was incredible."

"Indeed it was," said Mrs Goodman. James hurried out of the pub.

"I don't know about that. I was terrified, to tell you the truth! I've never sewn someone else up, only myself," shrugged George. He took another drink. "Right. Mrs Goodman, I have to ask you this. Has your husband really gone to inform the authorities?"

"Aye, George, I'm afraid he has."

"Then it is my duty to at least try and worn my comrades who still march towards Nottingham. So I must go. Goodbye, Mrs Goodman. I cannot thank you enough." He held out his hand.

Mrs Goodman shook it. "Please. Call me Ann. And I can promise you this. When the authorities ask me what happened, I shall not hesitate to tell them of your bravery this night. Goodbye and good luck, George."

"Thank you. It is much appreciated. Sadly though, I think it will do little good. I am beyond redemption now, I fear."

"Thank you George, I owe you my life," said Walters, he raised his hand shakily. George shook it and left.

The Gilt Brook, Nottinghamshire. Dawn, June 10, 1817.

What remained of the Derbyshire rebels (for their numbers had almost halved through desertion) were now making their way along a footpath that ran beside what locals referred to as the Gilt brook. Although the worst of the storm had passed, the rain had stubbornly refused to abate in any way and the men were soaked to the skin and thoroughly weather beaten. The sun was coming up and the birds noisily informed them as such as they tramped ever onward towards Nottingham, which was now a mere seven miles away. As usual, Brandreth, Isaac and Will were at the front of the party. The chanting long over, the three men talked quietly as they walked.

"Not far now, lads," said Brandreth, "we can do it in an hour, I reckon."

"Not at this rate Jerry. Look at them," said Will nodding towards the rest of the rebels behind them. "They're exhausted. More like an hour and a half. Maybe two?"

"Well, they shouldn't have got so blind bloody drunk, should they?" Brandreth snapped.

"Well you did say it was time for an ale or two," added Isaac.

"An ale or two, yes. Lathered, no. No bloody self-discipline this lot. No determination." Brandreth was obviously short tempered. The trio fell silent for a moment.

Suddenly, they heard the sound of distant shouting from behind them. Idly, Will turned his head and saw a figure running towards them from the direction of Langley Mill. He turned. Walking backwards, he squinted at the lone figure running towards them, his breath streaming out behind him.

"Bloody hell," he said, grabbing at Brandreth's coat, "It's George!"

"By God, it is an' all!" exclaimed Isaac. The three men stopped. Brandreth held up his hand, signalling the men to halt.

"Listen! Everyone! Stop!" George gasped as he approached, "You need to listen to me!"

"Well look who it is, lads. Judas himself has returned to the flock," mocked Jeremiah. The men all turned.

George's lungs felt like they were going to burst and his heart hammered in his chest. It took all his concentration not to vomit. "The authorities..." he bent over, almost crippled with stitch and fighting for air. "They know where we are..."

"Did you hear that lads?" called out Brandreth. The men parted as he walked towards the exhausted George. "He's sold us out!"

There was a mixture of gasps and cries of 'traitor'. George managed to stand upright, clutching his side. A long string of spit cut loose from the side of his mouth and spattered the ground about his feet. "What?" he said, incredulously, "You think I..? No, listen! I'm no traitor."

"Well what *should* we call a man who goes against his leader's orders, colludes with the enemy and alerts the authorities?" Brandreth quizzed as he slowly walked towards George.

"Walters could have died! I'm no traitor!"

"Then how come they know where we are? I presume that's what you've come to tell us! Guilty conscience is it, George?"

George was beginning to regain his composure. He had come to thoroughly despise this man over the last twenty four hours. He had single-handedly destroyed all he'd fought for and believed in, in the space of one night. He decided it was time he let him know and to hell with the consequences.

"Why are you doing this, Jerry? This uprising, since you got involved, has become a personal crusade - though God only knows for what purpose! I'm no traitor, as you are no reformist! You've twisted this group into something I no longer recognise. You've beaten and killed innocent people, so if it's not parliamentary reform, what do you want, Jeremiah? Eh? Answer me!"

Brandreth remained stony faced but continued his approach. George waited until he was in striking distance. "I said answer me. You gypsy bastard!" he cried and before the Nottingham Captain could draw either of his pistols, George found his right fist connecting with his jaw.

Brandreth staggered back momentarily caught off guard. He seemed genuinely surprised that George had it in him to actually strike the first blow.

"For fuck's sake George!" Will cried from somewhere to his right. George looked round, distracted and in that moment Brandreth was on him like a frenzied animal. He grabbed George's sodden coat with one fist and used the other to rain a barrage of punches into George's face. He hit him with such force that he immediately lost his grip on the wet wool in his hand and George was on his back in the mud. Brandreth was on top of him immediately, but George was a strong man. After all, he'd carried logs and trees all his working life. With one swift movement, he tossed Brandreth to one side and hit him again, this time his fist connected with his left ear. Brandreth rolled over with the impact, giving George enough time to get back on his feet. Jeremiah lashed out with his foot, taking George's leg from under him. He fell on top of his opponent and the two men wrestled fiercely. Desperate to stop him taking one of the weapons in his waistband out, George pinned Brandreth by his wrists to the ground. Brandreth responded by head-butting him square in the face. George's nose exploded with a loud crack, spattering the two of them with blood. He instinctively reached up with his hands to his face, crying out in pain. Brandreth, although temporarily blinded, reached down into his waistband and found the handle of what he was so desperately searching for.

"Jesus Christ, No Jerry!" screamed Isaac. Still unable to see, he brought the butt of the gun to bear on George's temple with all the force he could muster. The hard edge of the gun instantly splitting his eyebrow, he was thrown sideways to the ground once more. George had guessed that Jeremiah had managed to draw a pistol, but the mud underfoot was making it difficult to stand.

Likewise, Brandreth was still desperately blinking his attackers' blood from his eyes while trying to find some traction. Both men struggled to right themselves at the same time. Unfortunately for George, however, Jeremiah was just a fraction of second quicker. As he finally managed to stand, he heard the tell-tale click of a pistol's hammer being cocked. It was over.

The two men face each other. They were both covered in a mixture of blood and mud. The rain seemed louder than ever. His arm out straight, Jeremiah placed the end of the barrel squarely between George's eyes. Both men were surrounded by the remains of the rebels.

"You asked what I wanted, Weightman," he said calmly. "So I'm going to tell you. Then I'm going to kill you. I want revenge."

"On who?" George hissed. Blood was running down the back of his throat and his mouth was full of it. He spat what he could out.

"On those who destroyed my livelihood and

reduced me to living on handouts. I was going to be a name in history. A leader of the triumphant Luddites! Not someone who scraped a living in a trade crushed by mill owners. I want revenge for my brothers who hanged. You have no idea how it feels to see someone you struggled along side kick their legs in blind panic as the life drains out of them, while you hide in the crowd, scared that you might be next." His voice trembled. In all the time he had known him, George had never seen him so emotional. His face contorted with contempt. "You're right George. Frankly, I don't care what you and your idealist friends do with Parliament after this is over! All I want to see is the government that ruined my life utterly destroyed and if anyone gets in my way, well that's too bad. And that includes, you, George..."

George closed his eyes, waiting for the explosion that would end his life.

"Jeremiah, wait!" screamed Will.

"William Turner, please don't tell me even you have lost your bottle now!"

"No! Look!"

There was a vague distant rumble of thunder. Or was it..?

The entire group all realised what they were hearing simultaneously, but it was Isaac who spotted them first.

"Royal Dragoons! On horseback!" he cried.

"Aye and they're coming from this way too! We're surrounded!" Will exclaimed.

Blind panic. The men froze. There must have been twenty or so horses in total, ten on each side, hammering towards them, with more troops running alongside and behind. Everyone turned in the direction of the brook in time to see more men striding across the fields towards them, rifles aimed directly at them. They turned again but the view to the south was identical. Will was right. They were completely surrounded. Within moments, they were on top of the rebels.

"Hands in the air where we can see them, gentlemen!" cried their captain. "And drop your weapons. As you can see, I have a full platoon on both foot and horseback surrounding you and your sorry rabble, so you won't get far if you're thinking of running."

Pikes and guns alike thudded into the mud. The rebels raised their hands. Jeremiah was the only one still holding a gun.

"The game's up Brandreth. Now drop your weapon, or we'll take that filthy head of yours clean off your shoulders!"

Reluctantly, he obliged. "Excellent," the captain smiled, "Right men! Time to round up Oliver's sheep!"

"Did he say Oliver?" Isaac hissed.

"This doesn't make sense," exclaimed George.

"What do you mean?" said Will.

"They came from the direction of Nottingham! But the messenger told me -"

"That Nottingham was taken?" scoffed the captain. "You got the message then!" The rebels all looked at each other in disbelief. "Right men! Mr Oliver and Mr Allsopp want as many of these low life traitors captured as possible, so on my mark -"

"It's a trap!" exclaimed George, "The whole thing's been a trap from the beginning!"

Seizing the moment, Brandreth suddenly threw back his frock coat, pulled his second pistol from his waistband and fired it into the air. The captain's horse, now mere feet from him, reared up, whinnying in shock. Brandreth dropped to his knees in an instant, grabbed the pistol he'd dropped and fired that skywards too. "Scatter!" He screamed, as loud as his lungs would let him. The rebels didn't need telling twice.

Men ran in every direction. Some of them followed Brandreth's example, scrabbling at weapons dropped and firing them randomly into the air in order to add to the chaos. Horses reared. Some splashed into the brook and ran upstream back towards Langley Mill. Rifles began to ring out. Some fell immediately, their legs shattering from the devastating impact of being shot at such close range. Smoke billowed everywhere. Many were captured before being able to make a run for it. Rifle butts and bullets flew about the place. Screams and shouts were mixed with barked orders. Brawls broke out. It was unclear in the chaos just how many had effected an escape, as men scattered across fields in every direction, pursued by cavalry.

Within minutes around thirty or so men were on their knees with their hands clasped behind their heads. The remaining soldiers that had not given chase herded them like cattle into a group which they surrounded.

As the smoke cleared, Captain Frederick Philipson of the 15th Regiment of the King's Light Dragoons surveyed the devastation. This was a definitely a job well done on the part of him and his men. He'd been a little reticent of the task in hand – after all the rebels had outnumbered his troops at least five fold and he knew they were armed and the worse for wear from alcohol. It could have gone either way. Just enough booze can make men more dangerous, reckless even. But too much makes reactions slow and decision making poor. Fortunately, it had been the latter – the ambush had been timed to perfection.

"Sergeant Wheeler!" he barked from his saddle, "Recall your men."

"But, sir, quite a few have slipped the net," the Sergeant replied from his mount.

"It's of little consequence. The rest of the patrols will round them up soon enough. We have plenty here to lead us to the others. We'll soon beat the names of the rest of the rabble out of them. I need to make sure we can hold on to our quarry, in case they get any more ideas," he sneered.

"Very good Sir," nodded the sergeant. He took a small bugle from a saddle bag and sounded the recall.

11. Hunted

Will Turner was running for his life. The oxygen rushing into his lungs with every breath burned like fire. The muscles in his legs felt like hot lead as he tore across field after field, pausing only to hurdle a fence or leap across the odd entrance to a badger set or rabbit hole. He had no idea if he'd been running for minutes or hours, but it felt like the latter. As he stole a glance over his shoulder, suddenly the ground fell away beneath him and he tumbled headlong, cartwheeling down a hillock. Desperately he tried to catch hold of any random bramble he could as first the sky and then the grass flashed past his eyes over and over in rapid succession. Then, in an instant, the ground was gone and there was only sky, before the sudden gut-wrenching impact. The wind was smashed out of his chest and his head met the ground with a sickening thud.

He tried to breathe, but couldn't. Suddenly

there were hands around his torso. Wheezing feebly he clawed at them as someone tried to turn him over.

"Will! It's me! Edward." Will relaxed his grip at the familiar sound of his brother's voice, letting himself be rolled over.

It was broad daylight, but he was seeing stars, probably from the lack of oxygen as much as the impact. A face swam into view. Finally, with a ghostly rattle he drew breath. His face blue, he wretched hard. He just managed to roll onto his side before he wretched a second time, vomiting a mixture of ale and frothy sputum into the dirt. He looked up again. A wall of earth rose up in front of him, while a second pressed damp and cold into his back.

"Where are we?" he asked, confused.

"Drainage trench by the looks," his brother said. "I practically did the same as you. Came out of nowhere, it did. Funny that we both ran in the same direction." Edward grinned.

"I kept hearing the crack of rifles," Will gasped, "I kept thinking any moment now, I'll be hit and that will be it. But somehow, I wasn't. God only knows how."

"Yes. Same here. Perhaps God is on our side after all?"

Will nodded. "Unlike George bloody Weightman. Can you believe it, Ed? He sold us out. One of our own, a traitor. Wait 'til I get my hands on him. He'll get the hiding he deserves and no mistake."

"You really think he did?" Edward looked shocked.

"Well who else could it be?"

Edward shrugged. "I don't know, but I really

don't think it was George. He came back for us. Why would he do that?"

"I dunno," Will shrugged, "guilty conscience?"

"No. Didn't you hear the Captain? He said we were Oliver's sheep. William Oliver. I reckon this was a setup from the beginning."

"But what about Nottingham?"

"I'm reckoning they never even got started. Rounded up before they even made a single move."

"They must have arrested Oliver then. At one of the meetings. Probably a Nottingham one. But we heard from them only yesterday, so it must have been last night, sometime after we started out."

"It's impossible to say," said Edward, shrugging his shoulders.

"Where are we, do you think?" asked Will.

"No idea. Somewhere between Langley Mill and Codnor I think. I've lost all sense of direction to be honest. Can you walk? Are you hurt?"

"Don't think so. I'll be right as rain in minute or two, little brother." Edward smiled.

"What? I'm as fit as you and you know it!" said Will. "Besides, I think it would make more sense to stay here for a while. These fields will be crawling with troops for the next few hours."

"I never said you weren't. You're probably right though. Were they chasing you?"

"I don't know. I only looked back once and that's when I found myself in here with you."

"Lucky for you, eh?"

"Any idea who else got away?"

"No. I did the same as you. I just ran and kept running, waiting for that bullet that never came." He shook his head. "What were we thinking? What was Jerry thinking?"

"What do you mean?"

"The pubs. Getting us drunk. It was the worst decision ever. We should have been ready for a fight, not half soaked."

"I think Butterley rattled him. We looked like timid cattle. He kept saying this'll put some fire in our bellies. Dutch courage, I suppose."

"But it went too far! We became a drunken rabble. Hardly a force to be reckoned with. I'm beginning to wonder whether he was the right man for the job. He seemed reckless at times. And he shot Widow Hepworth for Christ's sake. Should we have trusted him?"

Will's temper was immediately obvious. "What are you saying Ed? That he sold us out?"

"Well, we can't rule anything out at this stage. We hardly knew the man," said Edward.

"Listen to me. You know nothing. He was a good man and a brilliant Captain. We spent weeks going over the campaign, looking at the maps, planning the route, Butterley, the barracks, everything!" shouted Will.

"Keep your voice down!"

"Or what?"

"Or you might just get caught?"

There was a series of loud clicks from above, as the two of them realised that it wasn't the other who had spoken.

The brothers looked up. Several cavalry men were pointing their rifles straight at their heads.

The soldier who had spoken spoke again. "Come on you two. On your feet. Hands above your heads. Move!"

The two Turners slowly got to their feet.

"You run that way, I'll run this," Will

whispered, indicating each way the trench ran, "They might not be able to shoot us both."

"Don't be stupid Will. It's over," growled Edward, "Though we might have been fine if you could have kept your trap shut!"

Two of the three soldiers jumped down into the trench. While one kept his rifle firmly trained on Will and Edward, the other one produced wrist irons.

"Hands out front," barked the one still above, "do it now, or I'll take your bloody heads clean off."

The two captured men did as they were told. As they were cuffed, the soldier above said "Gentlemen. I am arresting you for high treason. The penalty for which, if found guilty, is death. You will now come with us. If at any point, you attempt to escape, or do not comply completely with my instructions, I will not hesitate to kill you. Is that clear?"

The two men nodded.

"Good. Now move it!"

Utterly dejected, the two Turners clambered out of the trench.

St. Matthew's Church, Pentrich. Mid-morning, June 10, 2017.

"Our Father, which art in heaven, hallowed be thy name. Thy Kingdom come, thy will be done, in earth, as it is in heaven. Give us this day our daily bread and forgive us our trespasses, as we forgive them that trespass against us. And lead us not into temptation, but deliver us from evil. For thine is the kingdom, the power, and the glory, for ever and ever. Amen."

Reverend Hugh Wolstonholme made the sign of the cross over his chest and let out a huge sigh. Never had the Lord's Prayer seemed more poignant. He remained kneeling at the altar. It was mid-morning and the beautiful summer sun was streaming through the windows of St. Matthew's church in Pentrich, illuminating the tiny particles of dust that floated idly in the air. As a child, he'd always imagined that they were tiny angels keeping watch over him as he watched his father commune with the Lord, just like he was now.

He had never seemed stuck for words. He always seemed to know exactly what to say when talking to God. Whereas Hugh felt he was the total opposite. He knew he'd always take his father's place as curate of St. Matthew's – it's what you did. But he'd never felt quite as if he'd had the calling in the same way. Perhaps it was the fact that growing up, he'd struggled to come to terms with how the world was changing for what seemed the worse. As he transitioned from man to boy, he'd watched parishioners lose loved ones fighting the French and be forced to seek sustenance via the slavery of the mills or workhouses of the rich just to stay alive. Children had starved. Those who had come back from the fighting were shadows of their former selves, haunted by the atrocities of war, driven to drink. It had made him question the divine design. Would any God, who lived in a kingdom of eternal peace and sacrificed his only son really stand by and let this happen? He believed not and therefore, logically, he had come to the conclusion that there was no God.

But he took solace in the fact that his role was more than just being a conduit to the creator for the people of his parish. Even if he had had his faith shaken, there were plenty in his flock who had not and they often came to him for advice, guidance and comfort. He still believed in the words of the bible. How could he not? They taught you to love thy neighbour, be kind to those around you, respect others and be humble. But more and more he'd grown to feel that the bible was not the word of God, but the word of man. So he had vowed that even if he had forsaken the Lord, he would not forsake his fellow man. And yet here he was, still praying, every day. Well, it was part of his job, he mused and who knows, he might be proven wrong one day...

He was roused from his thoughts by the clatter of the church door handle followed by the tell-tale creak of its hinges. He calmly stood and turned to see who had entered the vestibule. As the figure stepped from the shadows and he realised who it was, his jaw dropped and he could barely contain his surprise.

"My dear Lord! It can't be! I thought you'd been captured!"

The door swung shut and the haggard looking figure of George Weightman staggered down the aisle towards him.

"Reverend. I couldn't think of anywhere else to go." George whispered hoarsely.

Walstonholme went to him. He was clearly unsteady on his feet. He looked tired. "Please, sit. You look exhausted," he said, taking George by the arm and steering him to a pew. George collapsed into a seat. "How did you escape capture?" he asked.

"I honestly don't know. The cavalry... they ambushed us. Jerry fired his gun and I ran. And kept running. I turned my back and fled, Reverend," he gasped, "I let them down," he croaked. At that moment, tired of running and more emotionally drained than he'd ever been in his life, he broke down.

"I'm sure you did your best George. I can't imagine what I would have done. Besides, I heard about what you did for Charles Walters. Young James Turner told me you saved his life this morning. It sounds to me like you've let no-one down."

Wolstonholme, not knowing quite what else to do, sat down beside him and held George's hand.

After a few minutes, George managed to compose himself. Using his sleeve, he wiped a mixture of sweat, blood and tears from his face. "Reverend. I need your help. I have nowhere to go. They will be looking for me. I cannot go home. I need somewhere to hide. Please. I know you helped Uncle Tommy. Might you be able to help me? Has anyone else managed to make it back?"

"I've heard that there are a few men already hiding in a hayloft not far from here. I was going to try and organise a collection around the village. Food, I mean – just bread or anything the villagers can spare. It's the least I can do for the cause."

"Which hayloft? Where? Perhaps I can join them?" George looked excited.

Wolstonholme shook his head. "George. No. Think about it. If they are caught, the worst they are looking at is a spell in Derby Gaol, charged with rioting or something similar. You are one of the leaders. They will undoubtedly know that you, Will, Isaac and that Brandreth fellow are the ringleaders. You'll be held up as an example. Charged with treason. You did all the planning, the organising.

You know what treason means, don't you George?"

George nodded. "Aye. I do, Reverend. The gallows. But where can I go? Where is Uncle Tommy?"

"I can't tell you that, George. If they capture you, they'll make you talk. If you want to keep your Uncle Tommy safe, its best you don't know anything of his whereabouts," he said.

"I would never tell those scum anything!" said George, defiant.

"You say that now, but when they're branding you with hot irons, George, the lord himself only knows what will come from your mouth to end the pain. No, I can help you. But I can't tell you where your Uncle is. I promised him I wouldn't tell anyone."

"Is that because he betrayed us?"

Reverend Wolstonholme looked puzzled. "Old Tommy Bacon? A traitor? Listen to what you're saying George! You know I support the cause more than I ought for someone in my position. No. He's not a traitor. He's a good and honourable man who fights for what he believes in and I intend he stays that way, hopefully until the day he dies. While Tommy Bacon is free, the working men of England still have a chance. I truly believe that. And that's why I will help you, like I helped him. Now, I have cousins in Yorkshire who are part of our movement. I can deliver you to them safely, but not right now. This parish will be crawling with soldiers for the next few days. You can stay at my cottage until the searching dies down. They would never suspect my involvement as a man of the cloth so my home will be the last place they'll think to look. That will give me time to make some arrangements."

George nodded. "But what about Becky? And the children? Can I see them first?"

Reverend Wolstonholme was silent. He seemed reluctant to look George in the eye.

"What?"

"George, think about it. That will be the first place they will go. If she even admits that she's seen you, even if she knows nothing about where you've gone, she will be tortured until they have the information they want."

"But I won't tell her anything, I promise!"

"That will not matter. They will be convinced she knows where you are and they will not cease trying to extract that knowledge from her until she is no more. No. For all we know, they might even be watching your house right now, waiting for you to come home. For your children and your wife's sake, George, you must not see them until all this is at an end. Do you understand?"

Reluctantly, George eventually nodded.

"I'm thinking of you and your wife and your children George. You know that. If they are to survive this, no-one must know where you are. Agreed?"

"Agreed."

"Good. Now, let's get you safe before the King's troops turn up."

Reverend Wolstonholme stood up and offered his hand to George once more. Wiping the silent tears from his eyes, George took it and let the curate put his comforting arm around his shoulders and lead him out of the side door of the church.

Nottingham Magistrate's court. June 10, 1817.
2.10pm

Lancelot Rolleston was a typical magistrate. Long in the tooth, short of temper and a stickler for time keeping. His face contorted into something resembling a British bulldog that had accidentally swallowed an angry wasp. He sighed heavily as he consulted his pocket watch for what seemed like the hundredth time. As he snapped it shut with disdain, there was a timely knock on his office door.

He immediately recognised the signature timid rapping as that of his fellow junior magistrate, Lewis Allsop. He rolled his eyes and decided to make him a wait a few moments – he took great pleasure in adding to the man's already uncomfortable demeanour. After what he deemed was probably long enough, he cleared his throat.

"Come." He bellowed.

The door creaked open just enough to accommodate Allsop's head.

Rolleston didn't look up. He didn't need to. Instead he pretended to study some papers on the desk in front of him. He knew perfectly well that Allsop would procrastinate in the doorway until he at least made eye contact. Eventually, he obliged.

"Well?"

"It's after two, Mr Rolleston. I'm here to discuss the uprising."

"Mmm. You're late, Mr Allsop. If there's one thing I measure a man by, it's his punctuality. You should know that by now."

"I know. I cannot apologise, enough. It's just that I had some problems rousing Mr Oliver."

"You mean he's not with you?" Rolleston's face was one of abject incredulity.

"He'll be along in a moment. He was, er,

otherwise engaged."

"Staying at the Blackamoor's Head no doubt, then. We really ought to send a constable to have a word with the landlady about her daughters and their lack of discretion."

"We did, Mr Rolleston. I think he ended up owing the girls about a week's wages."

"Why does that not surprise me? No wonder syphilis is rife in Nottingham. For heaven's sake man, stop prevaricating. Close the door and take a seat."

"He's here now in fact, sir."

"About time. Now, can we please get on with this? I have much to do."

A figure appeared behind Allsop, throwing the door open.

"William Oliver at your service. I assume you are Mr Rolleston?"

Oliver wasted no time in taking command. He strode into the room and hung his cloak on a nearby hat stand.

"I apologise for my tardiness, gentlemen, I had some business I needed to finish before coming here that took somewhat longer than I anticipated."

"Yes. I had gathered as much." Said Rolleston.

Without waiting for an invite, Oliver parked himself in a chair opposite Rolleston's desk. Allsop seemed momentarily annoyed, probably due to the fact he now had to find a spare chair from somewhere else in Rolleston's chambers. Oliver didn't wait.

"So. Do we have them?"

Rolleston waited until Allsop was seated, before turning to him. "Where are my manners. Mr Allsop, would you fetch the scotch from my cabinet? I expect Mr Oliver would like a drink."

Rolleston's eyes met Oliver's. Oliver smiled wryly.

"I see you and I cut from the same cloth," he said under his breath. Allsop returned with a decanter of whisky and three glasses. He poured three large measures and sat down.

"I presume we are toasting a job well done?" said Oliver.

There was an uncomfortable silence. "Not exactly," said Rolleston eventually.

"Please tell me we captured them?" Oliver's tone had changed.

"A sizeable proportion of the marchers were apprehended yes. I oversaw their internment myself this morning. However, once we had established exactly who was and who wasn't in our custody, it was immediately apparent that we still have some work to do."

"What do you mean?"

"Unfortunately, three of the four ringleaders of your little operation seem to have eluded us."

"For the love of God! It was hardly the most challenging of missions. I knew I should have taken charge of matters!" Oliver was clearly agitated.

"Well, perhaps if you hadn't been 'otherwise engaged' things may have gone a little more to plan?"

Oliver downed his scotch and held the glass under Allsop's nose. Rolleston indicated his fellow magistrate should refill it with a nod. Allsop obliged.

"So who are we missing?" said Oliver after taking another slug.

"William Turner was taken this morning. Unfortunately, as of this precise moment in time,

Messrs Weightman, Ludlam and Brandreth are still at large."

"Some forty men were taken at the scene," interrupted Allsop, "and we have troops tearing Pentrich apart as we speak."

"I don't care about the rest. They are the puppets of puppets and will be easy to apprehend. My mission will not be deemed a success until we have all four leaders' necks ready for the noose. You will prioritise finding them above all else, or you will have to answer to Westminster directly. Is that entirely clear, gentlemen?"

Rolleston smiled. "Mr Oliver, I can assure you. They won't get far."

"Do not underestimate your quarry. These men know that they face the gallows if caught and they will do everything in their power to evade you. I wouldn't be surprised if they have contingency plans for their evacuation already in motion. They are well connected in reformist circles. I'm already fully aware that you have no leads for Thomas Bacon. You will send memos to all major ports. Especially those with vessels bound for the Americas. Leave no stone unturned. Start with their homes and the homes of their relatives. Do whatever is necessary to make them talk. I will supply you with the names and addresses of their collaborators in Yorkshire. Send armed troops to them. Do not rest until you have these men in your custody. Hunt them down. Inform all local authorities that they are dangerous killers who have conspired against the crown - traitors of the most despicable kind. Offer sizable rewards. Do whatever it takes. Is that clear?"

"Perfectly, Mr Oliver. Most of these precautions we have already taken. Isn't that right,

Mr Allsop?"

"Indeed it is. My colleague Mr Enfield has a man on the ground. An informant who moves freely amongst the reformists as if he were one of them. With six children to feed and little work coming his way from trade, we made him an offer he could not refuse. He is well trusted and plans are in place that will enable him to draw them out of the shadows like moths to the flame."

"Good. Do not fail me. Believe me, there are more than just your livelihoods at stake if you do." With that, Oliver finished his whisky and stood up. "Now. I must bid you good day. I will leave you to get on with these somewhat pressing matters. I myself will be heading back to London forthwith." He threw his cloak back over his shoulders curtly. "Good day gentlemen." The door slammed shut and William Oliver was gone.

"What a vile man," said Rolleston. There was another awkward silence while he shuffled some papers on his desk. Allsop felt uncomfortable. Eventually Rolleston looked up, giving him a stare as if he were something unpleasant he had stepped in. "Well, what are you waiting for? You've been his lapdog in all this from the beginning. Might as well see the damn job through."

Allsop nodded.

"So get to it, man!" barked Rolleston.

"Of course, Mr Rolleston, right away," he fawned, backing out of the room. The door closed again, this time the clicking of the latch barely audible.

"Bumbling idiot," said Rolleston under his breath, "he didn't even have the decency to put my scotch away."

That afternoon, the manhunt began in earnest. The majority of the more inebriated men were rounded up relatively quickly, found hiding in various fields and ditches between the Gilt brook and Pentrich while trying to sober up. By early evening, Asherfield's barn was stormed by a small garrison of troops, exactly as Reverend Wolstonholme had predicted and a further twenty or so men were seized and promptly taken to Derby Gaol. That night, while children slept in their beds and wives, worried for the whereabouts of their spouses darned by the fire side, soldiers dispatched by Allsop arrived in Pentrich and South Wingfield. They were ruthless and doggedly determined, turning over every house, cottage and dwelling that was listed as home to a marcher. Women, children and siblings were dragged from their homes and beaten, regardless of whether they knew their husband's, father's or brother's whereabouts. Those men who had been foolish enough to return to their homes were chained, dragged on to the back of a waggon and extradited. Within forty eight hours, most of the Regenerationists were in custody at either Derby or Nottingham Gaol. But still the whereabouts of George Weightman, Isaac Ludlam and Jeremiah Brandreth were a mystery to the authorities.

12. The Net Closes In
Cock and Bull Coaching Inn, Uttoxeter. June 11, 1817.

"You there! Coach driver!" The call came from somewhere over his shoulder. Benjamin Buxton sighed. He had already been stopped by soldiers at several roadblocks on his journey from Derby today. It had made him late by over an hour and consequently a couple of his passengers had missed their connection here in Uttoxeter. He was not a happy man. As he uncoupled the right hand horse, he glanced momentarily back down the courtyard – a group of four troops were approaching from the side door of the coaching inn. He turned to his co-driver who was uncoupling the second steed. "Carry, on, I'll handle these," he said, nodding towards the approaching soldiers. His co-driver tipped his peaked cap in acknowledgement and continued his work.

"Gentlemen. How may I help you?" he said, forcing a false smile.

"Landlord says this coach is from Derby. That right?" said one of the soldiers.

Buxton clocked his stripes. "Aye, Sergeant, that's right. Already an hour late an' all. Been stopped three times by the King's men today."

The sergeant ignored him. "They your passengers? The ones that have just gone in the Cock and Bull?"

"Aye."

"Just them three?"

"Aye."

The sergeant nodded. "We've already checked them. Your stories match."

"What's this all about, sir, if you don't mind me asking?"

"We're looking for fugitives. Men from Derbyshire. Guilty of treason, they are. After some very dangerous fellows in particular. Do these names mean anything to you?"

The sergeant held out his hand and one of the other troops handed him a sheet of paper that looked like a warrant. He unfolded it, held it up and read out the names. "George Weightman. Jeremiah Brandreth. Isaac Ludlam. Thomas Bacon." With each name he read, he looked Buxton squarely in the eyes, gauging his reaction.

Buxton waited for a moment and then shrugged. "Can't say I've ever heard of any of them."

"You've carried no passengers of those names these past few days?"

"No sir. I don't believe I have. Could've signed up for the journey under false names, though, like."

"Indeed. What's your name, coachman?"

"Buxton, sir. Benjamin Buxton. I'm a

registered coach driver. I have my papers, if you need to see them."

"No. It's fine. We already know who you are. Who is this?"

The sergeant indicated his co-driver, who was now leading the uncoupled horse to a drinking trough.

"My co-driver. Mr Brunswick. But then, if you know my name, you'd already know that."

The sergeant smiled. "Aye. That we do, sir. Now, if you receive passengers going by any of those names, or know of any driver that does over the next few days, you must inform a constable or a magistrate immediately. Is that clear, Mr Buxton?"

"Aye sir, it is."

"Good man. You may go about your business."

"Thank you sir."

The sergeant saluted, turned on his heel and led his men out of the coaching house's courtyard. Buxton continued to uncouple the remaining horse in silence for a moment, then when he was sure the soldiers had left, he said in a hushed tone: "That was another close call, Isaac. I've had my fill to be honest. It's one thing to support the cause, but I'm no good at this sort of business at all."

Isaac Ludlam removed his cap. "Ben, I can't thank you enough. I'm so sorry. As soon as we've sorted the horses, I'll take my leave of you. I didn't mean to involve you, but it's all I could think of. When I got back to Pentrich yesterday afternoon, I'd remembered chatting to you at the White Horse the other day and you telling me that Brunswick was sick. I knew if I tried to just get on a coach, I'd be caught. But I thought if I pretended to be Brunswick, I might just slip through."

"Aye, well, let's hope I don't get stopped on the way back to Derby. They might work out my co-driver is missing and put two and two and together."

"It's unlikely they'll stop someone going into Derby as opposed to out. I reckon you'll be alright."

"Aye, well let's hope your right, Isaac. When was the last time you had owt to eat?"

"Two days ago. The night of the march."

"Here," said Buxton, handing Isaac some coins, "go and get yourself some bread and broth. Not in here, mind. Go to another inn. Then for the love of God bugger off as soon as you can. Where you headed?"

Isaac shrugged. "My cousin lives a few hours walk from here. I'll rest up for a day or two, then head south. Hopefully the searching will have died down a bit by then."

"I hope so. Get going now, before they come back asking more questions."

"What about getting the horses fed?"

"I can cope with that. I was going to drive today's run on my own anyway without Brunswick. I've done it before, I can cope. Go on, get going."

"What will you say if they do come back?"

Buxton shrugged. "I'll say you've gone to tell the new passengers we're running a bit late. It'll be fine. You go."

"You've been so kind, Ben. I won't forget this."

The two men shook hands. Isaac donned his cap, pulled it as low as he could without looking too suspicious and made his way out on to the main street.

Furtively, he crossed the road and headed

along the high street. The first inn he came to, The Red Lion, he went inside. The pub was crowded and hazy with smoke. It was lunchtime and many of the local market workers were in search of ale and sustenance. He weaved his way through the crowd and made his way to the bar. Once there, he quickly managed to attract the attention of the bar maid and ordered himself a mug of ale, a bowl of broth and a sizeable chunk of bread. As soon as it arrived, Isaac began to devour his meal where he stood.

"Not eating at the coach house?" said a voice behind him. He turned round in shock. It was the army sergeant.

"I, er, don't care for their food much," replied Isaac turning back to the bar, his heart in his throat.

"Typical coach house, eh? Bet they do all the old tricks. Serving the soup late so it gets left by passengers not wanting to miss their connection - so they can pour it back in the pot and use it again. Too much salt so you buy more ale, believe me, I've travelled enough – I've seen 'em all."

Isaac smiled and nodded nervously. His mind was doing somersaults. He couldn't leave, that would look very suspicious. But was the sergeant on to him? No, surely not, he would have just arrested him right there and then. The sergeant caught the eye of the barmaid and she came over. He ordered himself a mug of ale. Moments later, she returned with his order. As she moved to collect payment – some coins he had stacked on the bar – he reached over and grabbed her hand. She automatically tried to recoil, not expecting the physical contact, but he held her hand fast.

"Just a moment, miss. Sergeant Raynor. Royal Dragoons," he smiled. The barmaid didn't smile back. "What's your name?"

"Eliza," she replied, nervously. Isaac felt uncomfortable. She was a young girl, not even out of her teens and quite clearly intimidated by the burly officer and his demeanour.

"I need to ask you one or two questions Eliza," he said quietly.

"What about?"

"I'm looking for someone. Strangers. Dangerous men wanted for high treason. Do you see anyone in this tavern you do not recognise?"

Isaac was filled with panic. He briefly caught her eye. Would she give him away? He continued to eat. Momentarily she stared at him, trying to interpret his look. He could feel her eyes on him.

"Miss?"

He could hear his blood pounding in his chest. Every muscle in his body tensed. He wanted to run, but he knew that would be the worst thing he could do right now. Instead he glanced up at Eliza and shook his head.

"Well?" the sergeant tightened his grip round her wrist.

"Please, you're hurting me sir!"

"Sorry miss. I need to know." Without faltering, he moved his eyes towards Isaac and then back towards the girl. Silently he tightened his grip further. She nodded, wincing.

Isaac wasn't prepared to wait to see if the game was up. He didn't like the sadistic way he was manhandling the barmaid anyway. Without a moment's hesitation, he upended the contents of his broth bowl over the Sergeant's head, pushed him to the floor and turned to run. Two other soldiers appeared in the doorway. No escape that way. In an instant he vaulted the bar, before anyone had time to react, pushing his way past Eliza.

"Help me!" she cried. Several of the nearest men lunged to grab Isaac, but he managed to dodge them and bolted in to the back room.

"He's a traitor to the King!" shouted Sergeant Raynor, stumbling to his feet, "There's a reward for his capture!" The room erupted. Men were suddenly falling over themselves to try and apprehend Isaac. In the chaos, Raynor was knocked off his feet again.

Isaac was already tearing down a narrow passageway, headed for the back door. He stopped dead in his tracks when he saw the door latch lifting. He caught sight of the fourth soldier's pistol coming round the door and immediately turned right into a pantry room.

He slammed the door behind him. Ale barrels were everywhere. He grabbed the nearest one he could and braced the door with it, almost dislocating his shoulders in the process, it was so heavy. He spotted a small window at head height. He might just fit. Isaac wheeled another barrel underneath it, just as someone started shoulder barging the door.

"Open this door, in the name of the King!" It was Raynor.

His fingers scrabbled at the window's catch. It didn't seem to want to budge. Suddenly it gave way and Isaac hurled himself at the gap. At that moment, there was loud crashing sound as the door gave way.

"Get back the way you came, soldier, he's going out the window!" he heard Raynor cry, as he fell into the room. "Isaac Ludlam, you are under arrest!" He was half way out the window when he felt hands around his waist. He kicked out blindly, catching Raynor square in the chest. The sergeant crashed to the floor as he forced himself through the gap.

Isaac had underestimated his momentum however and rolled awkwardly out of the window, dropping some six feet on to the ground below, feet first, into a tight alley way between two buildings. When he tried to stand, his ankle immediately gave way under him. In that second, he heard the click of a pistol. The soldier who had appeared at the back door was approaching him from the back of the tavern.

"Stop, or I'll shoot!"

Isaac tried to stand again. It was no good. He rolled round to face the approaching troop and kicked wildly at his torso in sheer desperation. Miraculously, his boot caught the soldiers pistol as he fired, sending the shot ricocheting off the wall of the building. He stood again, this time determined to run. The other two troops were now approaching him from the other end of the alley. Isaac turned, contemplating rushing the trooper who was fumbling with his pistol in a desperate attempt to reload it. He reckoned he had about three or four seconds before the other two arrived. That was when the butt of Raynor's pistol crashed into his head.

As he hit the ground, consciousness slipping away, he felt the full weight of Sergeant Raynor on top of him.

"It's over, Ludlam!" he sneered in his ear, forcing his hands behind his back. He felt the cold metal of irons round his wrists and then everything went black.

13. Gone to Ground
Sheffield Market, June 22, 1817.

"Reverend? Is everything alright?"

"Mmm? Yes. I'm sorry, my thoughts were elsewhere for a moment. I must apologise, I've had a long journey. It seems I'm a penny short, madam. I'll leave the cheese."

The stall owner smiled. "No. You take it, you look like you need it. I'm sure the good Lord needs you to keep your strength up if you are to do his work."

"Bless you. You're so kind. I'll mention you in prayer, when I get to a church. What's your name?"

"Elizabeth. Elizabeth Cole."

"Thank you, Elizabeth. I will not forget your kindness."

"I don't think I've seen you before, vicar. What brings you to Sheffield?"

"Oh, I'm calling on a friend to inform them of the passing of a relative. A bit sudden, I'm afraid, hence my lack of preparation."

"You look exhausted. Where have you come from?"

"Dronfield."

"Have you walked all the way? In this rain?"

"I did, yes. It's not too far, a good afternoon's walk."

"But not in this weather! You need to get yourself dry."

"Yes, I will. I'm looking for the Bull's Head inn, if you please?"

"It's over there, just off the market square. Next to the butcher's. You can't miss it!" the young woman smiled.

"Thank you. You've been more than kind my child."

The vicar turned to leave, but not before looking over his shoulder suspiciously. A second later, he had disappeared into the crowd.

"Beth? You alright? Something bothering you?" It was her husband, Tom.

"That Vicar. He said he'd walked from Dronfield this afternoon. But he looked like he'd not slept for a week."

"Righto." Tom shrugged, "So what brings him to Sheffield? Did he say?"

"Bereavement. Come to inform a relative, he says."

"Probably been sat by some old dear's death bed for days then. No sleep, I expect. Who'd be a vicar, eh?"

"I suppose. Though he asked where the Bull's Head was. I told him it was yonder, next to the butchers. He thanked me then went the other way. If I didn't know any better, I'd say he was trying to avoid them two constables over there."

Tom's eyes widened for a moment. Fortunately for him, his wife was preoccupied with arranging the remainder of the produce on their stall.

"Tell you what," said Tom. I'll see if he needs help. He sounds lost..."

"Aye, he does!" Beth laughed. "In more ways than one."

"Back in a minute my love, you mind the stall."

Tom slipped into the busy market crowd. It didn't take him long to locate the mysterious vicar – the black cassock stood out in the crowd like a sore thumb. Keeping his distance, he followed him through the throng. He seemed to be trying to keep as many people between himself and the constables, but with one eye on the public house he'd asked Beth about.

Suddenly the two constables turned on their heels and headed off towards a different area of the busy square. Tom saw that the vicar had spotted this and had immediately changed direction, this time heading for the pub directly. From where he stood now however, he had a distinct advantage over the supposed emissary – he could see the front of the Bull's Head, but the errant vicar's line of sight was blocked by a group of chatting housewives. What he saw caused him to curse out loud. "Bugger," he said, quickening his pace to intercept. Two soldiers were questioning a couple of men, sipping ale in the tavern's doorway. At that moment the group of ladies dispersed, causing the vicar to stop in his tracks, a look of terror on his face – he had seen the soldiers. Tom seized the moment.

"Reverend!" he exclaimed, striding forward, his hand held outstretched, "So good to see you!

Beth told me you had arrived!"

The vicar turned, his face turning from a look of fear to one of total puzzlement. Tom shook his hand. "Tom. Tom Cole. You bring news? Of dear old uncle Richard?" he winked.

The Vicar nodded. "Yes, yes, erm, not good I'm afraid. Sadly he, er, passed away just this morning. I'm so sorry."

"We knew it wouldn't be long. Please, let me take you to my father, I'm sure he'd like to thank you for sitting with his brother these past few days." Tom gestured for the Reverend to follow him down a narrow alley between the butchers and the pub. Once out of sight of the soldiers, he turned and in a hushed voice said: "George? George Weightman? My old man asked me to look out for you. Said you'd be dressed as a man of the cloth. Quickly, we'll go in the back way!"

George nodded. "I thought I was done for then. Constables and soldiers everywhere, it seems!"

"Yes, they've been looking for you for the whole week. I'm afraid I don't know if they know you're coming here, or they're just searching all over. Those two constables are new though. Definitely not from Sheffield. You look exhausted!"

"I am. I daren't risk taking a coach. I'd heard a rumour that my friend Isaac Ludlam had been caught at a coaching house in Uttoxeter. So I've walked all the way from Pentrich. Slept in whatever I could find along the way – barns, outhouses – trees even! I'm pretty sure I recognise those two constables. I think they might actually be from Pentrich."

Tom nodded. "Well, you're in safe hands now. We'll get you to out to Joe Wolstonholme's later tonight. But for now, let's get you fed and watered." He opened the side door of the pub.

"I can't thank you enough –"

"No need, George. They might have crushed the uprising – for now, but they'll never crush the reformist movement. We're everywhere! I'll take you to a room upstairs then let Dad know you've made it here safely." George smiled. The two men went inside.

Bristol Docks, June 23, 1817.

"Stop or we'll shoot!" Jeremiah Brandreth ignored the cry. He threw the false travel documents in the face of the boarding clerk, turned and ran to the gangplank of the cargo ship bound for America that he was so desperate to board. Several crewmen tried to bar his way, but he was already at full tilt, using his momentum to barge past the first two. The third somehow managed to get a grip on his coat, bringing him down. Further along the deck, two yeomen raised their weapons.

"No, no, no, you idiots, you'll hit the sailors! Wait 'til I give the order – we need to get a clear shot. And for the love of God, aim for the legs! Do not kill him! We are under strict orders to bring him in alive," the Customs officer cried. He gestured to the sailor wrestling with him to stand clear. But instead the man just looked confused, unsure of what was being asked of him.

Brandreth seized the moment. Slipping out of his coat, he threw the rest of the garment over the man's head and bolted.

Another man appeared at the top of the ship's gangplank, blocking his way. In a split second, he was vaulting the rail, bypassing the interceptor. The fall was a good six feet, but he hit the gangplank square in the centre, behind his would be captor. The impact was enough to bring him to his knees, but he had already spotted another guard approaching the foot of the walkway and so used the rest of the momentum to barrel roll off the ramp on to the quayside.

A group of passengers sorting a pile of luggage were caught totally by surprise as he crashed through their suitcases. He grabbed one by the handle and threw it into the face of the guard at the bottom of the ramp who had now changed direction. It hit him in the square in the chin, taking him off his feet.

Although the quay was extremely busy, he was now on open ground and he estimated it was some twenty yards to the first alley way that could offer him any kind of cover. He had no choice but to run for it.

"We have him now. Open fire!" the cry came. Unfortunately, the gentleman whose luggage was now scattered across the cobbles had other ideas. Inadvertently he stepped into their line of sight, pointed at the customs officer and cried 'You Sir! What is the meaning of this outrage?"

"In the name of the King I order you to get out of the bloody way!" the customs officer boomed. Fortunately, the guard who had almost swallowed the man's suitcase was now back on his feet. Drawing his pistol he cried "I have clear sight, sir!" and opened fire.

Brick dust exploded around Brandreth's head with a deafening crack, but he did not stop. The irate passenger had bought him just enough time. He was now in the labyrinth of back streets that surrounded Bristol docks. As long as he didn't choose a dead end, his chances of escape were now greatly increased. In the distance, he could hear the cries of his pursuers. On the first ship he'd tried to board bound for the Americas, they were not really ready for him and he had managed to give them the slip reasonably easily – the element of surprise had been on his side. This time, however, as he now realised, he had been very foolish to try a second time. He chuckled at his own brazenness. He made a mental note that if he ever visited his sister in Brighton again, he would track down the forger who'd supplied him with the false papers and personally remove his silver tongue – preferably with the rustiest knife he could find. The self-proclaimed 'best forger in the south of England' couldn't even spell Philadelphia.

Unfortunately, any thoughts of recompense for the situation he now found himself in would have to wait. He could hear that the melee of sailors and government troops behind him were already gaining ground – he had run out of what sustenance and little money his sister had given him several days before now and his energy levels were desperately low. He'd only been running a minute or two and his legs already felt like lead. It was the busiest time of day – almost noon and so whichever way he turned, onlookers were only too happy to join in the sport clearly unfolding before them with cries of "He went that way!" as the soldiers arrived at yet another confusing junction.

No. If he was to escape this time, he was in desperate need of somewhere to hide. But where? He bolted down a cobbled alley that two rows of tightly packed slum cottages backed onto. Dockers and shipyard worker's homes, no doubt. Could he hide out in someone's back yard? Unlikely – he could be seen from any of the upstairs windows and if anyone saw him from the house itself, they wouldn't think twice about stepping out and giving him a beating for being on their property – these were hard men and this was a hard neighbourhood. He could tell this from the lines of washing that spanned the narrow alley way like some bizarre form of street bunting. In a street like this, no-one dared steal anything from anyone, so you could happily leave your smalls unattended on wash day.

That's when it struck him. He stopped, turned and looked about him. At that precise moment, there was no-one to be seen. The tight rows of linen and drying garments provided him with just about enough cover. He turned to the nearest line, selected the largest ladies' dress he could find and threw it over his head. Although he'd shaved off his beard during his visit to his sister's home in Brighton in order to better his chances of passing unnoticed, he did now have a few days whisker growth about his chin, but his hair was certainly long enough to pass as a woman's from a distance… he grabbed a shawl, placed it over his head like a scarf and tied it under his chin. He checked his reflection in a nearby window. He looked ridiculous in all honesty, but his pursuers were under the impression they were chasing a man in a white linen shirt and grey breeches, not a woman in a brown dress and knitted shawl.

"In for a penny, in for a pound," he muttered. A nearby back yard gate stood ajar slightly and through the crack he saw a broken wicker basket, obviously awaiting repair or relegated to use for collecting in the washing. He tucked the basket under his arm, hiding the hole in its side against his chest. Taking a deep breath, he strode confidently back the way he came, doing his best to look like a sailor's wife going shopping, albeit in hobnail boots.

Brandreth arrived back at the entrance to the alley just in time to see the troops go running past. He paused to let the last of them go by. None of them gave him a second glance. He turned left out on to the street and headed back the way he had come.

It seemed his every attempt to leave the country would be blocked and the net was closing in as the government forces were scouring the land for him. Time for a change of plan, he thought. He needed to go to ground and somewhere they'd least expect to find him…

Eccleston, Yorkshire, June 23, 1817.

It was under the cover of darkness that the horse and trap secreted George to his hideout. Pulling up outside the entrance to a carpenter's yard, the driver, Tom Cole's father Charles looked about him cautiously and then leaned back towards the cart, which contained a large tarpaulin covered consignment of timber.

"George," he whispered. There was no response. He reached out with his hand and fumbled at the tarpaulin covering until he felt something slightly softer than wood. He shook it vigorously. "George, wake up, we're here. This is Eccleston."

George stirred and stuck his head out from

under the covering.

"I'm so sorry, I must have fallen asleep. I've not had much this last week. And when I have managed to grab a wink or two, it's been with one eye open in case I was found."

Charles smiled. "Well, you'll be able to get some proper rest once you're set up at Joseph's place. I'll let him know you're here." Charles clambered down from the driver's seat. "Keep your head down a minute while I sort things out."

George dutifully retreated back under the canvas, The smell of freshly cut wood was comforting – the smell reminded him of safer, simpler times.

All that seemed a lifetime ago now and he felt a pang of sadness. Would he ever see his wife and children again? Would his life ever return to normal? Had he made the biggest mistake of life getting involved with reformist movement?

His train of thought was cut short by the sharp rapping of a fist on a door. After a moment or two, he heard a latch followed by the creak of hinges. There was a brief exchange of hushed voices. He strained to hear the conversation, but it was too faint. Then approaching footsteps. The canvas lifted again. It was Charles Cole once more.

"He says we should shift the cart into his yard and close the gates. That way no-one will see you and you can help unload the wood," he said. George nodded silently. Charles climbed back into the driver's seat and with a loud cry and a sharp snap of the reins, he began to turn the cart around. George heard the rattle of wooden gates being opened at the same time as he felt the cart manoeuvring. Eventually the gates banged shut. Then silence. A moment or two later, the cloth was pulled back completely to reveal Charles and a somewhat nervous looking man in his thirties with a beard.

"George," said Charles, "This is Joe Wolstonholme. Joe, this is George Weightman."

George held out his hand. "It's a pleasure to meet you, Joe. I can't thank you -"

The man tentatively shook his hand. "Not here. Inside. Let's get this wood off and into the store first, then we can get properly acquainted," he whispered. George nodded.

The three men worked quickly and silently, taking the long freshly felled trunks into the wood store by oil light. George was in his element and it felt good to be doing something normal again. He had no problem shouldering the heavy loads and worked twice as fast as the other two men. He was determined to earn his keep from the off.

Soon they had finished. "Right, gentlemen," said Charles, "I'll take my leave of you two. Otherwise Mrs Cole'll be wonderin' where I've got to."

"Of course. Thank you for everything, Charles. I won't forget you."

Charles chuckled. "I'd prefer it if you did. What happened with you lot has got all of us reformists looking over our shoulders. Joe 'ere especially."

"Really?" mused George, "Why's that?"

"I'll explain inside," said Joe, nodding towards his house. He then shook Charles' hand. "I'll be seeing you in a few days, Charlie. Keep safe." George shook him warmly by the hand too.

"Good luck," Charles smiled and clambered back on board the cart. Joe opened the gates and a moment or two later Charles and his cart were gone. Without another word, Joe gestured for George to follow him into the house, which he dutifully did.

14. A Sanctuary of Sorts

Joe filled a tin kettle and hung it over the fire in his kitchen. George stood and watched in silence. Once or twice Joe went to the window at the front of the house and tentatively peeked out between the tired looking net drapes. He seemed to settle once the kettle came to the boil. There was also a pot of some kind hanging above the heat. "Would you like some stew, George?" he said eventually, breaking the silence.

"If it's not too much trouble," he nodded gratefully.

"Where are my manners?" said Joe, smiling for the first time. "Please, take a seat. At the table over there."

George sank down into one of two wooden chairs that were at the tiny kitchen table. Though the kitchen itself was small, he got the impression the house itself was quite roomy. Oil lamps flickered somewhat pitifully – the kitchen was mostly lit by the fire. Joe dished up two bowls of broth and placed them on the table. He then poured two mugs of what smelt like coffee to George and brought them over. He sank into the chair opposite him and let out a huge sigh.

"You made light work o' that wood, my friend." He said, tucking into the stew. "Sorry there's not a great deal in this. Mainly taters. Bit a' meat. It'll serve, I hope."

"Honestly, it's fine."

"Not much of a cook, see. The missus usually sees to that, only she's gone callin' on her sister for a day or two. Help out with her baby, see. It's all she ever talks about if I'm honest. I ain't been able to gi' er one of her own yet. She were also none too pleased 'bout you bein' 'ere, but a promise is a promise, so here you are and there she be."

"I won't be here long, as soon as I've had time to sort myself out I'll be moving on."

"No, it's fine. She's just worried, you know, 'bout the authorities n' that. She'll be fine once things settle. Besides, way I reckon it, you ain't got nowhere you can go."

"To be honest, Joe, no."

"Exactly. You best sitting tight, I think."

The two men finished up their stew and sat drinking coffee silently for a few minutes. "Reverend Hugh's my cousin, see," said Joe. George nodded. "He's a good man. Virtuous. But he puts himself in danger helping you lot out. He's got a good job, a man of the cloth. My brother, Bill. He knows your Uncle Tommy. He was always at your meetings. One of the big noises at your Wakefield gatherings. Not anymore. Arrested him, few weeks back. So you see why I'm nervous?"

"Course. I take it you're not a supporter of the cause then?"

"The complete opposite George. I was. Still am, but I'm scared. We all are. I mean, I'm not a leader, or an organiser should I say, but that doesn't mean I don't believe in what you're doing and haven't done my bit. But having you here is a big risk. But it's also an honour. You're a hero."

"I'm not so sure about that."

"Oh you are, my friend. Me, I'm a coward. I sit at the back and pray someone will stand up, take action. But I'm too afraid to stand up and be counted with my fellow working man. I envy you, George. Envy your courage."

"More like stupidity, I reckon," shrugged George, "I'm beginning to wish I'd never got involved. The whole thing was a setup from the beginning, I reckon."

"Mmm. There are others starting to think the same, me included. Tell me what happened."

"Do you know of William Oliver?"

"The gentleman reformer? Aye."

George paused, awkwardly. Although Joe was not necessarily active, the cause of the working man was clearly close to his heart and Oliver was seen as something of a figurehead – a champion of the poor with one foot in the ruling classes – one of the very few who could help them change opinions amongst the rich. To slur him could still cause upset in reformist circles.

"I think he was a spy. In fact, I think he was more than a spy. I think he was sent amongst us to trick us into an uprising that the government could publicly crush. As a show of strength."

Joe nodded solemnly. "Go on."

"We were gaining political ground. Even sympathy. Our meetings were becoming a serious concern, discussed in Parliament. I think they thought it time to act. If they just started arresting those folk who were at reformist meetings, the Hampden clubs and the like, it would have only helped our cause, not hindered it. I think they sought to goad us into rising."

"I see. But that could easily have gone very wrong for them, surely?"

"Yes. So they made sure they put a madman in charge of the campaign. Someone with a taste for blood and violence rather than political gain. Someone who could be relied upon to whip men up into a frenzy. Someone who would kill without a second thought. Someone who could destroy the reputation of our organisation in a single night."

"Jeremiah Brandreth?"

"Aye. A man none of us knew. A man already with a reputation for mayhem and destruction. An anarchist, not a reformist."

"You think Brandreth was paid off by Oliver? To bring your uprising down, from the inside?"

"It's possible. The man was poor. A known troublemaker. One of the bloodier Luddites, known for smashing heads as much as looms. He admitted as much himself. And proudly, I must add. I think he might have been offered money and immunity from prosecution in return for carrying out this task. He is a murderer and a traitor. I have no idea of his whereabouts, but I've heard nothing of his capture which only strengthens my theory. He might be in hiding, protected by the government. But mark my words Mr Wolstonholme, he has destroyed my life and everything I hold dear and for that reason, I shall hunt him down. And when I do find him, I shall take the greatest pleasure in slitting his throat and watching the life drain out of him."

Joe was visibly shocked. "George. I understand how you feel about what has happened. But you don't know any of this for sure. You need to tread carefully. I am willing to listen, but there are those amongst us who equally would not. What you're suggesting could split our movement apart. Right now, you are a hero. A beacon of hope that things are going to change. As one working man to another, I beg you, do not throw this away. Don't you see, lad? That's what they want. They want us to fall apart, our organisation shattered by hatred and mistrust."

"So what do you think I should do? Because I think both those men need to pay dearly for what they have done."

"George, I know your Uncle Tommy. He wouldn't want that. He believed strongly in bringing about change through as peaceful means as possible."

George sighed. "Aye. I wish I knew where he was now. He could help me. Guide me."

"Aye, that's as may be. I expect he is hidden away, plotting our next move. Out-plotting the plotters of London that seek to destroy us," smiled Joe. "He'll be back, when the time is right. Might have a different alias, but he will soon be back championing the cause and that's what you should do too."

"What do you mean?"

"So we lost this battle. Walked into a trap, possibly. But you still walk free and while you do, you're a danger to them and a symbol of hope to them what believe in what you stood up for. Don't let this end how they want it to."

"So what do I do?"

"Bide your time. Stay here with me. Let these government ants give up and scurry back to their nest. They will do soon enough. Then spread the word that you'll be trying again. That we are not beaten. Go to Wakefield and Sheffield and tell them what you think the government tried to do to us. Mark my words, George, do this and we will rise up stronger than ever."

"Stay here, with you? But what about your wife?"

"She'll come round. Once things quieten down. And I've got work for you. That wood won't cut itself."

"Thank you. But I'm no leader. The peace keeper, Uncle Tommy called me."

"A leader needs to keep the peace n' all. You've got it in you. I saw how angry you were a moment ago. Use that. Brandreth and Oliver, they're not the real enemy. The government is. Don't lose sight of that. Channel that anger. Not at Oliver and Brandreth, but at Parliament. You say you've lost everything. So you've nothing to lose. You can't go home until this war on the ruling classes is over. They may have betrayed us, but while them lot are still in charge, you will have no chance of proving that. If you truly believe they did and you want to bring them to justice then you need proof and you can only do that by dealing with what is rotten at the root of this country, not pruning the branches. Do you understand what I'm saying to you, George? The fight isn't over. You have to go on. And win. Only then will you get back what you have lost."

George nodded, albeit reticently. "Aye. You're right. Otherwise all this will have been for nothing."

"Exactly. You need to get some proper rest. Things'll seem different when you've had time to rest and think. And I need you in good shape an' all. Got lots of work for you George. You need to earn your keep,' smiled Joe.

"Course. I'm a good worker, me," said George.

"I don't doubt it. But let's get some rest, eh? Early start. Come on, we've got a bed to make up!" said Joe, standing up and slapping George heartily on the back. George grinned and followed Joe upstairs.

With a sharp tug on the reins, Charlie Cole brought his horse and trap to a stop, outside his cottage on the outskirts of Sheffield. It had been a long day and he was feeling exhausted. His belly rumbled at the thought of the cheese, bread and ale his wife had waiting for him. He jumped down, opened the gate and uncoupled the horse. He pulled a carrot from his pocket, which the beast consumed in seconds. He began to lead it to the stable round the back of the house, when suddenly the front door opened. It was Mary, his wife. Even in the dim oil-lit doorway, he could see she looked troubled. Still worried about harbouring a fugitive, no doubt. He rolled his eyes. He could do without this.

"Charlie, could you come inside please?"

"Aye, let me just get the horse indoors, I'll not be a minute."

There was an awkward pause. "Right. Well, could you hurry up. I need to talk to you about somethin'," she said. Strangely, he thought she would close the door and leave him to it, but instead she just stood there not moving, as he led the horse to the stable. "Bloody hell, Bess," he whispered in the horses' ear, "I thought we'd knocked this on the head. Oh well, looks like I'm in for a bit more ear ache before this night's done."

Once inside the stable, he topped up the horse's feed trough, closed the door and headed for the house.

"Charlie? You comin'?" Mary shouted. Her voice seemed odd, wavering somehow. Something wasn't quite right. As he reached the door, she stepped backwards awkwardly.

"Right, I'm here woman, what is it now? I've had a long day so I really could do without any more ear ache about -"

As he closed the door behind him he heard a click and felt something pressed against his head from the side. Mary let out a whimper of terror. "Hands up, Mr Cole. Where I can see 'em," commanded a voice from behind him. Simultaneously another figure stepped out from behind the tallboy in the hallway, where he'd been pointing his gun at Mary from the whole time.

"Don't you hurt her! Believe me, whatever you're after we ain't got nothin' worth takin'. I knew summat was up," he said as he placed his hands in the air.

The man behind him moved the gun into the middle of his Charlie's back. "We're not here to take anything, Mr Cole. We just want to ask you a few questions, is all."

"About what, exactly? And who the bloody hell are you two anyways?" The man with the gun pointed at Mary produced a piece of paper from inside his jacket with his spare hand, which he held out for Charlie to examine.

"Officers of the King's government, Mr Cole. You'll see our papers are in order. We're here on a matter of the gravest importance, sir. We have reason to believe you might know the whereabouts of a terrorist and a traitor," he said, gesturing for Charlie to inspect the document he was holding aloft.

"I have no idea what you're talking about."

"Really?" said the man behind him. "Only your wife seems to think differently, Mr Cole. It's amazing what information one can ascertain with the right persuasion."

"You cowardly bastards! You threaten a lone woman with a gun? You should be ashamed of yourselves!"

He moved as if to lunge at the constable in front of him, who responded by seizing Mary by the arm and placing his pistol firmly in her ribs. She gasped.

"Charlie, please - tell them!"

"That's right, Mr Cole, please tell us," said the constable nearest him. "Might I remind you at this conjecture that harbouring someone wanted for treason is in itself an act of treason, which, if found guilty of, is punishable by death. So, I'm going to ask you only once, Mr Cole. Where is George Weightman?"

"This better be good news, Mr Allsop. I grow tired of this endless catalogue of bumbling and trails gone cold," said Rolleston with a sigh.

Lewis Allsop stood fidgeting nervously in front of Rolleston's desk. He bit his lip as he rummaged about his person for the memo he had eagerly brought to read out.

"For God's sake, man. If you can't remember where you've put a piece of paper how on Earth are you going to catch a couple of fugitives?"

"Here it is, sir. And it is most certainly good news."

"Good God man, don't tell me the pair of them are in custody?"

"Not quite, sir, but -"

Rolleston slammed his fist on the desk. "Then what man? Out with it! We are running out of time. If we don't find Weightman and Brandreth soon, the King will have our balls on a spike!"

"Weightman is in Eccleston, near Sheffield. We have intelligence that he is at a relative of Wolstonholme's."

"The curate of Saint Matthew's?"

"The very same, sir."

"Excellent."

"The two constables on his trail have called for support."

"No, no no, Idiots. Must I do everything myself? Seriously, if they turn up anywhere near a village like that with half a garrison trampling about the place, believe me, he'll soon know. By the time they've blockaded the area, he'll be long gone. He's not stupid. Half of Nottingham's Dragoons surrounded him and his men and he still got away. No. Get them to watch him and report back. Stealth is the key. What of Brandreth since Brighton?"

"We have a report of him trying to board several ships in Bristol bound for America. Soldiers gave chase and shot at him, but he escaped."

"Imbeciles. No bother. Like I said before, I've had some juicy bait on the hook for some time now where that scallywag is concerned. Time to reel him in, I feel. This has gone on long enough. I need you to take a letter to the Mayor. This particular job doesn't require troops or espionage."

"Then what?"

"Hard cash, Mr Allsop. I was hoping I wouldn't have to dent the coffers any further – I've already had both my ears chewed about how much this is costing Nottingham. And someone will have to do some creative accounting, but that's not my problem - it's the only language these ne'er-do-wells understand. Now stop fidgeting and sit down while I write this."

15. Full Circle
Sutton-in-Ashfield, Nottinghamshire, Saturday, July 19, 1817.

Ann Brandreth straightened up, let out a sigh and placed the bucket down on the ground by the well. She paused and wiped the sweat from her brow. She arched her back, straightening her aching spine as best she could.

"Ann?" The shout came from the back door of the cottage. "What have I told thee 'bout fetchin' and carryin' in your state? You'll bring that baby on early, carryin' on like that!"

It was her father. He had obviously woken from his nap.

"That's just an old wives tale. I've had two children already tha' knows. Besides, this bairn in't due for six months. My back's hurtin' from fetchin' this water all the time, not carryin' a baby."

"That's as may be now, but it will – if you keep doing chores like this. You should have woken me!"

"I thought I'd make the most of the quiet. It's not very often that you, 'Lizbeth and Timmy are all asleep at the same time. There's clothes to be cleaned and that floor needs a good scrub. I said you'd all be worn out, playin' in the garden all morning. I'm young and fit, but a man of your age – well, you ain't quite got the stamina you used to have!" she smiled.

"You're not too old for a hiding, you know, young lady. 'Man of my age' – the cheek of it. Now, go inside and let me get that for you," her father smiled back at her.

"I can look after meself. And besides, me and the children – well, we owe you for lettin' us stay. I have to make myself useful – at least while I still can."

"Nonsense. I can manage. If this is about your mother, God rest her – I've managed until now and let me make this clear – I didn't invite you to stay here to cook and clean for me. I invited you here because you need to be safe."

"I know, but it ain't right. Please, it's the least I can do."

"Listen, if you want to make yourself useful, you can cut some of that bread and cheese for our supper – leave this kind of thing to me." He picked up the bucket and strode towards the cottage. "Now come on girl. In the house with you and get them little 'un's some snap sorted out."

Ann rolled her eyes and shook her head as she watched her father carry the wooden pail with almost no effort. He was right. He could look after himself, but she hated the idea that her father no longer had the guiding hand and company of a wife.

As she turned towards the house, she thought

she caught sight of something moving out of the corner of her eye. She stopped a moment, looking towards the outhouse, where they kept the feed for the chickens. No. She must have imagined it -

Suddenly there was a hand tight over her mouth and an arm round her waist. In a swift movement, her assailant pulled her backwards off her feet and was dragging her towards the back of the outhouse. Ann struggled to get free, her heart in her mouth as panic welled up. She tried to cry out, but nothing more than a muffled yelp issued forth from her throat.

"Shush woman!" hissed a familiar voice. "For once and for the love of God, let that wagging tongue lie still!"

She could hardly believe her ears. The man who held her tight, once he was sure they were out of sight, spun her round to face him, his hand still over her mouth. Her eyes clearly showed her mixture of shock and surprise.

He pushed her back against the stone wall, his left hand pinning her by the chest, his right hand still over her mouth. Sure that the shock was enough to keep her silent, he slowly took the other hand off her mouth and put his finger silently to his lips, indicating that she stay silent.

It was probably only a second or two, but it felt like an age to her. Eventually, she found her voice of sorts – albeit a hoarse squeak of one.

"Jerry!" She whispered, incredulous.

Brandreth grinned. "It's good to see you, Ann."

"Don't you smile at me, you bastard. We thought you'd buggered off abroad. Or dead."

"Keep your voice down -"

"Don't you dare think for a minute you can

come walking back into our lives without such as a -"

Suddenly, without warning, he turned her to him and kissed her firmly on the lips. She let it happen for a moment, before wrestling free and slapping him hard across the face.

For once Brandreth was speechless. He held his hand to his cheek for a moment, then grinned again.

"I told you to stop doing that!"

"You deserve far worse than that, Jeremiah." – it was Ann's father, from the doorway of the cottage.

Brandreth looked round. There was an awkward silence. The two men eyed each other. It was Jeremiah who conceded. He had decided he had enough enemies at this time.

"Mr Bridget. Good to see you, sir," he said calmly.

"Wish I could say the same, lad."

"I've come to talk with Ann. And you. Please. I'll not keep you long. The King's men are looking for me."

"Aye, I know. That's why your wife and family are staying with me. I should strangle you myself, save them the bother."

"Five minutes. That's all I ask. Please? Then I'll be on my way."

There was another awkward pause. Eventually, Bridget rolled his eyes. Stepping to one side, he nodded towards the open cottage doorway. "Very well. Five minutes and no more. Then I want you gone. Best come inside, lad, otherwise you might be seen."

"Thank you, sir. I'm indebted to you."

"It's not me you're indebted to, lad. It's your wife and family. Now get inside."

Brandreth did not hesitate. Hastily the three of them went inside, the old man closing the door behind them.

No sooner had the door shut than Bridget's hands were around Jeremiah's throat, pinning him against the wall.

"Dad! Please!" screamed Ann.

"Now listen lad. I might be an old man, but so help me God I'm sure I can find it me to crush the life out of you after what you've done to this family. Have you any idea? Soldiers tearing your home apart in the middle of the night. Your wife and children terrified for their own safety! Forced out of their own home. You have no idea."

"Dad! The children! Please. Let him go! And let him speak."

Eventually, her father conceded, letting go of Brandreth, he turned to a jug on the kitchen table and poured some ale into an old tankard. He gestured with the jug towards Brandreth before placing it back on the table.

"You might as well have a drink, lad. And there's some bread and cheese here too. You look like you've not eaten proper for a good few weeks."

"No, sir. I've not. Where are the children?"

"Upstairs. Asleep. Sit. Eat. And say your piece."

"Can I see them?"

"Sit first. And talk."

Brandreth nodded. Ann sighed with relief. She knew her husband to be a fearsome character to many men, especially those that crossed him. But somehow, probably because he allowed it, her father, despite his age and diminutive stature, still seemed to hold sway over him where others could not. It was for this reason alone she believed that whatever atrocities her husband was rumoured to have carried out on that fateful night, he still loved and respected her and the family. The three sat down.

Ann's father carefully removed a loaf of bread from its brown paper wrapping and began slicing it into door step slabs. Ann took the lid from a tatty old cheese dish and did likewise.

"Like old times eh?" said Brandreth.

Bridget ignored the comment. Instead, he calmly asked "So where've you been? We heard talk of you heading to Brighton. Your sister's place. Expect you'd be looking to leave the country from there?"

Brandreth nodded. "Aye. But once I was safe – settled – work and lodgings and whatnot, I was going to come back for you. All of you. I promise. You've got to believe me. Anyway, there's been a change of plan. I'm back in contact with the movement. I'm at a safe house. It's not over. There are plans -"

"Where?" Ann interrupted.

Brandreth shook his head. "I can't tell you that, my love. For your own safety. You cannot know where I am. But we are going to rise again. We are regrouping. I was betrayed. From the inside. There was a mole. And that mole was George Weightman."

"Are you sure? Bacon's nephew? Surely there was never a more loyal reformist than him?" said Bridget.

"I know it was him. He gave himself away. But don't worry. I've got plans for him an' all. Next time I see George Weightman, it'll be to put a knife in him."

"Jerry, please," said Ann.

"He deserves it. He's a traitor." The three ate silently for a few minutes. Eventually Ann spoke.

"So what are these plans?"

"No," said Bridget. "Don't tell us. We mustn't know. They'll come here, eventually. They're hunting you. I don't care what you've got planned or who is behind you. Eventually, they'll find you and when they do, it will be the noose."

"You're wrong. To the movement, I am a hero. A leader of working men. They need me. Don't you understand? I couldn't be in a better position! They need a figurehead. A man of action and I have proved that I am it. This is just a temporary setback. Just you wait and see. We will rise again, with me as their captain and my first job will be to find George Weightman and make him pay for what he did to us."

"No lad. I don't know who's filling your head with this nonsense, but you need to face up to the truth. It's over. Why can't you see that? It's been over since they rounded up your little gang of loom smashers and sent them to the gallows. Why didn't you learn your lesson then? God spared you then, but you wouldn't let it go -"

"God spared me then, because what we did was right and just. And I tell you this, old man. I will not rest until I've had my revenge for what happened to my brother luddites. And that revenge starts with George bloody Weightman! Now I would like to see my children if you don't mind?" Brandreth slammed his fist down on the table, causing cutlery, crockery and his wife Ann all to jump. There was a moment of silence. Brandreth looked first at Bridget and then his wife. "Well?"

Ann scraped her chair back and began to rise from the table. Suddenly Bridget's arm was across her lap.

"No." he said calmly. "Stay where you are, Ann." She sat down.

Brandreth began to boil. "Don't push me, old man, I'm warning you -"

"No! You listen to me Jeremiah, and you listen good. They are going to come here, looking for you. And when they do, your wife and I are going to have to lie and say we've not seen you. Like you've already said, we can't possibly know where you're hiding because, make no mistake, they will do terrible things to us if they think we know where you might be. As it stands, the only thing we will have to lie about is having seen you at all. If pushed, they might end up getting that out of us but whatever they do to us, they'll soon figure out we're telling the truth that we don't know where you are. But if we are to stand any chance of convincing them we haven't seen you, then I'm sorry Jerry, but you can't see the children. They won't be able to keep a secret like that, especially if they are witness to anything they're doing to me and Ann to get us to talk. So, no."

Brandreth began to shake his head.

"Damn it!" said Bridget. "Think about it lad! If you care at all about your family and what you're saying you believe to be true about this not being over, then you will honour what I'm asking of you now."

"Which is?"

"That you leave now, without seeing the children and only come back when all this is finally over. I don't care what you think of me, but you owe it to Ann and your children to keep them as safe as you possibly can."

Brandreth held Bridget's gaze for a moment. Then he looked at his wife. Finally he stood up. "In that case, I best be off. But I promise you, old man, this is far from over."

"I hope you're right lad. Believe me, I'll be the first to pat you on the back if you're successful. I wish you and your comrades the best of luck, because ultimately, I want the same as you. Call me a coward if you like though, but I'm not prepared to risk everything I hold dear for any cause. But the world won't change itself either. You are prepared to fight for what you believe in. That is honourable, even if I don't believe in what you do, I admire your resolve. But you must go, now."

Brandreth nodded. Ann began to cry. He took his wife in his arms. "Don't cry, my love. I will be back. I promise you. And when I return I will be a free man and a hero. And this country will be free. Understand?"

She nodded. Slowly, he drew himself away from her and made his way to the front door. Ann couldn't bear to look up, her resolve crumbling. Her father rose and stood between her and Brandreth, taking his daughter in his arms. He turned and nodded for Brandreth to go. Jeremiah turned on his heel and seconds later, the cottage door clattered shut. Ann buried her head in her father's chest, not daring to look up, she let out a stifled sob.

"Ann, my love, it's alright. You'll see him

again soon, of that I'm sure," Bridget said. He wasn't lying to her, he was certain of that much, but he didn't dare tell what he thought the true nature of their next encounter with Jeremiah Brandreth would be.

"If I correctly recall, Mr Allsop, I told you in no uncertain terms that I did not want to see you again unless you were bringing me some good news regarding our quarry. Please, for both our sakes, tell me you here to put me out of my misery."

Lewis Allsop nodded like an eager puppy while nervously shifting his weight from foot to foot.

Rolleston looked up from his desk and rolled his eyes. "Come on then, out with it, man."

"We're watching Weightman now, sir. You were right. He's lodging with a reformist sympathiser, in Eccleston, not far from Sheffield. A carpenter by the name of Joe Wolstonholme. As per your instructions, I sent a message to the two constables to keep him under observation and await further orders."

Rolleston smiled, catching Allsop off guard. "Excellent. I told you so. Are you absolutely sure he hasn't twigged?"

"Yes sir, seems pretty settled by all accounts, working for the man. Shall I send instructions to apprehend him?"

"Not just yet. Let him lie a little longer. He's not an idiot. He's cut from the same cloth as his uncle. If he gets even the vaguest whiff that we're on to him, he'll be off and Mr Oliver will be delivering our balls on a plate to Parliament. Make no mistake, he is more than capable of giving that pair of half-wits the slip. We know where he is. We need to let him feel comfortable, so he lets his guard down. I'm putting my neck on the line here, but we stand a much better chance of snaring him if he thinks he's safe. Send the two constables enough money to lodge in Sheffield for the next five days. Anywhere closer and he might get wind of it. Strangers don't go unnoticed in these isolated communities. But Sheffield is big enough for our men to remain undetected. But do your homework – put them somewhere that we know isn't infected by this wretched reformist network."

"Very good, sir."

"And where is this Cole fellow who gave us the lead?"

"He's being held in custody in Sheffield as a suspected terrorist and a traitor to the crown."

"Right. He'll have had long enough to stew. Offer him a substantial reward and tell him to keep his trap shut, then release him. Tell him there'll be a further reward if Weightman is apprehended without any further hitches. I don't know what a carter earns, but it can't be great deal, so make him comfortable, income wise, for the next six months or so. But make it perfectly clear that if Weightman absconds he'll still be facing the gallows. That should help him make his mind up where his loyalties lie. And get that release order out quickly. We don't want him missed. Is that clear?"

"As day, sir."

"Now, what of Brandreth? Any news on that front?"

"Indeed there is, sir. Our man has made contact and taken him in."

"Excellent. At last! You and I might actually

come out of this not looking like a pair of idiots. Is he there now?"

"No sir."

"What?"

"Our man says he has gone to visit his wife and children in Sutton-in-Ashfield, but is due back this evening."

"Perfect. We move in now and lay in wait for his return. Send a messenger on horseback immediately. Do not mess up, Allsop. We are so very close to crushing this revolt once and for all. Those men are now a hair's breadth away from the hangman's noose."

"Indeed they are, sir. Indeed they are. Will that be all?"

"You've done well, Allsop, though it pains me to say it. There's just one more job left to do."

"Of course, sir. And what will that be?"

"I want you to gather up all correspondence and paperwork that references Mr Oliver and burn it." The look on Lewis Allsop's face spoke volumes. "Problem?" asked Rolleston.

"Well, sir, you're asking me to break the law. Speaking as one magistrate to another -"

"This is by order of the government itself, Mr Allsop. All papers residing within this building carrying Mr Oliver's name are to be destroyed. Do not worry. This will not compromise your position in any way. You have my word. Now get on with it man. Time is short and we must make our kill."

"Understood, sir," Allsop said, somewhat twitchily. With that, he turned and was gone from Rolleston's office.

"Wretched little man," whispered Rolleston quietly to himself. "Thank God you're as spineless as I always thought you were."

He grinned smugly to himself. Today had indeed been a good day. He reached for his decanter.

Pentrich – England's Last Uprising

16. The Death of Freedom
Bullwell, Nottingham. July 22, 1817.

"Jerry! Jerry! Rise and shine me old mate. Come on. There's work to be done." Henry Sampson rapped on the door to his spare room loudly for the second time.

"What time is it?" came the muffled reply from within.

"Breakfast time!"

The door swung open to reveal a bleary eyed Jeremiah Brandreth in his long-johns.

"Funny. I meant what hour?"

"Just after six. It's a lovely morning Jerry."

"Tha' could have let me sleep in. It's a long walk from Sutton to here tha' knows. Me feet are still aching now."

"You walked all the way?" Sampson asked incredulously.

"Well I could hardly get a coach, could I? Has tha' forgot I'm a fugitive? A wanted man?"

"Of course I haven't! But someone might have

took pity and g'en you a lift. A Passing carter?"

"Not at that hour. I had to wait 'til dark before setting off, man. I can't be seen, can I?"

"No. Course. There's eggs and a bit o' porridge downstairs."

"So what's the plan? Did you sort it? You said you were going to see some contacts while I went to see Ann."

"Aye. I did. All in good time. I'll explain while we eat. Now get dressed and come downstairs."

With that, Sampson turned and headed down the narrow stairs of his tiny cottage. He paused by the front window and peered nervously out into the village. There was no-one to be seen. He frowned and then began serving up two bowls of what looked like wallpaper paste. He placed both bowls on a tiny table by the window and carefully scooped two boiled eggs out of a pot of boiling water on his battered old stove.

Brandreth appeared at the foot of the stairs.

"Coffee?" asked Sampson. "It's not the best, but it serves."

"That's fine comrade. Times are hard for us all. Don't worry, that'll change soon enough," grinned Brandreth.

Sampson gestured towards the table and Jeremiah took a seat. He poured a couple of mugs of tarry black liquid and sat down opposite him. The two of them ate in silence for a few minutes. Brandreth, clearly the more ravenous of the two, was already washing down the mixture of boiled egg and grey goo with the murky contents of his mug while Sampson had barely started.

He banged his cup down dramatically, wiped his mouth free of residue with the back of his sleeve and said "Right then. I've waited long enough Henry. Tha' knows time is of the essence. They could be coming for me right now. What's the plan? You do have one don't you?"

"Aye. Aye. I've made arrangements for you to be taken to Wales. Swansea. There's a supply cart arranged. It won't be comfortable, but it'll serve. You'll be the driver's mate, with a false name. Some papers are being made. There's a reformist group there who'll take you in – one of 'em works on the ships. He's going to get you on a ship to America. He knows what he's doing, he's helped many a fugitive such like yourself out of the country."

"Marvellous work. So when?"

"This morning. They should be on their way now I reckon. That's why I had to wake you so early, Jerry. Sorry, but you did say you needed to move as quick as possible."

"Aye. Still, I'm surprised you managed to sort all this so quickly."

"I arranged a letter to be sent ahead of you yesterday, so they'll know you're coming. There'll still be some talking to be done when you get there, but trust me, there won't be a problem. They're used to doing this. You're looking like you don't trust me, Jerry. What's the problem?"

"You just seem a bit -"

Brandreth was halted mid-sentence by a sharp rap at the door. He froze, looking directly at Sampson, who gestured for Jerry to be quiet with a finger to his lips. Instinctively Brandreth reached for the place in his belt where he kept his pistol, but silently cursed himself when he remembered he'd long since sold the weapon for food during his exile. Sampson edged to the front window and tentatively leant forward, straining to see who was at the door. After a moment or two, he let out a huge sigh of relief.

"It's alright Jerry, it's them."

Brandreth grinned. "You've done well my friend. Very well. I'll get me kit bag." He hurried upstairs.

Sampson opened the door.

"Is he here?" a man on the other side whispered. Sampson nodded silently, and gestured for the two men to step inside. They entered cautiously, the one who hadn't spoken looking behind the door before closing it. At that moment Brandreth reappeared at the bottom of the stairs with a small duffle bag over his shoulder.

"Gentlemen. Am I glad to see you!" he beamed, holding out his hand.

"Jeremiah Brandreth?" said one of the men stepping forward.

Brandreth nodded eagerly. "Aye that's me."

Smiling, the man took Brandreth's outstretched hand, but instead of shaking it, he suddenly twisted it violently up his back. Jeremiah dropped the kit bag and fell to his knees, gasping in sharp pain. Before he had chance to do anything with his free fist, the burly stranger had forced his other arm to join the first in the centre of his shoulder blades. With a swift flourish, Brandreth was in wrist irons. He rolled over and lashed out with his feet, but his captor nimbly sidestepped.

"Sampson, you bloody weasel! I trusted you!" Brandreth cried, staggering to his feet.

"I swear Jerry, I thought it was them! We've been set up!"

It was at this point the second man, who had

been guarding the front door, stepped forward producing a short wooden truncheon from his overcoat. He raised it above his head. As the first man neatly swept Brandreth off his feet with a single sweep of his boot, the second made swift work of applying the thick wooden baton to the back his head.

Jeremiah Brandreth lay in an awkward crumpled heap on the stone floor, unmoving. A single rivulet of blood ran out of his hair and down the side of his ear.

The second man put his truncheon back inside his jacket and knelt by the side of his bounty.

"You did good, Henry," said the first.

"But when does 'ah get paid?"

"There's a pulse. He's just sleeping like a baby," the second man said, taking two fingers off of Brandreth's jugular.

"Good job an' all Constable," said the first, "otherwise, if you'd killed him, none of us would get paid."

"So when does 'ah get me money?" Sampson asked again.

"Nowt to do we us, I'm afraid. You'll have to ask Mr Rolleston that y'self."

"Right, and when will that be?"

"In about two hours' time I should reckon, cos you're coming with us, Henry Sampson."

"What for?"

"To give a statement of course. The magistrates 'll need to know that we had no choice but to render the suspect unconscious due to his violent nature."

"But he barely had time to -"

"Look, Mr Sampson, if you want to get paid

like the rest of us, be a good lad and do as you're told, otherwise constable Preston here will have to take his wood to you an' all. Now, gi' us' hand getting this lump on the cart will ya?" said the first constable, gesturing toward Brandreth's body.

Between the two of them, Preston and Sampson hoisted the unconscious Brandreth on to their shoulders.

The first constable grinned as they carried him out of the cottage. "And that, Jeremiah Brandreth," he chuckled smarmily, "Is the end of your precious revolution, forever."

Glistening with sweat, George Weightman put down the large bow saw he was brandishing and collapsed on to a nearby log, panting.

Joe appeared, carrying two mugs of ale and parked himself next to George on his makeshift bench.

"Tha's made swift work 'o that lot, George. I was expecting it to take all day. It's only lunch time and it looks as if tha's about done already."

"I told you I was good!" grinned George. Joe handed him one of the mugs. "Anyway, there's still a few left, look." George gestured to a small pile of timbers.

"Aye. Not many though. And they all look bang on to me. Did you measure them?"

"Nah. No need. I knows what six foot looks like, God knows I've cut enough timbers in my time. Tha' can measure 'em if you like."

"No need. I can see for me self," he grinned. "Now, let me get some bread and cheese and we'll make a lunch of it, eh?"

"Let me finish these few first, Joe."

"Don't be daft. At this rate I'll have run out of work for you by Wednesday! Have some bloody snap and be done wi' it."

"Well, if you insist," George grinned. He reached for his shirt, which he'd hung on a nearby woodpile.

"Here's to doing a fine job!" said Joe, and he clanked his mug against George's. "Right I'll get that bread and cheese," he said patting George on the back and heading back to the cottage.

After watching Joe head back, he put the shirt back down and reached for the saw. 'No harm in doing one more while I wait," he mused to himself. He was just about to make the first cut when he heard a crash from the house. He looked up. The door stood agape, but the yard was silent.

"Joe?" he called. Silence. "Joe?" he called again louder. Still no response. Something felt wrong. He tightened his grip on the bow saw handle and cautiously approached the house.

Arriving at the front door, the hairs on the back of his neck stood on end. He tentatively pushed the door open, but could see no-one. He stepped inside the kitchen and suddenly the door was thrown shut by someone from behind it.

George span round, raising the saw. A tall man stepped out of the shadows, brandishing a truncheon.

In that instant he heard the click of a pistol being cocked, coming from behind. George span round again. Framed in the doorway to the pantry was Joe, with a pistol resting on his temple.

"I wouldn't if I were you, Weightman," a voice said sternly, from behind Wolstonholme. "Drop the saw, there's a good lad."

"Show yourself!" said George.

"With pleasure!" came the voice, pushing Joe into the kitchen in front of him.

"On Your knees in front of me, please, Wolstonholme."

Joe knelt. "Hands on your head. Do it," the man ordered calmly.

George's jaw dropped. "Martin?"

"Constable Bartlett, if you don't mind, George," the man said, stepping into the sunlight streaming through the kitchen window, his gun still trained on Joe's head.

"But you're one of *us*. A working man!" said George.

"Aye, but I'm also a constable for the parish now and I'm afraid I'm here to bring you in, my friend."

"But you believe in what we stand for!"

"Aye, but I also believe in upholding the law. Which you've broken multiple times, making yourself an outlaw and a traitor to King and country."

"You won't shoot. Do you know who that is? He's a cousin of our vicar."

"George, I have orders to capture you by any means necessary and I'll use whatever force I have to."

"Does that include on me?" George shouted and raised the saw, as if to rush the man. But George had forgotten the second constable behind him who had closed the door. Suddenly the truncheon was across his throat, dragging him backwards off his feet. He clawed at it, but it was futile. The second constable was a giant of a man.

Bartlett remained calm. "Constable Marsden's

a big lad, George, so I wouldn't try anything, or he'll snap you like a twig."

"It was you, wasn't it? Who I saw in Sheffield," George spat.

"Aye. It was. We've been tracking you since you left Pentrich. We were just waiting for the order to apprehend. We've now received that order. So you're going to have to come with us now. The game's up. Now be a good lad and drop the saw."

"Bartlett! Listen to me. The Government you work for is corrupt. They set us up from the beginning. They wanted to stop the growing support for us in its tracks. To make us look like rabble. Criminals. You can help us. We could use men like you. You have principals. You have to listen to what I've got to say. I promise, I won't do anything stupid, just lower your weapon."

"Not a chance, George. You're a terrorist. There was a time when I thought you lot stood for something. I wanted to be part of it. But that was before you started shooting innocent men and smashing up people's property."

"I had no part in any of that. It was all down to a man called Jeremiah Brandreth. He was unhinged and deliberately put amongst us to sabotage our cause. You've got to believe me!"

Bartlett shook his head. "No George. You all let us down. You and your gang of wrong 'uns. Did you not stop to think about the impact on our community if your ridiculous scheme failed? They have torn Pentrich apart looking for you lot. Wives, children, brothers, sisters – arrested, beaten even. They've ripped our community apart. I've heard talk of pulling down the houses belonging to the families of those involved. I'm here to put an end to that. By bringing you in. You say you did what you did for the working man - so that the people of Pentrich could have better lives. Well answer me this George, how can you say that when what you've done has brought us misery and destruction? That's why I'm here. Because I *do* care about our community. It's the only way I can bring this terrible, terrible business to an end. Any hope we have of saving our village lies with me bringing you in, because until you're in the hands of the magistrates, they will not stop their campaign to wipe Pentrich off the map of Derbyshire."

"He's lying, George!" said Joe.

"I am not George. You know me. And you know Marsden here too. Have done all your life. Look at yourself, George. They say one man's freedom fighter is another man's terrorist. And you may well ask who's side am I on? Yes, I think the same of the government as you, but there comes a time when you question what is the right thing to do for your people. Your family and friends. Well I think this is the right thing to do George. To end the suffering that you have brought upon the people of Pentrich. I truly believe what I'm doing is right, just as you did I'm sure. And like you, nothing is going to stop me standing up for what *I believe* will put this situation right – and that's bringing you back with me to Derby, alive or dead. Now, don't make me prove it, George. Drop the saw and come with me. I'll even let Joe go. He will not face any charges, you have my word. But please. Do the right thing. Come with me now of your own free will or I will take both of your bodies back in a couple of sacks. It's up to you." Bartlett gestured for Marsden to release George. He did so.

George stood in silence for a moment. Bartlett raised an eyebrow. "Well? What's it to be?"

George looked at Joe, who nodded. He released his grip and the bow saw clattered to the floor.

17. From Persecution to Prosecution
County Hall, Derby, August 18, 1817.

"Good morning, gentlemen, I trust your lodgings were more than adequate and that you all slept well. Apologies for my tardiness, I was waiting on my clerk to finish adding a number of key addendums to the briefs," William Lockett announced cheerily as he swept into the room, slamming the heavy wooden door with his posterior because his arms were stacked high with legal bundles.

He was a weasely looking man, with rodent like features and beady eyes, but was always immaculately turned out. He barely glanced at the impatient congregation before him.

"I think you will find everything in here is now in order and that we are more than ready to do our duty for the Crown."

He scurried to the head of the long oak meeting table, dropping the tower of papers with a dramatic thud. Immediately, the six other men seated round the table rose to their feet and one by one exchanged formal handshakes with him while Lockett continued to orate. "Well, I'm sure you've all already met, but just to make sure everyone is familiarised, we have present for this meeting Attorney General to the Crown, Sir Samuel Shepherd, Solicitor General to the Crown, Sir Robert Gifford, Sergeant Vaughan, Sergeant Copley and my appointed learned colleagues Messrs Clarke, Gurney, Reader and Reynolds and as I'm sure you are all aware, I am William Lockett, the solicitor acting for the prosecution on behalf of Derby County Court."

Lockett paused to allow a second flurry of handshakes and head nods across the table, before handing each man a bundle, leaving the last one for himself, which he opened dramatically. "Please," he gestured, "be seated." There was a brief scraping of chairs as everyone sat down.

"Now, as you know we are here by the appointment of his Majesty's Government to represent the Crown as prosecutors against the rioters of the Pentrich and Wingfield districts, who on the night of June the ninth -"

"Yes yes yes, Mr Lockett," interjected Shepherd, with more than a hint of tedium in his inflection. He was a tall, chiselled looking man with a serious face and piercing eyes. When he spoke, it was with the unnerving authority of someone with a distinguished legal background. "We are all familiar with the purpose in hand and I'm also familiar with your methods and how in particular, that you like to do things 'by the book'. I don't doubt everything here is watertight, cross-referenced and comprehensive. We can apply our attention to the minutiae at a further engagement but let's get one thing perfectly clear from the beginning. These men, these self-styled 'regenerators' were not rioters. Their intention was to destroy the democracy and governance of this land and I have strict orders from Parliament that these men will all be tried as protagonists of high treason. Myself and Mr Gifford's sole objective regarding these proceedings is that as many of these men as possible are found guilty of the highest betrayal possible and that they are sentenced accordingly. I'm sure I don't need to familiarise your good self with what that entails?"

"No sir. You do not. I can assure you, nothing will give me greater pleasure as I've been in pursuit of every last one of these miscreants since the entire debacle took place some two months past and -"

"Good. So without ado, I'd like to bring to your attention some key details on exactly how this is going to work. You will follow myself and Mr Gifford's instructions to the letter. We are very much under the scrutiny of not only our paymasters, but every newspaper, journal and political commentator throughout the land. What is discussed here today in this meeting room does not leave the four walls of this County Hall under pain of death. Is that clear?"

"Very much so Attorney General, yes, we have all sworn an oath -" Lockett could feel his mouth becoming dry.

"Forget your oath. The future of the country and those who govern it hangs very much in balance. If we mess any aspect of this trial up, we could be facing anarchy and insurrection on a grand scale, which brings me to my first point regarding jury selection. I want as many men of wealth as you can find. Land owners, profitable farmers, mill owners. As many men as you can gather that will not look favourably, or with pity, on the plight of these wretched fellows. I want you to do everything in your power to make sure that the trial is held off until the harvest is completed."

"May I ask why?"

"Because firstly, they will be both reluctant and distracted participants if they think this trial is likely to interfere with their profits. Secondly, if the harvest has failed, they are more likely to be sympathetic to the plight of their work force, many of whom are represented here, with their pleadings that poverty and starvation drove them to it. I've done my research here and pending a complete turnaround with the weather of the next few weeks, all should go well where mother nature is concerned. But if not, we will need time to be able to change our tack accordingly."

"Very well. I will make every endeavour to see that hearings begin in, say early, October? Around six to seven weeks from now?"

"No endeavours, just see to it."

"Very good, Attorney General, consider it done." Lockett made a note on the front of his bundle. He could feel the sweat collecting on his brow. He took a kerchief from a pocket under his gown and mopped it away. "Anything else?"

"Indeed there is. I wish to discuss the role of Mr William Oliver in these proceedings."

"Very well..."

"There is to be no mention of his involvement whatsoever. If any of this documentation makes reference to Oliver I want it removed immediately. He is not to be called to court by the prosecution in any capacity."

"Why?"

Shepherd shot Gifford a glance and a nod, motioning him to speak.

"There is this, shall we say, somewhat absurd notion that Oliver was a government plant. A spy. Some are going further and suggesting that he was an agent provocateur. All completely unsubstantiated, of course."

Lockett nodded. "But he is well known in Parliament to be a sympathiser for the rights of the working men. It's also common knowledge that he has travelled the land speaking with groups of disaffected labourers. A wealthy voice for the struggles of these men is one thing, but a spy? Or even worse? Surely such talk would be thrown out of court as nonsense. But he has attended these groups and meetings. What if the defence wishes to bring Mr Oliver to the stand as a character witness? Or even worse, to confess that he was indeed some kind of fire starter?"

"I've already got wheels in motion to make sure that does not happen," continued Gifford.

"Meaning?"

"Meaning that I've had, shall we say, persuasive words in the right ears that rather than help their cause, legally it will be seen to totally hinder it."

"In what way? If rumours are circulating that Oliver was a spy and he is called to give evidence this could look -"

Shepherd held up his hand, halting Lockett in his tracks.

"Let's just say that I've planted the seeds that if the defence plan to out Oliver as a government agent then it will make them all appear completely guilty of treason. Not rioting, or protesting and therefore the consequences for them will ultimately be much worse."

"I see," grinned Lockett. "Most wily indeed. But if that's the case, why not just give them enough rope?"

Are you familiar with the trial of Folly Hall, Mr Lockett?"

"I am indeed, sir."

"The crown versus Watson, Hooper, Thistlewood and Preston."

"Aye, it took place not two months hence."

"They should have been found guilty of high treason, but instead the trial collapsed because of accusations that a member of that party was in fact a government plant, who incited their behaviour. That the powers that be were seeking to make an example of these reformist groups."

"But it wasn't proven either way -"

"Let's just say I'm double bolting that particular stable door. Mr Oliver will not appear nor be mentioned. If, in the unlikely event that the defence mentions his name we will divert them away from the subject as irrelevant conjecture. Furthermore, I am making arrangements for Mr Oliver to be brought to us on commencement of the trial under a secret identity. He will remain in our custody until the proceedings are closed. That way, if we need him to, say, suit our needs, we can make use of him as we see fit and also, more importantly it will ensure there will be no surprise appearances of Mr Oliver on behalf of the defendants."

"Very good," said Lockett, hastily scrawling another note and placing the piece of paper back into his bundle.

"Now, to the matter of the ringleaders. I am of course referring to Messrs Brandreth, Weightman, Ludlam and Turner."

"Of course. What of them?"

"I trust they have been placed in solitary confinement to avoid evidential contamination?"

"Yes. We've not been able to do that with the others and if I'm honest with you, Derby Gaol is rapidly becoming untenable due to the recent influx of marchers. We've rounded more or a less a hundred of them up in the intervening months."

"But these four reside alone?"

"They do indeed."

"Good. I want the four of them ironed and sustained only on bread and water until the trial. They are to have no contact with one another – not in the exercise yard or anywhere else until the trial is over. Is that clear?"

"Yes sir."

"I want any rebellious intent totally squeezed out of them. I want them starved both of will and of body. I care not what happens to the rest of the rabble and their testaments are almost irrelevant. But these four must be in a state of total despondency by the time we come trial. They must not have their wits about them. Not one bit. And finally, as for the trial itself – all eyes will be upon us as I stated earlier, so I want swift justice. The longer this persists, the more opportunities will arise for things to go awry. This trial should last no more than five days. Is that understood?"

"It is."

"Good fellow."

"Is that everything, Attorney General?"

"For the moment, yes."

"Very good... Now, I have a question for you, sir. Do we have any idea who is to represent the riot - I mean the insurrectionists?"

"Yes. It will be Mr Thomas Denman and Mr John Cross."

"I see. Denman has track record in these parts for representing Luddites in these recent, somewhat unsettled times."

"I know and that's why I can't think of anyone more suited for the role. It will all appear exactly as it should, don't you think Mr Gifford?"

"I do indeed."

A knowing look passed between them.

"Very good," Lockett scribbled the names down, eagerly. "And Mr Cross?"

"Neither use nor ornament, Mr Lockett and therefore a somewhat large fly in Mr Denman's ointment, I rather think…"

Shepherd and Gifford both let out a hearty laugh.

Lockett beamed. "Well, that's the important parts of the agenda out of the way. How about I arrange for someone to fetch something medicinal to help ease us through this lot?" he said, indicating the bundles placed in front of each of them.

Derby Gaol, August 20, 1817.

"Your visitor has arrived, Mr Eaton, sir." Derby Gaol's commander in chief looked up from his desk towards his open office door. The eager young clerk standing in it raised an eyebrow indicating mild surprise at what was clearly bafflement on the face of his superior. "Thomas

Denman, sir," he offered, "The counsel who is to represent the Pentrich men."

The penny dropped. "Ah, of course. I'm afraid I was not tracking the passage of time with the vigour that I ought, Wilson. Where is he?"

"He's at the gatehouse, sir. Shall I bring him up?"

"Yes, most definitely, yes."

With a nod, the clerk disappeared, returning a moment later with a tall, immaculately presented, chiselled looking man with neatly cropped her in his late thirties. Eaton rose from behind his desk and immediately offered his hand, which Denman shook firmly.

"A pleasure to meet you finally, Mr Denman. Would you like a seat? Might I offer you some refreshment?"

"No, thank you, Mr Eaton, perhaps later. First and foremost, I'm keen to familiarise myself with the accused – the leaders in particular."

"Of course, of course. The four gentlemen in question are in the solitary wing. I will escort you myself. Wilson, will you be so kind as to take the gentleman's overcoat and baggage?

Wilson held out his hands. Denman handed over a large leather bag clearly stuffed with documents and turned his back to the young clerk who hung the bag on a nearby coat stand, then slipped the pristine frock coat from the solicitor's shoulders in a well-practiced manner.

"Right, if you'd care to follow me, Mr Denman, I'll make sure one of the guards accompanies us, just as a precaution, you understand..."

George Weightman was jolted awake by the loud echoing clank of a key turning in his cell door. Almost in reflex, he tried to rise from his cell's meagre wooden bunk. The single brown hessian blanket that he'd been provided with slid to the floor revealing the painful reminder of why he couldn't just sit up. Both wrists and ankles were bound in irons, joined by a heavy linkage chain. He winced and let out a gasp of pain. His breath hung in the dank air about his head, causing him to shiver. He tried again to rise from his supine position, this time with more caution, to avoid his restraints removing any more flesh from his joints. George dropped his stockinged feet to the ground, the weight of the irons dragging him upright, just in time for him to see his cell door swing open.

He squinted in the gloom. A single barred letter-box like window above his head was the only light source. Eventually, his eyes adjusted and he recognised his captor.

"Mr Eaton. I'm afraid I have no idea what hour it is..." his voice was hoarse.

Eaton stepped into the cell, accompanied by a single armed guard. "It's a little after seven in the morning. Get up, Weightman. Someone here to see you."

George struggled to his feet. A third man appeared in the doorway.

"George Weightman?"

"Aye. Who's asking?"

"My name is Denman. Thomas Denman. I've been appointed by his majesty the King to be your brief for the forthcoming trial." But George didn't hear him. He was suddenly overcome by an overwhelming wave of light headedness and began to topple forward.

"Guard!" Denman cried, indicating that he steady George. "Sit him back down." he commanded. The guard complied, taking George by the shoulders and lowering him back on to his bunk.

Denman shook his head. "This man is in a miserable state. He hasn't even been found guilty yet. Who ordered these irons?"

"Mr Lockett of County Hall, Sir. He presented a letter from the Home Office stating the four leaders were to be ironed, sir." said Eaton.

"I see. And what sustenance is provided to them?"

"Bread and water only, sir."

"Also an order from the Home Office?"

"Aye sir."

"This is simply disgraceful. I shall be petitioning strongly against this. These men will be in no fit state for the trial if their current circumstances persist. Now leave us. I wish to talk to my client in private."

Eaton hesitated. "I'm afraid I can't do that Mr Denman, these men are being charged with high treason. They're considered highly dangerous enemies of the Crown and therefore -"

"Highly dangerous?" snapped Denman. "Look at him. He can barely stand. You're insulting my intellect by trying to claim any of these men are in any way a danger to me or the constitution right now. Now please leave me and my client in private, as is my right as this man's legal representation. I'll knock when I'm ready to come out."

"As you wish, sir. But I'll leave the guard on the other side of the door," said Eaton.

"If it pleases you to do so, yes. Now leave us."

Eaton nodded, then gestured to the guard. The two men left the room and the iron clad door swung shut with a loud clang.

"George. Can you hear me? My name is Denman. I'm going to represent you at your trial, along with another colleague. A Mr John Cross. Can you understand what I'm saying?"

George, his back against the cell wall and his eyes closed, nodded. Denman filled a battered looking metal cup with water from a small bucket on the floor by the door.

"Here, drink this. You look dehydrated. Take a minute to steady yourself, there's a good fellow." He placed the cup to George's dry lips and he drank eagerly.

"They leave the water by the door... it makes it so difficult to fetch even a sip, especially with these on..." George whispered, indicating his bindings.

"I will try to get these removed. And hopefully arrange something more substantial to eat. This is monstrous. At this rate, none of you will make it to court, let alone sentencing."

"Are the others here? Will? Isaac? Jerry?"

"They are, yes. Though you're the first I've seen. I take it you've not seen them at all?"

"No. I'm taken to the exercise yard once a day. I've seen some of the other men. But I'm made to walk out on the other side of the yard as far away from any of them as is possible. If anyone tries to talk to me, they get the baton."

"The others will be exercised at different times to you. I'm afraid you're not allowed to see them until the trial, in case any potential examinations are contaminated."

"It's probably just as well," said George,

smiling weakly, "If I saw Jeremiah, wild dogs would not be able to stop me. I shall tear him limb from limb when I get the chance. When is the trial?"

"It won't be for several more weeks, I'm afraid. It's been vetoed to commence before the harvest is in."

George finally seemed to be lucid at last. "We were duped. Tricked into this. Pawns in a game. You need to find William Oliver. There will be no hope of justice for us unless you find William Oliver. I am convinced he was sent amongst us by the Government to trick us into rising. The cavalry were waiting for us. I think they paid Jerry too."

"I know. I certainly believe you about Oliver. But I'm afraid I cannot call him as a witness on your behalf. Even if I can find him, convince him to testify and he admits he was an agent of anyone, government or otherwise, it will harm your case, not help you."

"Why so? It will reveal corruption and trickery led to these events."

"It would, but it will also show that you're certainly guilty of treason. That you had full intention to rise up against the government. You will certainly go to the gallows if this is demonstrated to be the case."

"But this is not justice. This is a conspiracy of the highest order."

"George, listen. Your best hope for survival is that you plead that poverty and starvation drove you to this. Not political ambition. And you must also be of the opinion that your uncle, Thomas Bacon misled you."

"I can't do that. Uncle Tommy is a good man."

"It's your only hope George. Though things

look slightly better for you personally because you abandoned the campaign to save a man's life."

"He would have died. It was the right thing to do. And Jerry Brandreth had wrecked everything. If anyone is to blame, it's him."

"He was not the instigator by your own account, though George, it was your uncle."

"No. It was Oliver."

"I'm afraid I cannot call Oliver to the stand, you will all hang."

"So the government get their sacrificial goats, the movement is crushed and we are shamed. I'm not a fool. Every newspaper up and down the land will be eager to know the outcome of this trial, am I right?"

"Yes. Which is why we must proceed with caution. We need to be smart. You will carry no shame and won't be viewed as traitors if you plead poverty and starvation led you to desperate but misguided measures. If you want any hope of rebuilding a life for you and your family you must plead not guilty of treason. Even if it goes against everything you believe in, George. Think of your family. Surely your wife and children come first above all else?"

George nodded solemnly. "Tell me, what of them? Rebecca and the children. I write to them, but I hear nothing back. Can you find out if my letters are being sent? I must know if they are at least well and managing?"

"I will find out for you. Right. I must take my leave of you, George. I need to talk to the others. All of them. I will be back soon, I promise. I've helped others like you – Luddites. That is why I was chosen. But you must do what I say. I'll be back soon, I promise you."

Pentrich – England's Last Uprising

18. The Trial Begins
Port Macquarie, New South Wales, Australia.
October 21, 1822.

With the exception of my captors, Mr Denman and Mr Cross were the only other human faces I saw in the run up to the proceedings that led me to my current position in life. In the weeks between my incarceration and my trial I do not recall anything with any real clarity due to the continued deterioration of both my physical and mental state. It became difficult to track the days other than by daily routines of sustenance and exercise. Mr Denman told me that he had sent constables to our home to call on you and the children after my inquiry but you were not in residence. I can only hope that at the time, you had found sanctuary at your mother's. As time marched on inexorably toward the day we would finally know our fate I learned that the four of us who had led our campaign would be tried first and individually. The rest of the Regenerators would be tried as a group.

To my mind, this made it very clear that at least the four of us would be used to set an example to all as to what fate would be in store for anyone who dared to challenge the constitution of King and Country in the way we had. With just days to go, I learned that Jerry would take to the stand first, followed by Will Turner, then Isaac Ludlam and finally myself.

And so it came to pass that on the Wednesday the 15th of October, 1817, what the newspapers up and down the land had dubbed 'The Trial of the Failed Derbyshire Revolt' began.

Apparently, all of Derby was a hubbub and the whole of England were excited with interest to hear our tale of treachery and plotting in all its glory.

The chief solicitor for the prosecution, a Mr Lockett, had had a great deal of trouble finding accommodation for the four judges and their retinue as more than three hundred potential jurymen and two hundred and sixty eight witnesses for the prosecution were being held ready about the town.

Fifteen of our number who, until then, had been held in Nottingham were brought to Derby gaol and although this had caused an emotional reunion upon their arrival, it only added to the now cramped conditions of my fellow marchers. I of course was not party to any of this.

However, I did hear that the judges, along with other court house officials took themselves off to All Saints' Church to discuss matters of order, only to be met by the words 'Jurymen, remember Oliver!' scrawled in large script on the doors of the church. I heard talk that others had also seen similar messages in public places all about town. There had also been sympathetic rhetoric throughout the alehouses and taverns of Derby the night before, but all this was of little comfort to me as I languished half-starved in my solitary confinement. Especially as - as Mr Denman had iterated to me on numerous occasions - any indication that we had truly conspired to bring down the government would certainly lead us to the gallows...

Derby County Hall, Thursday, 16 October, 1817.

George Weightman woke with a start, roused from his troubled, restless slumber by the sound of a key clattering noisily in his cell door. Two guards entered, one carrying a bowl of water and a cloth. He was ordered to wash, which was no mean feat with both his hands and feet in irons, before being led out into the gaol yard. He stood there for a few moments, while his eyes adjusted to the almost blinding autumn sunlight, wondering where his fate now lay. Glancing around the yard, squinting, he counted seven of his brothers in arms gathered there, none of whom he had seen since they had scattered to the four winds on that fateful morning. He scanned the assembled group and his Uncle Tommy immediately caught his eye. His face was expressionless, but he acknowledged he had seen George too, with a single nod. George had never seen him so crestfallen, but at least he knew he was alive. Up until that moment, he had had no idea whether old man Bacon had been apprehended or not. The rest of the group were comprised mostly of other Turners and Ludlams who had been with them on the march.

He wondered if they were to be tried in groups of men who were related as he knew that there were at least sixty of the marchers held in Derby Gaol.

George desperately wanted to shield his eyes, but his irons made it impossible for him to do so. Had it been any other occasion it would have been an emotional moment, but he felt empty, drained and despondent - almost removed from the events unfolding. None of his fellow prisoners dared utter a word for fear of retribution from the armed soldiers that were guarding the group. Everyone, captors and captured alike, was on edge. Suddenly a murmur went up amongst the men and Will Turner and Isaac Ludlam were led out into the centre of the yard. They had obviously saved the ringleaders to bring out last. At that moment George saw him.

With a guard on each arm, Jeremiah Brandreth was led out. Bearded and dishevelled, but still somehow managing to look defiant. George burned with hate. Some of the men cheered. Why were they cheering him? He was the reason they were all in this predicament. Did they really still see him as their glorious commander in chief? If he had not been bound hand and foot – armed guards or not, George would have done his damnedest to get across the exercise yard and squeeze the very life out of him with his bare hands. A few swift rifle butts were issued to the more vocal of the men and the silence resumed.

At that moment, a flatbed horse drawn cart was led into the yard and the prisoners were all herded onto it as if they were cattle. The journey to the County Hall lasted only a few minutes but to George it felt like a lifetime. Armed troops escorted the cortège on foot. Eventually, the cart was led into the cobbled yard in front of the hall through two large imposing iron gates. Then once again they were herded off the waggon and directly into the court.

As George and his fellow prisoners trudged wearily between two wide open oak doors, guards on either side, he could only fixate his thoughts on one thing – that whatever unfolded in this building over the next few days, this was certain: they were to be his last days on God's Earth.

The atmosphere inside County Hall was taut. Although he had never seen the inside of a court in his life, George guessed that the enclosure at the front would be where the judges would sit, while the benches at the back were for him and his colleagues. Armed soldiers stood on either side. Facing into the room were two raised wooden pulpit type affairs, with a couple of wooden steps up to each. He presumed these were dock and witness box accordingly. The prisoners were filed in and ordered to fill the benches in an orderly fashion. A number of them began murmuring, until a soldier who was clearly of some rank and likely in charge told them to remain silent or risk physical retribution.

Men in gowns filed into the room, taking up their places at the two desks facing the judge's bench. There was something like eight men on the one side, while on the other there were only four. George recognised two of these as Thomas Denman and John Cross, which meant the other side must be the prosecution. He sighed – it was already looking like they were totally outgunned in every way possible. There were also men seated on chairs at the sides of the room – newspaper reporters, George surmised. Another long box to the side, yet to be filled, had several rows of seats. Undoubtedly for the jury. As they were led in, a total of twenty three in all, George fancied he recognised at least eight or nine of them – all land owners, mill owners or figures of local standing. Once everyone was in place and seated an usher was whispered to by another man in a gown that George guessed was the clerk. The usher scurried off through a side door, returning only moments later to give the clerk a curt nod.

The clerk raised his hand in a gesture for silence. The room duly obliged.

"All rise," he barked officially. Everyone did as they were told and with that four elderly gentlemen in robes and wigs entered and took their places at the empty bench. "The Right Honourable Lord Chief Baron Richards. The Honourable Mister Justice Dallas. The Honourable Mister Justice Abbot and The Honourable Mister Justice Holroyd," he announced. The four men sat down and the clerk motioned that the entire room may now also do the same.

Papers were handed out to the four judges. Some hushed words were exchanged between them, then silence. It was probably no more than a few seconds, but to George, it felt like forever. It was Lord Chief Justice Baron Richards who spoke first.

"Mr Attorney General, you may open."

The Attorney General, Sir Samuel Shepherd, rose immediately, the scent of blood clearly in his nostrils.

"My Lord and learned friends, it is my intention to proceed to the trial of Jeremiah Brandreth first."

"Very good. Please bring Mr Brandreth to the bar."

Jeremiah was escorted to the stand facing the

jury box.

"Mr Brandreth," Shepherd began, "I'm sure you've had this procedure explained to you already by your own counsel, but for the benefit of the court and the records of this trial, I shall explain what is about to happen. From the panel of men seated opposite you, twelve individuals will become the jury for the proceedings hence forth.

"Each in turn will stand, say his name and then they will swear an oath on the bible. As is your right, you may challenge whether that man is, in your opinion, a fair and just individual to serve on that jury. The same holds for the Crown. If you issue a challenge, that man leaves this court and takes no further part in these proceedings. You make your challenge via your counsel. You may do so thirty five times. If, by the time we have worked our way through this bench of proposed members and we do not have a jury, more representatives waiting elsewhere in these chambers will be fetched and the process will begin again, until we have a completed jury. Is that clear?"

Brandreth nodded.

"Very good. Then we shall begin. Mr Denman?"

Denman rose and went to stand by Jeremiah.

"Sheriff, if you please." Shepherd nodded towards the bench of waiting men. The Sheriff, bible in hand, stepped towards the first man on the front row.

"Please stand and state your name and occupation, sir."

The man stood.

"William White. Farmer."

"Place your left hand on the bible and raise

your right hand thus -"

"Challenged by the defendant," Denman announced.

The man stepped down and was led from the court. The Sheriff moved to the next man and the process began again.

"Please stand and state your name and occupation."

"William Morley. Farmer."

"Challenged by the defendant."

And so it went on. An elaborate game of cat and mouse. Occasionally and probably for no other reason than he knew he was close to the judges intervening, Brandreth nodded and the man standing was sworn in. To everyone in the room it soon became apparent that it was making little difference to the make-up of the men who ultimately would decide the defendant's fate. They were a seemingly never ending stream of land owners, employers and business men.

Eventually, Brandreth ran out of challenges and the final juror was sworn in. Lord Chief Justice Richards, stoically remained silent for a minute, while making some careful notes on his papers. Then he looked up.

"Gentlemen of the jury. I wish to have it understood that no part of the proceedings of this day or any day during any of the trials shall be made public until all this is concluded and if this notice which I now give is not attended to, the court must use the authority it has to bring any delinquent to punishment. I trust there will be no occasion for any further notice."

The twelve men nodded in silent confirmation.

"Very good. Attorney General, will you please proceed with the indictment."

Shepherd rose and began to stride slowly and purposefully in front of the jury as he addressed them.

"Gentlemen of the jury. We are assembled in this place upon a most solemn and important occasion and you twelve gentlemen are placed in that box to perform one of the most solemn and sacred functions that men can be called upon to perform, namely that of deciding by your verdict, upon the guilt or innocence of one of your fellow subjects charged with the highest crime that any man can commit. There are other crimes to which human nature at times is prone, of a very great and enormous magnitude, but those crimes are striking generally only at the safety and happiness of certain individuals.

"Yet in the class of civil crimes, they fall far short of the crime of high treason, which is in fact committed against all and each of the community who belong to the state and society where that crime happens to be committed."

He paused dramatically, taking time to look each jury member in the eye before speaking again.

"Gentlemen. My duty upon this occasion consists in this: in stating to you, with as much accuracy as I am able, the law, as it affects the particular case in question, and the facts by which, I conceive, I shall make out the guilt of the prisoner. I have no other duty to perform than that."

He paused momentarily, looked Jeremiah up and down for a moment then began again. "Gentlemen. It is necessary that I should state to you what I conceive to be the law upon the subject, which I will do very shortly, as applicable to this indictment and this charge. The indictment has, upon the face of it, three charges. All of them amounting to high treason. The first charge is that this man..."

He turned and pointed dramatically at Jeremiah. "Together with persons, some of whom are named on the indictment, levied war against His Majesty and that in levying war, did arm themselves and march through the country in hostile array. The second count, which was founded upon a statute which was passed in the thirty sixth year of the present King, charges the prisoner and his colleagues with compassing and imagining to depose the King.

"Compassing in this legal sense meaning to carry out open and overt acts, which in this case, were done by the prisoner and other men named in this indictment, as supporting evidence that he and his fellow conspirators intended to depose the King. Not just imagining to depose the King, but the actual devising of plans and means to carry out this purpose – not only assembling, meeting and conspiring to stir up, raise, make and levy insurrection, rebellion and war against the King but also to subvert and destroy the constitution and the government. Evidenced by him and his fellow conspirators providing arms and ammunition in order to effect this purpose."

Shepherd paused again, to let the first two charges sink in.

"The third and final charge imputes to this man the crime of conspiring to levy war against the King in order to compel him to change his measures by means of certain overt acts, which are the same acts as those stated in the first and second count of the indictment. War. Gentlemen. War intended to end the life of the King, subvert the constitution upon which our country and the very foundation of our society is founded and to destroy the government.

"War. Subversion. Destruction. By definition of the law of this land, levying war against the King is any number of persons combining themselves together by hostile open force with or without arms for the purpose of overturning or destroying the government. *The graveness of this I cannot make any clearer*. Also, and this is of the utmost importance with reference to this case – it is not necessary that the parties who have begun this process have arrived at any level of success for their acts. If men of any number assemble themselves together with the treasonable purpose of overturning the government by means of the use of arms to do so then it is as much levying war as if they had a hundred thousand men in battle in the field. You will therefore consider this when deciding if this man, Jeremiah Brandreth, together with his colleagues, are guilty or not guilty of the highest crime in all the land – high treason.

"What was the exact object this prisoner and those concerned with him had when they carried out the acts they did in the weeks running up to, as well as on, the night of June the ninth? Gentlemen. I will now present you with the details of those events in order that you decide if these men, however successful, however numerous they were, wished, by means of the most deplorable and evil acts to murder and depose the King, wage war and totally destroy the governance and constitution of England..."

19. Defences Breached

And so the case for the prosecution was clear from the beginning, following the same pattern for all four of the ring leaders. High Treason. There was no higher crime in the eyes of the law. Beginning with Jeremiah Brandreth, Sir Samuel Shepherd carefully related the entire misadventure from beginning to end, starting with the early meetings at Hunt's Barn as led by old Tommy Bacon and progressing onto how, as the numbers grew so did the scale of the plot. Men from all over the north of England would join the cause and their numbers would swell as they converged on Nottingham where they would take the army barracks by surprise and win their first victory over the King, before making their way in their thousands to London on stolen cargo barges via the canal system.

He moved quickly on to how a leader, a figurehead with hatred for the government and no fear of authority – Jeremiah Brandreth, was chosen to lead them into battle on the night of June the ninth.

He told of how they repeatedly and openly talked of revolution – not protest or even rioting, but revolution - and that his witnesses would prove that beyond any shadow of a doubt.

How, on that fateful night, they began to sweep through Wingfield and Pentrich, press-ganging men and acquiring fire arms which culminated in the cold blooded execution of Mrs Hepworth's manservant who had dared to defy these wicked men.

Onwards they marched to Butterley ironworks with the intention of seizing control of the forge and its arsenal, but thanks to being forewarned, Messer's Outram and Jessop's men had sent them packing with naught save more anger in their hearts and even more determination to wreak havoc. He told how they ransacked the inns at Codnor and then, at Langley Mill, drunk on stolen ale, they even managed to shoot and seriously wound one of their own men – clearly a sign they wanted to spill blood and as soon as possible. Onwards they marched, dealing out terror and chaos in equal measures until, as dawn was approaching, they were ambushed by the King's Hussars by the Gilt brook, a mere seven miles from Nottingham.

Witness after witness was called and questioned exhaustively – Pentrich villagers who had hid in fear when the men came knocking, or who had been forced to hand over their weapons in terror. Employees of Butterley iron works who had defended their livelihood from tyranny. Patrons of the White Horse public house who had heard the men plotting, seen the maps of the campaign. The owners of the inns they had ransacked along the way - even Mrs Mary Hepworth herself took to the stand to relate how her family home was terrorised and her manservant was brutally murdered by these evil monsters that had lost all sense of morality. The final witness called was Captain Philips of the King's Hussars who had been in charge of ambushing the marchers. The evidence seemed overwhelmingly damning. Denman and Cross made several attempts to challenge, mainly on points of law, bias, or opinion but the panel of judges and the prosecution quickly overruled or crushed them.

When it came to putting the case for the defence, Denman took the pre-determined angle that the uprising had been a protest march born out of poverty and desperation that had got out of hand and become a petty riot. Character witnesses were called to paint the picture that Brandreth was a family man pushed to the edge of desperation by the need to provide for his family, but to all in the court it was clear that it was failing to garner the sympathy of the twelve men who were to decide Brandreth's fate.

Each one of them was cut down during cross examination by Shepherd and his entourage with examples of Brandreth's past escapades as a key player in the Luddite movement – some of them were even exposed as political agitators themselves.

The proceedings rattled along mercilessly with no let up. Clearly the Crown were determined to make this kill as swift and as clean as possible. The relentlessness was obviously wearing down anyone not used to courtroom protocol, Brandreth included, and any astute observer could be forgiven for thinking that this approach was deliberate.

"And so, gentleman of the jury," said Denman finally, "I ask you to consider this important question. Have any of you learned, informed and intelligent gentleman ever heard in any reign that rising with your fellow workers and marching to enhance wages was termed high treason? No. Of course not. Yes, certainly they did rise. Of that there is no doubt. But for what object? I fear I must admit that their object was to plunder their neighbours' larders and to fill their empty bellies.

"One says England, France and Ireland were all to rise together. Can you suppose that was said? Or if you believe it was indeed said, can you suppose they had any idea what they were saying? Another says 'We are going to Nottingham and shall take the barracks.' Another says the keys of the Tower are already given up to the Hampden Club. Another says 'We're going to pay off or wipe off the national debt.'

"I can see from your faces what you, sober in the cold light of day think of these absurd suppositions. There is no wild programme these poor deluded people did not state. But as to a defined object of any description I am at a loss to find such a thing from the beginning to the end of the evening, except for the object of a bigger loaf and going on a folly of drunken pleasure on the river Trent in Nottingham. Nothing more, nothing less. This was not high treason on three counts, but folly and fantasy driven by empty stomachs and desperation."

And with that final statement, Denman drew his case for the defence to a close. The room fell silent, all eyes on Lord Chief Justice Richards. It was probably only a few seconds while he finished writing some notes on his papers but to everyone present it seemed to last an age. Finally he spoke.

"Will that be all, Mr Denman?"

"Yes my Lord."

"Very good. Jeremiah Brandreth, if you wish to address anything to the jury, in your own defence, this is the time for you to do so."

Brandreth shook his head slowly. "No my lord."

Whether he thought it was a pointless exercise, that opening his mouth would only further serve the prosecution's condemnation, or that he'd had enough of the entire charade, no one could tell. He simply stood stony faced and expressionless.

Richards nodded his acknowledgement.

"In that case I shall summarise. Gentlemen of the jury. I now request your attention while I state to you the evidence that has been produced before you and suggest any observations as occur to me upon the subject. The prisoner at the bar, Jeremiah Brandreth, otherwise called the Nottingham Captain, is charged by the indictment before you, with the crime of high treason. That crime has been truly described to you as the highest known to the law of England and indeed it may perhaps be said that it includes every other crime and therefore it requires great patience and attention on the part of you, the jury."

He paused, before continuing with deliberate emphasis. "But it is to be tried by the same rules that govern other cases. You are to consider and weigh the evidence and you are to decide, according to that evidence, applying to it the law as you shall understand it. You will address yourselves to this duty with all the impartiality which I'm sure belongs to you and you will find your verdict according to that evidence, however painful that may be.

"If you should feel yourselves compelled to find the prisoner guilty, you should have no hesitation in doing so, for you are to find a verdict *according to the evidence*.

"If, on the other hand you find him not guilty, you will also satisfy your conscience and so will every person who hears you. The verdict, whatever it may be, will, I am satisfied, be agreeable to the *evidence*. The indictment, states that the prisoner, along with other persons present, was *traitorously* assembled and gathered together against our Lord the King, that he wickedly, maliciously and traitorously did levy and make war against him within this realm and did then, *with great force and violence*, parade and march in a hostile manner, through villages, public highways and other places and endeavoured by force and arms, to subvert and destroy the government and constitution of this realm, as established by the law.

"Now, Gentlemen, it is very important that you should understand clearly what is meant by levying war against the King in terms of the act of Parliament. I shall make the meaning and the consequences of it upon the acts you've heard evidenced here very clear to you.

"The act runs thus: when a man doth compass or imagine the death of our Lord the King, or if any man do levy war against our Lord the King in his realm, then he is without doubt, *guilty of high treason*. If there is an insurrection, that is, a large rising of the people, in order by force or violence to accomplish or avenge not any *private* object of their own, not any *private* quarrels, but to effectuate these acts against the general public with that purpose, that is considered as *a levying of war*. There must be an insurrection. Force must accompany that insurrection. And it must be for an object of a general nature. If all these circumstances concur that is quite sufficient to constitute the offence of levying war. If you ascertain, as has been contended by the defendant's counsel, that this rising was *anything but* an attack aimed at the authority of the realm, then that would *not* be treason...

"Gentlemen. That these people were in a low situation of life is *no excuse at all*. For a crime is not any less a crime because the man who commits it is poor. If they were in distress, of which there is no evidence, that can be no excuse. If – and this is key – if they intended to overturn the government, even if there was no real prospect of their success, *that is no excuse*. It is no less an act of treason if the design is unlikely to be concluded in the way they desire it. Now, gentlemen, the evidence as you have heard it - and there is no evidence to contradict it – is that throughout the proceedings, their stated object was to destroy the government. If you believe that that which they stated *repeatedly* was their actual intent and not bravado then you must find the prisoner guilty of high treason. If on the other hand, gentlemen, you can lay your hands upon your hearts and say that you are satisfied their purpose was anything but to destroy the government, a private motivation, *of which there has been no counter evidence presented*, then you must find him not guilty. I call upon you to consider it with care and integrity.

"You will put out of your minds all the consequences that can happen and attend only to the important consideration of your duty. You are to do justice and pronounce a verdict in the face of your God and your country in accordance with the law and the *evidence*... You will now retire to the jury room to deliberate your decision."

He nodded to the clerk and immediately began to collect together his papers.

The clerk stood up. "All rise."

Everyone did. He nodded to the judges' bench and then to the usher. The jury was promptly led out of the court while everyone stood in silence. It was a little after ten p.m. and it had been a very long day.

20. Verdict

After only half an hour's deliberation, the twelve men who had been selected to determine Jeremiah Brandreth's fate summoned the clerk. Nervously he knocked at the door of the jury room. The door was opened immediately by a tall, stout bearded gentleman.

"Are you the foreman?"

"I am indeed. Please inform Lord Justice Richards we have reached a verdict."

"Very good, sir," he said, and scurried off in the direction of the judge's chambers.

As they were led back in to court, every man present could feel the tension, the silence was deafening, especially amongst the prisoners. They all knew that whatever verdict was given now would set the precedence for all of them. It had been clear from the beginning that the day's proceedings had been a carefully orchestrated template which would be applied to everyone made to stand and face the bar over the coming days. The fact that it had only taken half an hour had added to the fear.

The clerk exchanged hushed words with the counsel for the prosecution and the defence, before hurrying out of a side door. He returned with the twelve jury men, all of whom were clearly not giving anything away. A single guard escorted Brandreth to the dock, his wrist and leg irons clanking noisily in contrast to the pin-drop silence. Moments later the usher returned to his seat at the side of the court as Richards, Dallas, Abbot and Holroyd entered. No sooner was the last judge seated than the clerk called "All Rise. This court is now in session."

The entire room stood once again. Richards gave a nod and the clerk indicated that everyone may be seated. The Lord Chief Justice seemed to be scribbling some note or other. Brandreth had a pained expression on his face. The anticipation mounted.

"Will the foreman please make himself known to me," Richards said eventually. The stout bearded gentleman stood.

"Have you reached a verdict, sir?"

"That we have my Lord."

"And is that verdict, in accordance with the law, a unanimous one?"

"It is, my Lord."

"On all three counts of the indictment?"

"Aye, my Lord."

"Very good. How do you find the prisoner, Jeremiah Brandreth, otherwise known as the Nottingham Captain, on the first count of the indictment, that of high treason by levying war against our Lord the King?"

"Guilty."

"And on the second count of the indictment, that of compassing and imagining to depose the King?"

"Guilty."

"And on the third and final count of the indictment, that of the crime of conspiring to levy war against our Lord the King in order to compel him to change his measures?"

"Guilty."

All eyes were on Brandreth. Beads of sweat had gathered on his now pallid forehead. The colour drained from his cheeks and his shoulder sank. He seemed to try and steady himself in the box momentarily.

"A chair, please, for the prisoner," said Richards, almost matter of fact. "And if he smokes, a pipe of tobacco if you be so kind. This man has probably had the shock of his life."

The usher came over, producing a pouch of tobacco and a clay pipe from under his gown.

"This trial is now at an end. Sentences will be passed at the end of these proceedings, though I am sure you are all aware of the penalties in place for being found guilty of High Treason. We will reconvene tomorrow with the trial of Mr William Turner. This court is now adjourned. If any man of the press present wishes to ask any questions of the prisoner - and should he wish to answer, now is the time."

Chaos ensued. Several men armed with paper and quill rushed the dock. The rest of the prisoners began chattering nervously. The two opposing counsel teams shook hands and the four judges began to gather up their things and leave.

Questions were barked at Brandreth, but he just shook his head and refused to answer. George couldn't take his eyes off him – in all the time he had known him, he had never seen him in this state. As the noise in the room reached cacophony, he stared at the man he had grown to hate, trying to reconcile his feelings. On the one hand he was pleased that the man whom he viewed responsible for his current situation was now visibly broken. Finally he'd had all his bravado and arrogance knocked out of him. But at the same time, he was filled with dread because he knew that in a couple of days' time, his fate would almost certainly be the same.

21. Facing the Inevitable
Friday, October 23, 1817.

There was a loud clank accompanied by a sharp creaking sound and George's cell door swung open. It was Denman, just as he had expected. Immediately, the guard closed the door behind him, leaving the two men alone in the cell. George lay on his bunk staring at the dank stone ceiling.

"Good morning, George. It's almost time for you to face the bar, so I thought we'd better discuss some things."

"What's the point?" George didn't bother to make eye contact.

"What do you mean?"

"You know exactly what I mean, Mr Denman. My trial will go the same way as Jerry's, Will's and Isaac's. They've all followed exactly the same course, the same witnesses have been called, the same accounts given and the same points emphasised every time. The jury is composed entirely of employers and wealthy sorts and you've clearly told the other three that when asked, you say nothing, so that we go to the gallows without any danger of political scandal. The whole thing has a very bad smell an' no mistake."

"We've been over this, but yes, you're right. Although you are given the opportunity to speak, trust me, it is in your best interests to remain silent. I know it sounds wrong, but you must understand – one wrong word to either the jury or the judges, who, as you've rightly observed, are far from sympathetic, and you could easily make the situation much worse."

George laughed. He swung his legs down to the floor and sat up, looking Denman square in the eyes.

"How could it possibly be much worse? It's clear as day that all four of us were to be found guilty of high treason come hell or high water - no exception."

"You've yet to be sentenced, George. There' still hope of some justice for you four, but you need to show remorse and humility. These are learned men. You are ignorant. If you say the wrong things, they will not look favourably -"

"I'm uneducated, Mr Denman, but not ignorant. I know exactly how this works. We are to be made an example of, in a carefully orchestrated circus. It's a show and a sham, designed to give the government and newspapers exactly what they need to keep anyone else with ideas like ours right where they belong – cap in hand at the rich man's table."

"It's not a circus George. These trials are being followed to the letter of the law and I am doing the best I can to represent you and see that you're tried fairly."

"Oh, yes, I'm sure they're watertight legally. I wouldn't expect any less, when all of England's eyes are upon us. But I'm no idiot. The whole thing is being carefully guided. I've seen you, shaking hands with Shepherd and his cronies at the end of every single one of these charades."

"It is customary to do so, George. We are men with a duty to uphold the judicial system and the law of this land. Part of that is recognising that we are just doing our jobs and showing that we are professional and courteous with it. It is not a charade, I can assure you."

"Then why no mention of Oliver? Everyone knows about him. His name is scrawled on walls all over this town, so I'm told. He is conspicuous in his absence. I wouldn't be surprised if he were here, in Derby, right now, whispering to them afterwards. Probably sits with those newspaper folk, in disguise, advising them what to write. Telling them exactly how to make us look like traitors."

"It is not in your interests to bring up Mr Oliver's involvement, which is merely speculation on your part anyway."

"That's absolute nonsense and you know it. Not in our interest! Ha! It makes no difference now, I'm going to be hanged – we all are and that's the end of it."

Denman sighed. "We don't know that yet. Your fate is in the hands of the King and God and you would do well to be mindful of that."

"Fuck the King. What sort of King sits on his thrown, knowing that his subjects are starving? The likes of Will Turner fought Napoleon for him and he didn't even get paid. I still believe in what we aspired to do and why, Mr Denman, so it's probably just as well that we say nowt to them up there, because if I open my mouth I am afraid of what might come out of it!"

"Then I must implore you one last time not to do that. If you have any desire to survive this, for the sake of your wife and children, you say nothing."

"If there's one thing I've learned this week, Mr Denman, it won't make the slightest difference to the outcome of this trial if I speak out or remain silent. I have no hope of truth or justice prevailing as I see it, so all that remains left to me is that at least my family are not ashamed of me or made pariahs because I stood up for what I believed in. What I still believe in. So for that reason alone, I shall keep my mouth firmly shut. And I hope that what we stood for somehow survives and is passed on, that it resonates with the working men of tomorrow and that one day, because of us, justice truly does prevail, because if it doesn't I can't begin to imagine what that world will be like to live in."

The cell door opened with another clank, bringing their conversation to an abrupt end. It was the head gaoler, Eaton.

He seemed to have a slight sneer to his demeanour.

"Weightman. They're ready for you…"

"God be with you, my friend," said Denman, holding out his hand.

"He can fuck off an' all," said George, heading for the door, deliberately walking straight past Denman's outstretched hand.

"Guilty." Once again, the word resonated round the courtroom. George didn't even bother to look up. Lord Justice Richards recorded the fourth guilty verdict in his notes solemnly, before turning to address the twelve men who had delivered it.

"Gentlemen of the jury. Your labours are over and I think I should not be doing justice to the jurymen of this country if I did not, in my own name and in the name of the learned judges who surround me, render our thanks to you for your great attention and care. I may venture to say that I never saw jurors to whom I am more obliged to pay every kind respect and gratitude than those who have assembled here on this occasion."

He then promptly turned his gaze back towards the four men who stood before him. "All that remains now is for me to pass sentence on the four prisoners whom have been identified as the ringleaders of this uprising. Please bring Jeremiah Brandreth, Isaac Ludlam and William Turner to the bar to stand alongside Mr Weightman."

With a guard each, the other three were brought before the four judges, their irons clanking loudly as they shuffled into the space in front of the bench. George was led down from the dock to join his former colleagues. Richards nodded to the clerk who turned to formerly address the four prisoners.

"What have you to say for yourself, why the court should not pass sentence of death upon you, according to the law?"

Surprising George, it was Brandreth who spoke first and with some confidence, too, possibly because he had had a few days for his verdict to sink in.

"I would ask for mercy, if mercy can be extended towards me and I would address you in the words of our saviour. If it be possible, let this cup pass from me – but not my will, but your will."

Nodding, Richards turned his attention to the next man in the line, Isaac Ludlam.

"May it please your Lordships, if you can show mercy, do, for the sake of my wife and family, whom, I hope, your Lordships will take into consideration and show mercy unto me. I hope the court will, in pity, remember me and spare my life! It will be a life corresponding to the will of God and man. I shall take it as one of the greatest favours my God can grant to me."

Again, Richards nodded. "Mr Turner?"

William Turner was visibly shaking. "Well? Mr Turner?"

When he finally spoke, his voice was audibly wavering.

"I hope… I hope your Lordships will have mercy upon me," he said and began to sob. Richards remained stony faced.

"And you, Mr Weightman?"

George was transfixed by Turner's state. With the exception of Brandreth, whom he now believed to be deranged, Will was undoubtedly the strongest willed of the four of them. To see him like this was deeply disturbing. He struggled to raise his arm and place it on Turner's shoulder, only to have it knocked off by one of the presiding guards.

"Mr Weightman?"

But George just couldn't find his voice. How had it come to this? He looked at Jeremiah who remained composed, his face blankly staring ahead.

"Final chance, Mr Weightman," said Richards, sternly.

George shook his head.

"Very well," he began, "Prisoners at the bar. To see so many persons, especially of your description, standing in the miserable condition in which you stand now before me, is indeed most melancholy. You exhibit to the public a spectacle as afflicting as it is uncommon. I thank God that it is very uncommon. It must be most satisfactory to the world and I hope it administers some consolation to you that you have had *every assistance* and *every advantage* that any man labouring under any charge could have wished for. You have been defended by counsel who used every exertion in your favour which their experience, their learning and their great abilities could suggest to them. You persisted in a plea of not guilty and were tried by several juries, of great respectability who were patient and as attentive, as ever appeared in a British court of justice.

"Those juries were compelled, by the clearest and most irresistible evidence, to find the four men they tried guilty of high treason, the highest and greatest offence known to the law. Your insurrection, I thank God, did not last long, but whilst it continued, it was marked with violent outrages and by the murder of a man who did not offer even the least appearance of provocation to you.

"That conduct showed the ferocity of your purpose. Your object was to wade through the blood of your countrymen, to extinguish the law and the constitution of your country and to sacrifice the property, the liberties and the lives of your fellow subjects - to confusion and anarchy and the most complete tyranny. God be praised, your purpose failed. Let me beseech you to weigh well your conditions. Your lives are become forfeit to the violated laws of this country. Make the most of the small remnant of those lives. Endeavour to make some compensation to the society which you have injured and pray God fervently for his forgiveness. I hope others, by remembering what passes today may avoid the dreadful situation in which you are now placed."

He paused, as if to let the gravity of what was about to be said sink in. "I cannot trust myself," he continued, "with speaking more upon the subject, but I hasten to pronounce upon you the last and awful sentence of the law. That you, and each of you, be taken from hence, to the gaol from whence you came and from there, thence be drawn on a hurdle to the place of execution. Once there you will be severally hanged by the neck until you be dead and afterwards your heads shall be severed from your bodies and your bodies divided into four quarters to be disposed of as His Majesty shall direct. May the Lord God of All Mercies have compassion upon you."

22. An Unexpected Turn of Fate

"Right, all four of you, inside," said Chief Gaoler Eaton, motioning to the cell door the guard had just opened.

"What? All of us? In one cell? But we've been kept separate 'til now. Why put us together now?" said George, eying him suspiciously.

"Trial's over for you lot. No need to keep you apart now. Besides I need the room. Now get inside." He replied.

"But we can't spend the rest of the trials cooped up in here. There's barely room for four men to lie on the floor," said Ludlam, nodding at the tiny cell before them.

Eaton smiled. "Don't worry it won't be long. They're trying the next twelve all at once and I've already heard that Mr Denman and Mr Cross have persuaded them to plead guilty. There'll be no need for all that to-ing and fro-ing now they've nailed you four."

"Aye. They've got exactly what they wanted with us. Why waste any more tax-payer's money, eh?" smirked Brandreth.

"You can't coop us all up in here. Like sheep in a pen!" said Ludlam.

"Or lambs to the slaughter? Like I said, it won't be for long. And besides, you'll have plenty of room to stretch your legs on them gallows, lads. And your necks! Now get inside before young Machin here has to show you the back end of his rifle. Stop complaining and get to it! At least them irons can come off now."

"Well, that changes everything, don't it lads?" snapped Brandreth sarcastically. He gave Eaton a hard stare, before trudging into the tiny cell. Weightman and Ludlam followed. George held back a moment, staring at the back of Brandreth's head.

"Come on Weightman. In you go."

Reluctantly, George did as he was told. Eaton and the guard followed them in, closing the door behind them.

"Right," said Eaton, producing a set of keys, "Let's get these off. Now don't get any ideas – Machin here is under orders from me to shoot any of you who try anything daft. Got that?"

"Not really much of a threat that, is it?" quipped Brandreth. "Shot now, or hanged in a couple of days."

Eaton ignored them. Instead, he systematically went round each of the prisoners, keys at the ready and one by one, four sets of irons clattered to the ground.

Scooping them up, he said 'There you go lads. At least your last few days on Earth will be slightly more tolerable, now." The cell door slammed shut and Eaton and the guard were gone.

"Together again at last, eh lads?" said Brandreth, breaking the silence as they all rubbed their red raw ankles and feet.

"Why do you keep this up, Jerry? This... I dunno, this pretence, this, defiance? We all saw you in the dock. You were as terrified as the rest of us when they read out the verdicts. You can drop it now." said Will.

"They might have broken you, Will, but they won't break me. Got to look the part ain't you? Remorseful. If you're to stand any chance of them deciding that we might not go to the drop."

"Did you not hear the sentence, Jerry? We're going to be hanged, that's the end of it," said Ludlam.

"It ain't done until Denman comes in here with a warrant. There's still time for the King to show mercy," said Brandreth.

"Don't you realise? Are you really that stupid? We've been hung out to dry. The whole trial went exactly how they planned it. They wanted to make examples out of the four of us. A clear message to the people of England," said George, exasperated. "This is how it ends for us. We will hang. If the other twelve change their pleas to guilty like Eaton says, they'll go to Australia. They'll be the example of how the King can show mercy, certainly not us. Denman tricked us into pleading not guilty. The rest of them will be jailed here."

"You don't know that for certain George. It's happened before – the King, or the judges might yet show leniency. Let's not forget they're Christians," said Ludlam.

"No. The newspapers will all be writing about us as I speak – labelling us as traitors, villains..." George turned his gaze to Brandreth. "Murderers even. That should never have happened! We stood for something. A cause. The freedom of the working man. Reform. Distribution of wealth. Justice! Equality! I wanted my children to have a future - an education, instead of scraping a living, cap in hand to the Mill owner! But you! You, Jeremiah Brandreth! You destroyed any hope of that!"

Suddenly George leapt at Brandreth, unable to contain his anger any longer. It was the last thing Brandreth had expected from George and so, totally caught off guard, he crashed to the ground, George landing on top of him, hands tight round his throat. Immediately Ludlam and Turner moved to drag him off.

"This solves nothing, George!" Ludlam cried, once the two men were separated.

"You think?" growled George, "It will solve everything for me! I'm not the one who killed an innocent man for no good reason! He did not want to join us. That was his right, his decision. The plan was to knock on doors and rally like-minded men to join us, Jerry! Not shoot them dead if they chose not to!"

"He was fetching a gun George. Jerry and I both saw him through the window!" barked Turner.

"Probably to give it to the cause!" George retorted.

"You know what I say. What I always said from the beginning, George. You're either with us, or against us," Brandreth sneered, "You have to show force. Resolve. If you are not prepared to shed blood in the name of freedom, then you might as well kiss freedom goodbye. No revolution, no uprising was ever won round the negotiating table. Even you are not stupid enough to think that!"

"Ha! This was no uprising. It was nothing more than a blood thirsty riot, whatever the jury thought!"

"No. It was a war. A war of class. A war of the have's against the have-nots. A war of rights. A war I'd been fighting for many years before you discovered your backbone, George!" snapped Brandreth.

"If he'd shot Jerry, we would've had no captain," Turner interjected. "The campaign would have been over before we started! You yourself said that we had to be prepared to spill blood -"

"Only if there was no other way! Only if it was your life or theirs!"

"Actually I was wrong. You never had a backbone!" scoffed Jeremiah. "That is why I was chosen as captain and not you! I have led many battles smashing looms – and the heads of their rich owners! That's why your uncle chose me for the job. Because he had no faith in you. Because he knew I would show men like that no mercy!"

"You didn't lead! You ruled by fear," spat George, "When you said 'you're either with us or against us', it was a threat, not a statement!"

"I was testing the men's resolve!" Brandreth exclaimed. "We needed men who were determined. Who would stop at nothing. Dedicated. I wanted to be sure we had strong minded men. We had one chance George. And you threw it away. Because of your lack of conviction!"

"He's right George," said Turner, solemnly, "we wouldn't have stood a chance with a bunch of cowards. We needed men with discipline. An

Army."

"Discipline?" George was incredulous. "You and your 'disciplined army' decided to ransack every pub on the way until they were all too bloody drunk to stand, let alone fight!"

"That's not how it happened, George -" Ludlam interjected.

"Really? That's not what it looked like to me -"

"You weren't even there, George!" added Will.

"Precisely! I was taking a message on horseback to our comrades in Nottingham. You were supposed to be taking the weapons from the ironworks at Butterley. But when I got back, you were taking all the ale you could from every tavern between Codnor and Langley Mill!"

"And that's when it happened, wasn't it, George?" said Brandreth. His voice was cold, accusatory.

"When what happened?"

"When you betrayed us to the authorities," Brandreth continued, "Went straight to the magistrate in Ripley, did you, George? When you realised it wasn't going your way! You denied it then and I bet you deny it again now."

"That's ridiculous!"

"Then how do you explain the fact that by the time we got to the Gilt brook, we were ambushed by the King's Infantry? Ever since your uncle picked me to lead the group instead of you, you've been jealous! You wanted him to pick you, but he knew you were gutless! So, when it wasn't going your way, to get your own back, you went straight to the magistrate in Ripley! Don't lie! I saw your face as you took to that horse!"

"I was shocked! You had just shot an innocent

man!"

Turner's eyes widened. He looked at Jeremiah and then back at George.

"Is that really what happened George?" he said, his voice now stern.

"That would also explain why you stood against me at the Navigation inn!" continued Jeremiah. "Stalling until the troops arrived. It all makes sense! I should kill you with my bare hands now!"

George looked at his three once-comrades in shock. They were all turning against him. Even now, Jeremiah still had power over Will and Isaac. "You intimidated the landlady and threatened the landlord with your pistol! It was utter chaos! Drunken revelry and rioting – looting even. Looting from people like us! Honest working people trying to make a living! The whole thing was completely out of control! And then Walters got shot! One of our own men shot! If I hadn't acted immediately and taken him back to the inn for help, he would have died!"

"He's got a point, Jerry," observed Ludlam. "He saved Walters' life."

Jeremiah shook his head. "I said at the time - they sent for constables from Ripley! That made them the enemy! So you were colluding with the enemy!"

George was shaking his head when Brandreth's punch landed squarely on his jaw. With a loud thud that took the wind from his lungs, he was on the floor before he realised what was happening. Without let up, Jeremiah was kneeling over him, raining blows to his head. It took the combined efforts of Turner and Ludlam to get him off.

"For the love of God, Jerry. Leave the man be.

He was just doing what he thought was right!" Ludlam cried. Somehow Turner managed to get Jeremiah in a headlock.

"Let me go! You pair of idiots! How can betraying his comrades and his precious cause be right?"

"He didn't betray the cause!" barked Ludlam. "You betrayed the cause – in fact you never stood for the cause in the first place! You just wanted to create as much misery and mayhem as possible. You betrayed us if anyone did!"

"Exactly!" said George, spitting blood onto the cell floor. "This uprising, from the moment you got involved, became a personal crusade, though God only knows for what purpose! I'm no traitor, as you are no reformist! You've twisted this group into something I no longer recognise, you've beaten and killed innocent people! You never wanted reform and you said so as much yourself, Jeremiah!"

There was an awkward pause. Jeremiah Brandreth seemed to stare into nothing. When he answered, it was slow, deliberate and somehow burning with hate and menace.

"That's right, George. Like I told you at the Gilt brook - I want revenge. Revenge on those who destroyed my livelihood. Revenge for my brothers who hanged. And like I said then, if anyone gets in my way, well I will snuff them out without a second thought. And that includes you!"

Brandreth took yet another step closer. The two men were nose to nose. Neither broke. Ludlam and Turner exchanged anxious glances. Was this the moment when one of these two men, who now clearly despised each other, would take the other's life? Brandreth slowly raised his hands…

At that precise moment, they were interrupted by a loud clanking sound - keys turned in the cell door and it squawked open. All four men turned. It was Denman. The door closed behind him. Brandreth turned to face him.

"Well, well, well... Mr Denman... Are you just here to gloat or do you finally bring word from your puppet masters?"

He rolled out some papers in his hand, ignoring Brandreth's comment. "Gentlemen. I bring warrants for the execution of the following men..."

Brandreth rolled his eyes and snorted. "Well, that didn't take long, did it?"

Denman, continued, still ignoring Jeremiah. His tone was officious and matter of fact as he read from the papers. "Jeremiah Brandreth. William Turner and Isaac Ludlam. On the morning of Friday, November the seventh, eighteen seventeen, you will be taken from this gaol and drawn on a hurdle to a place of public execution and there be severally hanged by the neck until you are dead. Your heads will then be severed from your bodies. His Majesty, the King has sympathy for the circumstances that drove you to your devilish acts and therefore, as an expression of his leniency, your bodies will not be divided into four quarters as is customary with convicted traitors. You will be buried in an unmarked communal grave in the grounds of St Werburgh's church, Derby." He paused and looked up. The four men were silent. George frowned, glancing at the others. As if to answer his silent question, Denman continued.

"George Weightman. Due to the testimonials of two key witnesses in your trial, your sentence has been given special consideration. Firstly, the testimonial of one Henry Tomlinson, farmer of South Wingfield. Mr Tomlinson stated in a letter to the judge that you showed him sympathy and considerable courage that allowed him to escape from being press-ganged into joining your mob. Secondly, the testimonial of one Mrs Ann Goodman, wife to the inn keeper of the Navigation inn, Langley Mill. She told the judge that not only did you show sympathy towards her and her husband when their premises was besieged by your mob, but you also displayed outstanding courage and character through deeds performed which led to saving the life of one Charles Walters, accidentally shot by another member of your party. As a result of these acts, Chief Baron of the Exchequer, Sir Justice Richards, the presiding Judge over these trials, together with his majesty the King, have decided that you will also be shown leniency. Instead of execution, you will be exiled for life to a penal colony in Australia. Are there any questions?"

The four prisoners stood in stunned silence. George's mouth opened and closed but no sound came forth. He looked frantically back and forth between his fellow prisoners and his counsel.

He sank to the ground. The other three exchanged glances of total disbelief.

"No questions?" Still silence. Denman continued in an almost scripted and slightly awkward manner: "Very well. I understand this must come as a great shock to you. I will leave you men to use the time you have left to consider your fate, hopefully repent and make your peace with the Lord, who may find it in his infinite wisdom to forgive you for your most heinous crimes and allow the condemned into the Kingdom of Heaven. As for you, George, it seems the Lord has already forgiven you for your part in this despicable folly. I suggest you praise him for your sparing and pray for your colleague's souls too.

"I would like to take this opportunity to thank you gentlemen for allowing me to be your counsel and co-operating with myself and my learned colleague Mr Cross so that we might serve your purpose to the best of our abilities. Good day, gentlemen and may the Lord God have mercy on your souls. If you have any further questions, please do not hesitate to request my presence via Mr Eaton. You may also wish to see the prison chaplain which, again, Mr Eaton will be more than happy to arrange, I'm sure."

George began to sob. It was difficult to tell whether it was relief, guilt or both. "Guard!" Denman suddenly called. The door opened and with that, he was gone.

Brandreth shook his head. "Well... Good job he didn't offer to shake hands. I would have broken the bastard's arm." He turned towards George once more. "So. I told you lads. Just as I suspected. The traitor is truly revealed. How does it feel, traitor? You'll have to watch us give our lives while you keep yours."

"For the love of God, Jerry. Leave the man be," sighed Ludlam. "He was saving a man's life! Doing what he thought was right and decent."

Jeremiah smiled and nodded. "I'm sure he was. Betraying his comrades and his cause. How can that be right? To me it's obvious what's happened here. A deal has been done."

George got to his feet, wiping the tears from

his eyes. "Just listen all of you! How easily we are divided. It doesn't matter why we all entered into this, or what we did. We were *all* betrayed by Oliver. It was a trap. A snare, set by the government to bring reformism into disrepute. And it worked perfectly. The rich being told what to do by the workers? Oh no, that just won't do. As if the great unwashed know what they want anyway! But they couldn't just carry on repressing us in the old way, because opinions and sympathies amongst their kind were changing. Respect from the ruling classes for the toiling man? No. That would never do. They wanted us shamed. They incited us. But wily old Oliver was worried we were too placid. We needed a figurehead, someone who could whip us into frenzy. Someone who wanted to settle an old score. Someone who would stop at nothing to get his revenge. Someone who could lead a group of working men into showing themselves up as the rabble they truly are. That someone was *you*, Jeremiah Brandreth!"

"I still think Oliver is a good man! I expect he was captured and tortured, same as the rest of us and that's how they got their information," said Brandreth, hastily.

"Then where is he now? Why was there no mention of Oliver in the trial? Why was he not called, even as a witness? Think about it, man!" pleaded George.

"You can try to blame Oliver all you like George, but the fact is you are responsible for this," Jeremiah sneered. "I hope they make you watch every last moment of our execution. Because I know what it's like. What you see on them gallows will eat at your very soul until the day you die. Like a canker. I know what you think of me. A maniac, hell bent on revenge – but there's more to it than that... You have no idea what I've been through. Well, we'll see if you think the same in ten years, George, when you've had plenty of time to live that moment over and over again.

"Every time you close your eyes at night, we'll be there, swinging. The ropes creaking. Suddenly you and me'll 'ave a lot more in common than you realised. Don't feel sorry for me George. Because I won't be suffering any more. No. If anything, it is I who feel sorry for you. To my wife and children I am finally a hero. A martyr. A man who fought for the people and died for the people. To your wife and children, you are a coward and someone to be ashamed of. An outcast. A pariah." He paused and smiled. "Good luck with your new life in Australia George. You're going to need it," he said, his voice laden with scorn.

There was a long pause. Finally, George let out a long sigh. He slumped to the ground and nodded, his face a picture of defeat.

"Aye. I hear you Jerry. And yes. You're right. I'll pay alright, I'm sure. Because I let everyone down. I should have been stronger. Insisted I was chosen as leader. But I didn't have the guts. I shied away from doing what I should have done and taken control. My Uncle Tommy said I was the democrat of our group. That I would help keep the balance. Ha! What future does democracy have? Parliament should be a government by the people for the people. And yet here we are, less than two hundred years on from the civil war and we have a government diseased with greed, riddled with corruption and poisoned with self-ambition.

"Where will our government be, two hundred years from now? Will angry disillusioned men be taking to the streets, rioting and looting lawlessly because they have no jobs and no future? Will rich men profit from war while the working men of our country are sent to kill in a foreign land? Will the men with money have one law for themselves while the working man is bound by another? I really don't know. But I do know the world is changing my friends. Machines in mills already dictate our working lives. Who knows what other machines they will invent in the future to enslave us with? Machines that will crush our spirit, suppress our will until we no longer question anything?

"I wanted and believed in something so much that I didn't even notice we were being carefully and cleverly controlled by what we wanted to destroy. And that's how it will be in the end. They will crush us before we have had a single revolutionary thought - because one day they will control the very way we think. You're right Jerry. I *am* the one who will suffer. Because as I live out my exile, I will see my beloved England become more and more divided and conquered. Just like we four have been. Look at us! Pitiful. We should be standing shoulder to shoulder, but instead we squabble like children, thinking only of ourselves.

"And as for your martyrdom Jerry, you can forget that too. The last thing they want is us to become martyrs. You mark my words. We will soon disappear from history. Forgotten. Smudged out. I wouldn't be surprised if, in ten years' time, no one outside of Derbyshire has heard of us. We will be wiped from the pages of England's history - after being on the face of every newspaper throughout the land today - because history is written by the winners..."

23. Execution
Port Macquarie, New South Wales, Australia.
October 21, 1822.

And that, my dearest wife, was how I came to learn that unlike my three comrades, my destiny did not lie in a noose outside Derby Gaol. True, my life was spared, but at that precise moment in time it was impossible to discern whether it was a miracle or the worst curse possible. I would now have to watch the three men who had been my closest companions these last eight months die, while I would live.

In their remaining days I was an outcast. They didn't say anything, but in their eyes, I felt sure that they believed I had betrayed them utterly, bringing their demise in the process. I prayed for the end. For them, because they were suffering, but also, somewhat selfishly, for me because I could not bear the crushing weight of the guilt I was carrying. We had stood shoulder to shoulder and acted together for the same cause, and now they would pay with their lives where I would not. Even Jeremiah, while he had clearly been hell bent on revenge so much that he had become a twisted, spiteful man driven by such anger and rage as I could not comprehend, had fought for the rights of his fellow workers and for what he believed was right for many years before he had met us. It is clear to me now the burden of this had taken its toll on his personage and was the true reason he was the man I had grown to despise.

I learned that Eaton had been correct in his supposing. The twelve men who were all to be tried together immediately after the four of us, Uncle Tommy included, collectively changed their plea to guilty and as a result, no evidence was heard against them. They were all sentenced to be transported, along with myself, to a penal colony in the new world continent of Australia, the place I now call home. The rest of the men, my brother Bill included, as I'm sure you're aware, all served gaol sentences of up to a year.

The remaining vigil, while it was but a short time, was unbearable for us all. We all wrote letters to our families and loved ones and Will, Isaac and Jeremiah all took visitors, which gave them some solace in their darkest hour. But, for what reasons I can only suppose, you did not come, Rebecca and I cannot pretend this did not break my heart.

Finally, the end came. But for me, and rightly so I suppose, there was no respite.

Derby Gaol, Derby. November 7, 1817.

Autumn was biting hard as the crowds began to flock into the town of Derby. A fog was clinging to the river Derwent and plumes of vapour rose into the air from out of the mouths of the crowd gathering at the gates of Derby Gaol, eager to see the traitors meet their fate. It wasn't even nine o' clock. The scaffold for the drop had begun construction at dawn – a gang of carpenters worked keenly while local constables gathered in number to guard them while they worked. William Lockett peered nervously from the window of Eaton's office at the activity taking place in the courtyard in front of him.

"Mr Eaton, look at this crowd. The execution is not due to take place until noon. I am concerned that things may get fractious and these local constables may not be able to contain any form of protest or outbreak of rioting."

"You think it might come to that?" said Eaton idly, attending to some paper work at his desk.

"I'd rather not take the risk, if I'm honest. I expect that as well as a large amount of blood thirsty rabble, there will undoubtedly be a lot of reformist types attending this event. It could get ugly."

"Don't worry Mr Lockett, I've been instructed to have some mounted cavalry here to keep order. They'll be in attendance before the morning is out."

"Before the morning is out? Look at that crowd, Mr Eaton. By mid-morning the streets outside this gaol will be crammed with thousands of spectators. Send someone to the barracks with a message – I think we'll need them here as soon as possible."

"Very good, Mr Lockett, as you wish."

"I do wish. I don't mind admitting that I will be glad when today is over. What is the itinerary for this morning? Apart from the obvious I mean."

Eaton chortled. "Well, Brandreth, Turner, Ludlam and Weightman were woken at dawn and given the opportunity to write any last letters for their loved ones. They all did, apart from the Weightman fellow."

"I see. And what state were they all in?"

"Well Weightman was in the strangest of moods, to say he's not going to hang. Been like it every day. Brandreth was his usual enigmatic self. Definitely not right that one. Turner was sobbing too much to write and I had to fetch his nephew to write it for him while he dictated – broke him, it has. Ludlam – well he's a lay preacher so his letter was full of what I can only describe as religious hysteria. In short, they are in the sort of state I would expect men about to die to be in, Mr Lockett."

"I see. And what of them now?"

"They'll be at the gaol chapel, with the chaplain. There's a service and prayers arranged for them and no doubt the opportunity to repent and make peace with God will have been given. The usual stuff for condemned men."

"This is far from usual, Mr Eaton. Be on your toes today. This is going to be all over the newspapers by this time tomorrow and hopefully for all the right reasons."

"And those reasons are?"

"That these men are wicked, rotten traitors to King and Country and are an example of what happens if you aspire to raising anarchy, chaos and violence in order to destroy democracy. If there is so much as a single incident that might be reported in a sympathetic light for the reformist movement I will have your balls, Mr Eaton. This day is long overdue and hopefully it will see the death of the reformist movement, the silencing of trouble makers up and down the country and order restored to the constitution. So do not mess it up. Am I clear?"

"As day, Mr Lockett. As day," said Eaton, rolling his eyes.

"Excellent, now get one of your lads to fetch those cavalry if you please."

As the morning drew on towards noon, the crowds swelled. Thousands now lined the streets outside Derby gaol. The noise was so overwhelming, it could be heard all over Derby.

"Do you hear that, George?" said Brandreth, sounding somewhat sardonic. "They're chanting our names. Can't hear yours though. They must know you're the traitor in our midst."

George refused to be baited. The cell door suddenly shrieked open. It was Eaton, flanked by a four prison guards. Three of them were holding a set of irons.

"Good morning gentlemen. I'm afraid it's time," he grinned.

"Irons? I thought we were done with irons?" said Will.

"He is," said Eaton, gesturing to George, "but you three will be grateful of these."

"What do you mean?" said Ludlam, looking puzzled.

"It's the weight," said Brandreth, "of the irons – it'll help snap our necks quicker. It's their idea of 'being humane'".

The four men were led out into the exercise yard. George was separated from Brandreth, Turner and Ludlam and led over to join the rest of the convicts gathered to watch. A Horse drawn hurdle waited in the middle. As the other three were man handled on to the back of it, George shuffled between the ranks of convicts until he found his Uncle Tommy and his brother, Bill.

"George! We heard you were to be spared," Tommy whispered.

"Aye. But I wish I wasn't. They're all saying I'm a traitor."

"Oliver was the traitor. The papers know this. This isn't over. The reformists will rally and gain favour because of this. We will win – and soon – I know it."

"Oi, you two, shut it!" snarled a nearby guard. They fell silent.

The cart pulled away and was drawn in full circuit of the yard past all of the prisoners gathered there. Some held up their hands and Brandreth shook as many of them as he could. "You were good men, be strong!" George heard him cry.

The cart then sped off towards the tunnel that led to the courtyard. The remaining prisoners were then herded on foot through a side gate, into the same arena.

They were immediately greeted by a huge roar from the massive crowd gathered there. Hundreds of faces were pressed up against the railings. Armed cavalry were everywhere on horseback and on foot, keeping the crowd under control. A large group of constables were lined up in front of the gallows. Three ropes hung down, ominously. A burly looking man meticulously checked the knots on the nooses.

A slow, repetitive drum beat began to be played by a single infantryman, literally beating out the seconds now left for the three men. George looked on in frozen horror, unable to comprehend the scene before him.

Brandreth, Turner and Ludlam stepped down

from the cart and stood in the archway that led into the court yard. Ludlam began to whisper a prayer once he caught sight of the monstrous wooden construction some fifty feet in front of them. Time itself seemed to slow down and an uneasy silence fell over the crowd. The sky was grey and heavy. Brandreth glanced at Will and saw his face streaked with tears. He was visibly shaking.

"Come on, Will," he said softly, holding out his hand, "We'll go together. Comrades. Martyrs. Shoulder to shoulder." Will took his hand. Brandreth leaned forward and kissed both their foreheads. "We fought as brothers and shall die as brothers."

There was a nod from the executioner that he was ready and the three men were led across the yard, past three crude wooden coffins with their names chalked on the lids.

Murmurs grew into a frenzied hubbub as the crowd realised this was the moment they'd waited for all morning. The atmosphere was tense.

The single bass drum boomed even louder, in order to be heard over the crowd, ringing out over and over in time with the three men's steps. A single guard flanked each prisoner as they mounted the wooden stair case slowly and steadfastly due to the weight of the irons round their ankles. Each laboured footfall was one step closer to the end. Still the drum rang out across the courtyard.

Turner was led to the far left rope, Brandreth the middle and Ludlam the last of the three.

The executioner slowly placed a hood over each man's head. Eaton and Lockett appeared and made their way up the steps.

"This better go off without any form of public affray, Eaton or we might be next up there!" Lockett hissed in his ear.

At that moment the crowd seemed to surge forward as more and more people scrambled to get a good view of the spectacle. The huge iron gates at the front seemed to buckle inwards from the sheer weight of the people against them. Lockett, his voice shaking with fear barked to Eaton "The troops! Give the order!"

"Captain! Bring this mob to order if you please!" Eaton barked.

An officer on horseback nodded, then gave a pre-arranged hand gesture to several of his mounts positioned strategically in front of the gates, who drew their pistols and pointed them into the air.

"Fire!"

There was a series of ear splitting cracks as the designated men fired skywards. It did the trick and the crowd fell silent.

Lockett took his pocket watch out with fumbling urgency. Glancing at the dial, he nodded to Eaton. He clearly wanted this over as quickly as possible. Eaton signalled the executioner with a single downturn of his thumb.

At that precise moment a clock somewhere nearby – probably the cathedral - began to chime. It was midday.

As the executioner placed the rope over Brandreth's hooded head, he suddenly cried out "God Bless You All! And Lord Castlereagh too!" Some members of the crowd let out a gasp at what was clearly a defiant jibe at the presiding leader of the House of Commons.

Ludlam joined in, though he seemed to sound somewhat more sincere as the noose closed around his throat. "I pray God bless you all and the King upon his throne!" he warbled in terror.

William Turner had other ideas, however. As the rope pressed against his gullet and the loop was tightened he suddenly wailed "This is the work of the government and Oliver!" A now clearly divided crowd roared in a juxtaposition of astonishment, approval and outrage.

Lockett's face was suddenly a mixture of panic and anger. He spun round, gesturing profusely at the huge lever that would release the platform under the convict's feet. The distant clock struck the first of twelve, before being drowned out by a surge of boos and hisses from the crowd. A horse whinnied and skittered. "Now man! Do it now!" he hissed.

The drum beat stopped, replaced by a deafening clunk followed by several gruesome snapping sounds as the executioner activated the drop lever and the three men's necks were instantly broken.

Stifled gasps gave way to a haunting quiet in an instant. Ropes creaked. The three men kicked frantically for a few seconds, as they dangled over the abyss that had opened up below them. Someone, it was difficult to tell who, let out a blood curdling choking sound. Then total silence. It began to spit with rain.

George couldn't bear the terrible sight any longer. Tears stung his face as averted his gaze and looked down at the cobbled yard in shame.

He closed his eyes tight, trying to block out the horror of what he had just witnessed. He was overwhelmed by a feeling of dizziness and nausea. Falling to his knees he felt the acid searing in his nose and throat momentarily before showering the cobbles in front of him with vomit.

It must have only been a minute or so but it seemed to last a lifetime. The distant clock had finished striking. The ropes creaked in the wind. Eventually, the three men became completely still as even the wind dropped to nothing. The executioner felt for a pulse in each one's neck. When he'd checked all three, he nodded to Lockett and Eaton.

Lockett grinned a nervous grin of relief. He turned and shouted to the huge, silent, crowd. "The traitors are dead. Long live the King!" The majority of the crowd cheered in rapturous ecstasy. Some booed and hissed – sympathisers no doubt, but he didn't care now. It was over. The spitting rain swelled into heavy drops and moments later the heavens opened. Lockett looked visibly relieved – the coming downpour couldn't be better timed – it would certainly aid the rapid dispersal of this volatile looking audience. They'd probably hang on until the three corpses had had their heads removed and then make a dash for the nearby ale houses and taverns in order to avoid a soaking.

The drop was reset and the lifeless bodies of Jeremiah Brandreth, William Turner and Isaac Ludlam were cut down and left in crumpled heaps on the platform. The executioner turned to a huge block of wood by his side, from which he drew a large axe. Grinning, and fully aware that all eyes were upon him, he ran his finger along the gleaming blade in theatrical manner, before heading over to the three lifeless bodies. In an almost ceremonial gesture, he raised the weapon slowly above his head, then slammed it down with the same mixture of force and practised precision that a butcher might use to cleave a particularly stubborn side of beef.

Epilogue

Port Macquarie, New South Wales, Australia. October 21, 1822.

...The sound of those ropes creaking in the wind will haunt me 'til I die. Every morning, I wake with that sound in my head, gnawing at my very soul, like the gibbet gnaws at the rope as it swings with the weight of a dead man... I know not how long I knelt there, on the cold wet cobblestones of Derby Gaol's courtyard, with my eyes screwed tightly shut. I endured the sound of each sickening thud, one after another – each blow felt like a knife to my heart as the hangman casually severed each of their heads without a second thought - in much the same way that I have cleaved timber all of my daily working life – he was simply doing his job.

Each head was raised as a trophy to justice and the crowds lapped up every moment, overjoyed that finally, the ringleaders of a dangerous rebellion who had threatened their community had been given their just deserts.

I'm certain the trapdoor had opened at that precise moment in order to cut short Will's outburst about Oliver - but what few words he did get out had managed to do their job. Soon the papers were rife with talk of a conspiracy. I heard William Oliver mysteriously disappeared abroad shortly after – with a healthy reward for his efforts no doubt. Rumour has it he took a governor's position in South Africa for his part in bringing down the reformist movement. Whether that is true, I cannot say, as soon afterwards I was aboard a prison ship bound for Botany Bay. I had a long time to think aboard that vessel.

On finally arriving in Australia I decided to put everything from my life in Derbyshire behind me and start afresh. Everything that is, except you my love. I have carried hope in my heart that one day you would forgive me and understand why the events of June the ninth, eighteen seventeen happened. I've been a virtuous man since I arrived in the New World. I volunteered to help build the new penal colony. I've worked hard these past four years in the hope that not only I repay my debt to society, but also to you, Rebecca.

It took me a long time to realise this, but I now truly believe that God spared me for a reason and I believe that reason was you. Because your love for me was always true. He spared me to give me a chance to put right the wrongs I have perpetrated to you and the children. Today, I believe my penance is at an end – I have been awarded a ticket of leave for all my hard labours in this community. Yes, I am a free man again! Able to work, have a home of my own and be reunited with my family.

In due course it is customary to apply for a pardon, but for now, I am only interested in making arrangements for you to finally join me here in my new life. I have applied for your passage grants from the governor, so it should simply be a matter of time. I am sure that together we can make a new and happy life for ourselves. There is good work for a skilled sawyer like me and a wonderful sense of opportunity. The chance to begin again anew. But my final redemption is in your hands, Rebecca.

Please, find it in your heart to forgive me. My enquiries via others' letters home to their loved ones tell me that you have not found another husband and that you and the children still reside in Pentrich, struggling to make ends meet without a man by your side. I am sure it is because deep down, you still love me. That is why I am writing to you this one last time. I await your reply with hope in my heart. I pray that your wounds have finally healed and that we can soon be happy and together again.

Your ever loving husband,
George.

AFTERWORD

Sadly, for reasons unknown, Rebecca never joined George in Australia, despite wives and children of other transported rebels doing so once they received their ticket of leave.

Rebecca died in poverty in Pentrich after working as a tea lady as well as receiving parish relief. She never married again. George never remarried either, but was eventually given a full pardon. He played a key part in the building of the new colony in Australia, working as a sawyer, providing the much needed timber required to build the growing colony. He came to be known as an upstanding member of the community. George outlived all of the transported rebels, passing away in his home, in the seaside town of Kiama in 1865. He was 74. His son, Joseph, emigrated to Australia as an adult and became a successful sheep farmer –

whether he was reunited with his father at any point is unclear.

Thomas Bacon died unpardoned and still living as a convict in 1831, aged 77.

The Pentrich uprising was a substantial national scandal at the time and despite attempts to cover up the true nature of William Oliver's involvement, many newspapers and journals alluded to his role as being an agent provocateur, employed by the government to bring the reformist movement into disrepute. It is believed that he was paid off and given a local governor's position in South Africa, under a new name, away from the scrutiny of the press. Though there is no evidence to support this, William Oliver did mysteriously disappear off the face of the earth following the trial.

Jeremiah Brandreth, William Turner and Isaac Ludlum were the last men to be executed for treason in England. Their bodies resided in an unmarked communal grave in the grounds of St Werburgh's church at the bottom of Friargate in Derby until they were exhumed and moved to the cities' largest cemetery in Chaddesden. This is believed to have happened sometime in the mid twentieth century - it is difficult to identify an exact date as numerous bodies were exhumed and transferred there over many years and no records were kept regarding the exact location that the Pentrich martyrs were finally laid to rest in.

If you're reading this because you're a descendent of any of the people that were involved in the Pentrich Uprising of 1817, I'd love to hear from you.

E-mail me at pete.darrington@hotmail.co.uk

Pentrich – England's Last Uprising